Extrasensory Deception

A Suny Davis Mystery

Book One

McLean Jacobson

CUSP books
2018

ISBN-13: 978-0-9912652-6-8

Printed in the United States of America

Chapter 1

I often observe that life is drudgery, which may be sad to say when one is sixteen years old, but I found myself reiterating that aphorism in the middle of Friday's Italian lesson.

Mr. Taintley was old, which in and of itself did not mean much, but he was nearly a relic and thought his advanced years brought advanced knowledge. Not so, as I have often observed. Mr. Taintley also taught French, Latin, and Spanish at the Broadman School for Girls. He fancied himself a wealth of culture to be genially bestowed upon the population of isolated females at Broadman, tucked away as they were, deep in the wilds of the Shenandoah Valley. However, his stumbling Italian was not what I would call a culturally enriching experience. I had told him so the previous week, unable to contain myself any longer.

The incident occurred just as I had begun my second term at Broadman. Although it was my second term, it was the beginning of an academic year for most, fall term, they called it, though the autumnal equinox was still a few weeks away. My academic life has never been what one could call traditional but, being used to that fact, I had arrived at my school of the moment, trunks and suitcases trailing me up the hot, humid stairs, steeled and ready for another year of painfully inadequate education. In that I was not to be disappointed.

During the first week of classes, in an attempt to draw in the less disciplined of mind, Mr. Taintley had set up our classroom like a bad set for a 1950's Italian bistro. He welcomed us with menus in hand, a steam table hissing by the blackboard. I tried to roll my eyes, a skill I have yet to acquire fully, murmured a choice expletive in Russian, and took my seat to the back of the class.

Mr. Taintley minced about the room, questioning the girls, who giggled and spat out answers in atrocious Italian, mixed liberally with English when their summer-sunburned brains failed them. I could smell overcooked calamari and sickeningly sweet Italian sausage stewing in the bubbling cart. The smell, an assault to my nose after six years as a dedicated vegetarian, only added to the indignation I felt at having to be put through an hour of an embarrassingly bad attempt at real-world education. When the door opened and one of the kitchen staff arrived with what looked like veal scaloppini, I could take no more.

Mr. Taintley had by then arrived at my desk, said desk covered in checked grease cloth. His face glowed with perspiration and delight at his little experiential lesson plan. His smile faltered a bit when he saw my face, but he still managed to squeak out his query.

"*Cosa ti piace mangiare, signorina?*"

"What would I like?" I asked in English.

"*Parla italiano, per favore*, Miss Davis."

"*Italiano? Se si desidera…*" And I proceeded to lecture him, in Italian as he wished, about the evils inherent in the traditional husbandry of veal calves, which he should know is currently in disfavor in most of Europe. He seemed not to understand the innately higher road of vegetarianism. I asked him pointedly how the veal in this case had been raised and, as he stuttered to answer me, I gave a brief evaluation of his Italian, and then left the room in protest.

It had been unfair to disabuse him of his notion that I knew less than a year's worth of Italian in such a manner, but when I reach a certain level of indignation, I find myself unable to consider the feelings of inadequacy my fluency in many matters must imbue in the adult in question.

I took myself off to the library and, so as not to be seen as eschewing the study of Italian entirely, made my way to the dusty room in which the older Broadman collection was now housed. There, I found a collection of Italian essays from the turn of the century and settled on a windowsill.

I was several pages along when I was joined, as I had expected to be, by Samuel Munston, the school's literature teacher, and my advisor. Mr. Munston was young, so young in fact that there were those on staff who worried about his effect on the adolescent females to whom he read stories of lust and greed and other failings of human nature as a matter of course. They were right to worry that he might inspire infatuations (several of the girls crooned over him regularly) but they were wrong to worry that he might take advantage of the fact. As the situation clearly presented itself to me when we first met, Mr. Munston was gay. Such was not the topic of our first conversations, but my observations as to his orientation were confirmed in my mind as we continually met to discuss my… well, my non-traditional approach to making use of the educational resources presented to me.

"Suny?"

I liked him further due to the fact that when we first met, he pronounced my name correctly, one of the rare people who did so, even after I explained that it was 'Soon-ee' like the New York State university system, not 'Sunny' like the weather forecast.

I looked up from my book and met his brown eyes. They were warm with understanding, a quality I admire in the rare adults who possess it in my presence. There was also something of a twinkle in them, though it might have been the sunlight from the window behind me.

"I am sorry, Mr. Munston, for leaving the classroom, but as you can see, I am still devoting my prescribed hour to improving my Italian."

"Suny, we talked about your diction, your word choice. It was you who came to me asking how to improve your social skills."

"I apologize. Still studying my Italian, Mr. Munston."

"I see that. Why didn't you tell us, tell me you're fluent in Italian?"

"I would not award myself the accolade of fluency. The level of which you speak takes years of exposure and I had only two months in Tuscany when father was researching the…

well, we were in Tuscany, but I found, as with other languages, that immersion for a short period followed by continued study, exposure to books, magazines, film, chat rooms…Well, much can be made of a single experience. Not to mention the fact that as a romance language, akin to French and Spanish, in which I had attained some fluency…"

"Suny, how many languages do you know?" Mr. Munston asked, taking the brittle book of Italian from my hands.

"Know? Could you be more specific as to what constitutes…"

"Suny–"

"Well, let's see. I came to my father knowing French and English– I was just two at the time. He was living in Honduras then, so naturally, one could add Spanish to the list. And the au pair when we returned to the States was German. Then there was Japan, though I still don't read or write so well, but that is perhaps because…"

"Suny, Suny! Stop! You're telling me you speak French, Spanish, German, Japanese…and Italian?"

"As well as English, of course. There was an assistant in Japan, a Russian with whom I tried to pursue that language. The Slavic languages…yes, well, to continue, he did not seem to wish to share his knowledge. The smattering of Russian I know is mostly profane, but my vocabulary in that vein is quite extensive. I continued to learn new curses as I continued to request his assistance, you see. Also some rather low romantic idioms because there was another assistant, a German female with whom the Russian was quite taken…"

"So Russian– a bit?"

"One might say so."

"Is that everything?"

"A bit of Swahili and a little Hindi. There was a six-month study in Kenya and an Indian restaurant in London above which we had a flat. The owners were kind enough to watch me while Father… uh… entertained on occasion."

"Well Suny, you have quite a gift for languages."

"Father has made the same observation, which is why he

sent me here to Broadman. He overlooked the time in Tuscany, and did not consult me about my knowledge of Italian. Frankly, I did not wish to remind him. The school I attended prior to Broadman lacked Italian and was co-educational and I find that, probably due to my non-traditional education up until my teenage years, I lack some social skills necessary to an American teenager. I thought, perhaps, that dealing with only the female sex might be somewhat easier than… Well, I was wrong on that account."

"Still having problems with your roommate?" Mr. Munston asked after a little sigh.

"This one is new this term, but I doubt she will be much better. It seems to me that women are so competitive between themselves that they will never reach full equality with men. If they focused more…"

"Suny, I have a class in ten minutes."

"Oh yes," I said, consulting my watch. "Be brief. In any case, I suppose my conduct will be reported to Father, and I will be restricted to academic activities," I ducked my head and awaited my punishment.

"Yes, that's right," Mr. Munston delivered, tucking the book of essays back on a shelf. Never mind that it was not properly catalogued. "Except for the mixer next Friday. I told Ms. Winston you needed the social practice."

I peeked up at him. His mouth threatened to pull into a smile.

"I wouldn't mind missing it."

"I had thought of that, Suny. I had even thought that you may have let loose on Mr. Taintley for just that reason, but no dice. A mixer is just what you need."

So here I found myself, enduring yet another Italian lesson, made ever more excruciating by how Mr. Taintley now took pains to be careful of his diction and pronunciation. It was much like listening to an Italian robot.

I missed being able to leave the grounds. There was a nice

library in town and I had discovered a few walks that led me through pastureland and into the foothills. I found that if I walked briskly, I could sit and reflect a while between the end of classes and the call to dinner.

But today, the last day (thank goodness) of my restriction, I was not allowed to leave the grounds. When Mr. Taintley dismissed us, avoiding my eye as I wished him a good weekend, I left the room and headed for the stairs. I turned there, letting the girls stream past me, excited already about the mixer this evening. I retraced my steps and found Mr. Taintley silent at his desk.

"Excuse me, Mr. Taintley."

He started, which seems to be the standard response of adults when made aware of my presence.

"Miss Davis, I...I didn't see you there."

"That is understandable as I just reentered the room." I smoothed my hair and continued, "Mr. Taintley, I would like to apologize once again for any discomfort I may have caused you and I would like to offer, as a sign of my positive future intentions with regard to this class, to introduce you to the Venicis, friends of my father's who operate a lovely Italian restaurant in Richmond. I am sure they would be more than pleased to arrange, well, an outing, a day of immersion, where the girls could enjoy Italian culture outside the classroom. Perhaps you will consider it."

He regarded me with a blank stare.

"Mr. Taintley?"

He shook himself. "Miss Davis– yes, thank you. I will consider it."

I nodded my approval and made my retreat. As I reached the doorway, I turned and said– appropriately, I thought–"*Pax sit.*"

Mr. Taintley blinked, then raised his hand to me, looking fatigued. Fridays were hard on teachers, I've found.

I mounted the stairs, flanked by portraits of headmistresses past. As I reached the midway landing, I let out, "*Gavno!*"

I had forgotten to tell Mr. Munston about knowing Latin. Oh well, perhaps dead languages don't count.

Roommates never made sense to me. By that I mean both individual roommates I have endured as well as the general convention of the having of a roommate. For the exorbitant fee one was required to pay for a boarding school, one might expect a private room. I, for one, would have paid much more for the privilege of a solitary retreat.

My present roommate had not yet taken over the room with her possessions, but I could see a tendency toward that when I entered the room. Clothing was piled on her bed; outfits already rejected were discarded randomly across the floor. My roommate, Morgan Virginia Stanfield, was wet and naked in the middle of the rug.

"Do you have any pink heels?" she demanded, more than asked. I felt her eyes scan me up and down. "No, I guess you wouldn't." She went back to digging like a small dog through her wardrobe.

I am savvy enough to realize she meant to be insulting. I knew from the moment I arrived that she did not intend to become friends with me. She took advantage of the fact that I liked to be off campus as much as possible by inviting half the dorm over every evening for facials, hair tips, and makeshift aerobics classes. She was quite stunning as a result of all her preening, and not dumb either. She accepted Bs and Cs without taking any time to study. I likened her to one of my father's wives: gorgeous, greedy, but not dumb.

Judging by the state of my own closet, Morgan had already ascertained that I did not possess pink heels. I also noted a few missing items for which I would have to search her own wardrobe before long. I reiterate my deep confusion as to the benefit of a roommate.

My wardrobe did not only lack pink heels, it lacked just about anything traditionally feminine. That truth was less the result of my dislike of traditionally feminine attire, than a reflection of the fact that I have been growing so quickly of late I haven't had time to replenish my wardrobe. Most girls my age have stopped growing, but as I neared six feet and size ten shoes, I doubt I would prove to be average in that regard either. Even my brassieres were perpetually too tight, an area in which I believed growth to be completely unnecessary. To have "a knockout body," as my present stepmother so crudely put it this summer, is not my goal in life. Hopefully her evaluation that it may be the only thing that would keep a boy in the room with me longer than ten minutes would prove to be incorrect when and if I desired any "boy" to remain. As yet, no one has stirred in me that desire.

My meager wardrobe had not been of concern until that moment. But I did want to please Mr. Munston, to show him I was trying to be more social. My eyes lit upon the small dressing case at the bottom of my closet.

As I retrieved it, Morgan stomped out half-dressed to continue her search for the ever-elusive pink heels. Storming through hallways unclad was just another benefit to an all-girls boarding school education. I should have remained co-ed. It had definitely been more civilized. Sometimes I wonder at my own judgment.

I was glad she had left. The case held some more personal and monetarily valuable items. I laid it on my bed, unlocked it with a key I kept in a compact of perfumed powder I never used, and surveyed the contents. In it I found a velvet pouch that held a pearl necklace, its larger pearl pendant encrusted with diamonds and sapphires. I hesitated, then took it out and laid it gingerly on my pillow. The blue of the sapphires was intense, deep in a mysterious way that attracted me like a siren's song. They stirred something in me: not precisely a memory, not exactly an emotion. Something. They had always been my favorite stone.

Aside from a diaper and a sheepskin flokati rug, the necklace was the only thing I had been wearing when I was delivered, sleeping in a rough French bicycle basket, to my father's hut/office. He remembered the necklace, even remembered having given it to some French girlfriend, but not exactly to which one of them.

The flokati rug lay across the bottom of my bed. I placed a few more things from the case on it before I found the item for which I was searching. I pulled yards of silk from the bottom of the case. Teal, gold, and orange, stitched throughout with beads, shells, and even some bits of mirror, the sari had been worn by our London landlady, Mrs. Paudwal's sister. Her unfortunate story only served to make the garment all the more romantic to me. She had been sixteen when killed by a truck that careened out of control into her parent's shop in India. Mrs. Paudwal had given it to me on the occasion of my eleventh birthday when my father failed to come home after a Paris weekend and I was left to make my own birthday cake. I had nearly ignited the building in its entirety before she arrived. Mrs. Paudwal put the fire out and then had taken pity on me, citing her sister's unfortunate demise as a worse situation than the one in which I found myself then. I had come to taking out the sari to wrap around me whenever my circumstances seemed particularly bleak. It is very interesting to me the things in which humans find comfort, but that is a completely separate matter.

On that long ago birthday, Mrs. Paudwal had wrapped the sari expertly around my already budding body. It had barely fit me then. It was hopeless to think it could swath my whole Amazon-like form now, but I stood in front of the mirror and wove pieces of its silk tentatively around my torso.

When my father had returned from that Paris weekend, he had with him a new bride. She was French and moneyed and he was not—moneyed, that is—at that juncture in his career, having lost quite a lot of assets to his last wife. He was also unable to procure new employment due to said ex-wife's libelous rumor-mongering. This new French wife quickly became bored while he was distracted by the writing of a book he thought might clear his name. Naomi, as she was called, took to me for

11

entertainment as I spoke more French than she had expected and I seemed to her a perfect life-size doll. Many a time she appeared in my London classroom, eyes wet, face puffy, purportedly removing me to visit someone on the continent who was ill, dead, or dying. The headmaster was fully taken in the first half-dozen times and Naomi absconded with me to Paris to visit houses of haute couture, or to drag me along to dinners where she felt some display of domesticity and motherly affection would come across as charming. Father was deeply buried in the writing of his vindicating tome and barely noticed.

As Naomi liked to dress me up so frequently, I couldn't help but pick up some of the nuances of form and flow of fabric that were key to the world of fashion. The sari fabric was enough to weave around my torso, unfortunately large breasts included, and up into my hair, whose shade the dyed silk complemented perfectly, if I do say so myself. The result was very pleasing, sexy without being revealing– mysterious, in fact. I applied some smoky-toned make-up quickly, but expertly (another skill forced upon me by Naomi) and pulled a few more copper-brown wisps of hair down to veil my eyes.

From the waist up, the effect was quite chic. White cotton panties did not enhance the outfit, however. I went to my wardrobe once more and was sadly disappointed by the options it held. As I said before, I have grown a bit since the last time I shopped and, aside from English tweed skirts, which were warm and practical, but looked frumpy at almost any length, the only possibilities that remained were the three short cotton skirts I had been wearing the last few warm September weeks and blue jeans. The jeans already looked too small, but I gave them a try. I finally managed to get myself stuffed into one pair after cutting off the waistband so it wouldn't constrict my intestines so severely. The ragged edge contrasted nicely with the shimmering silk of the sari. I gave the same treatment to the cuffs, elaborating on the fact that they rode too high above my ankles anyway. I efficiently painted my toenails with some enamel from my art kit, and wrapped my ankles in the jeweled foot chains that went with the sari, only needing to add a few necklace chains to stretch them around my man-sized feet.

I surveyed the results. Jeans and bare feet might not be exactly dress code for social functions at Broadman, but I thought I could get away with it. It was a kind of rough ethnic look that some designers might have appreciated. Overall, very satisfactory. I hadn't even needed to style my hair.

I was still trying to decide whether to add the pearls as a headdress or a necklace when Morgan returned, clicking through the door in coral heels, half-slip and a towel.

"No way!" she shrieked, apparently affronted by my appearance.

"You don't think the administration will allow jeans?" I began.

"That's not even available yet! How did you…" Her face suffused with purple. It was not a good shade with her bleached blonde hair and coral heels.

"I'm sorry, Morgan, but I don't understand…"

She flung a magazine at me. The glossy paper was heavy and I was lucky I caught it before it thumped into me. "Resortwear Preview," read one of the cover lines meant to entice. I began to leaf through but Morgan grabbed the pages from me and slammed them open on her desk to a dog-eared selection with "Demand this from Daddy for St. Thomas!!!" emblazoned across it in gel pen. The reminder, if you will, did not quite obscure an emaciated model wearing a plum-colored silk top, woven in panels across her enhanced chest, as well as blue jeans, raggedly cut at waist and cuffs, with the added embellishment of a pattern of beads and mirrors.

"Well, it's not the same exactly, is it? But I could see why you might…"

"You little bitch! You've been going through my things! How dare you look through my Vogue and steal my ideas!"

"First, it is not *I* who has been rummaging through the contents of *your*…"

"I can't believe I got stuck with you, you bastard daughter

13

of a freak!"

Her voice rang in my ears, stunning me to silence. My vision blurred.

I sank down on my bed and let the pearl necklace pool in my lap. It didn't register fully when Morgan left the room, nor did I truly hear any of the other inflammatory remarks she hurled at me before her departure. Her first hostile remark had been enough.

Chapter 2

The room slowly darkened as I sat, rolling pearl after pearl between my fingers like rosary beads. Doors slammed, girls called to one another, and heels clicked down the wooden stairs. I could hardly breathe, much less move.

Why Morgan's words affected me so strongly that evening, I cannot know for certain. Surely, I was used to hearing epitaphs hurled about regarding my father's chosen profession. And had I not consciously researched and decided that the abstract legal recognition of a couple's right to unite sexually and produce offspring did not add substantively to the worth of said child? To be born out of wedlock did not preclude one from valued contribution to the works of man, did it? Wasn't there a list of famous bastards in the Book of Lists?

Adolescence had hit me like a brick, or some such piece of masonry, and I had spent many hours reading philosophy, psychology, even self-help type books, all to determine that my identity, my value as an individual, need not be determined by the fact that my father chose to chase ghosts while not choosing to marry my mother.

Let me explain. My father, Eugene Fenimore Davis, was… is… purports to be– a psychic. He is world-renowned, sought after by kings and magnates, counselor to the powerful, the rich…the gullible. I did not have much faith in my father's chosen profession as a whole, finding gaps and paradoxes in the claims. Yet, my father was not a swindler like some, not a cheat…

Except when it came to women. Married four times to date, he admittedly had twenty times as many lovers through the years, and did not know exactly how many children he had fathered. That I was his, the necklace in my delivering basket clearly stated, and he did not deny it. He deduced from my ability to babble French and from my apparent age, that I was the daughter of any one of three young French women, or possibly one Canadian. Which one of the four was my mother never gave him pause. He accepted me as his responsibility without question and as I grew, my resemblance to him in features, in intelligence, in…well, in other ways, confirmed for him his paternity.

Several other claims were put to him in the years after he accepted me publicly. He was not only handsome and well-known, he also came from a three-generation family fortune, serving to make him an attractive target. He settled several claims of paternity without question, until the family's lawyers stepped in and decided he should be more cautious, discerning, and…well, discreet, about exactly how many women he'd been with and who, and when, and all other particulars. For the sake of the family name, they pleaded, if not for the sake of his own wealth. As if his profession were not enough of a blight on the family name already.

It should not have bothered me so much. So many claims showed that some people actually wanted to be recognized not only as bastard children (and their indiscreet mothers), but as bastard children of a charlatan "freak," as Morgan put it.

I don't know how long I sat in the dark. Eventually, I heard music, felt bass thrumming through the halls from the "ballroom." And then even that became background to my thoughts. I suppose I was just tired of being away at school. I much preferred a more self-styled education, and I was horrifically bored in this academically challenged finishing school.

A knock came at the door. Before I could decide whether or not I was ready for any human contact, a voice followed. It was Mr. Munston.

I called out unenthusiastically for him to enter. "I am sorry I have been remiss in fulfilling my obligation…"

"Suny–"

"I apologize. I'm sorry I have not appeared in the ballroom as yet."

"That's a bit better. What happened?" He came farther into

the room, pausing to switch on my desk lamp.

"Wow," he exclaimed.

"I know the room is somewhat untidy. My roommate is not the most conscientious…"

"Suny, that's not what I'm talking about. Stand up. You're gorgeous!"

I blushed despite myself, I must say. I did stand as he requested, but lodged my protest at the same time. "Mr. Munston, while I am capable of enhancing my physical attributes in a generally acceptable way—"

"Suny, your physical attributes have been enhanced very acceptably. Who would have guessed that under those baggy t-shirts of yours…Well, I'm sure there will be many appreciative young men downstairs." He offered his arm to escort me.

I hesitated.

"Suny?" Mr. Munston dropped the proffered arm to his side and his eyes softened in concern. "What's up?"

"Oh, just an altercation with my roommate."

"About?"

"Oh, silliness. She believes I illicitly perused her fashion magazine and 'stole' her outfit. As if a clothing design were patentable. If she ever read anything other than that magazine lying there, she would know that much money is made in the so-called 'knock-off' business of copying designer fashions."

Mr. Munston had taken advantage of my brief speech to leaf through the magazine in question.

"This one?" he asked, displaying the appropriate dog-eared page.

I nodded.

He whistled.

"And you didn't? No, no, don't get indignant. It's just pretty amazing that you…" He gazed at me speculatively. "Interesting coincidence."

"I'm sure statistically it would not be of any significance. It was truly coincidental and a product of my desperation over my meager wardrobe."

17

"Well," he said, slapping the magazine shut, "we can chat more about the situation Monday, if you'd like. Now, we have to get you downstairs so you can boogie with the boys."

As I mentioned previously, I have not yet mastered the teenage habit of eye-rolling, but I gave it a shot again right then and followed him out of the room.

Mr. Munston left me at the doorway of the ballroom. The ballroom at Broadman was small, used normally only for Parents Day Sunday brunches and other excuses for people to wear expensive clothes and talk quietly. The room was quite full on mixer nights. This evening was no exception. Boys from the neighboring Haydon School had been bussed in for the event. Inexplicably, they all seemed to be wearing costumes. I had forgotten this mixer was a themed event. World Cultures. Several tents were placed along the periphery of the room, and each was labeled with a country. Well, seeing as Mr. Munston hadn't objected to my "costume," I assumed that it passed as being culturally relevant.

I spotted Morgan heading my way in her coral heels and blindingly hot pink kimono. I ducked inside the nearest tent to avoid her.

"Oh, Miss Davis."

It was Mr. Taintley. At least, I thought it was he. He wore a gold lamé swami's turban and squinted at me from behind a table complete with crystal ball, looking quite unlike his normal self.

"Mr. Taintley."

"Uh– can I tell you your fortune?"

"I don't know– can you?" I checked myself, remembering the peace I had tried to make with him earlier. I supposed I should carry through with it and try to further mend the rift in our teacher-student relationship. "I mean, yes, of course. Please do."

I sat in the chair opposite him and tried not to sigh as he fumbled with a book– most likely a how-to book– hidden in his lap beneath the folds of fabric that covered the table.

"Yes, well, here we go. Your fortune to be told. Please stare with me into the crystal ball."

I acquiesced and did my best to appear intent on the hunk of glass.

"You…" much fluttering of pages "…you are a person of mystery…"

Oh, my. The things one must put oneself through for the sake of one's secondary education.

"You…please Miss Davis, look into the crystal ball…"

I pulled my attention back to the ball. It soon became apparent why he wanted my gaze to remain so attuned. A flickering of images stirred up from the smoky depths of the sphere. They grew and began to launch outward. A pair of deep blue eyes appeared, intense blue, the blue of… but they were gone, followed by a dark road, a lightning strike… a gull flying, struggling through wind and rain, dipping down and away… another road stretching on and on… foreign characters, an alphabet unknown floated… and then leaves swirling past hills dotted with figures…

I had never seen anything like it and that was saying a lot. Father had quite the collection of crystal balls, after all. I would have to ask Mr. Taintley where he had acquired such an object. There must have been an electric cord that ran through the bottom of the crystal ball's stand, and through the table. How else could the display appear?

Mr. Taintley was paying far too much attention to the book hidden in his lap and so was babbling something completely inconsistent with the images, something to do with good fortune and great deeds. Meanwhile, the leaves that had appeared swirled away… and then the images grew dark. A rapid thrusting of shapes… sharp angles, of glass and steel…

And then a skeletal face swam up to meet my gaze, jarring me back in my seat. All went black.

It took me a moment to gather myself. That skeletal face…

"Oh, good show, Mr. Taintley," I exclaimed with false but

hearty praise. "Especially that last bit with the skeleton."

"What? A skeleton?" Mr. Taintley peered intently into the crystal ball.

"Oh, yes. I'm sure Father would love to know where you found this ball. Quite a complex little toy."

Mr. Taintley still appeared confused. "You say you saw…"

"Oh yes, everything. And I can't even tell how you've hidden the wires."

"Wires?" Mr. Taintley picked up the ball from its stand, allowing me to see that the object was even more advanced than I'd thought. Apparently, it relied on some form of wireless transmission. What would they think of next? Although I put up a good front for Mr. Taintley's sake, I was, in truth, sickened by the thought that this item would make it all the more easy for a supposed soothsayer to trick the unwary.

"Well, thank you so much," I sang out as I pulled open the tent flap, leaving Mr. Taintley with a brow still furrowed in confusion. Perhaps he hadn't expected it to work so well.

I walked quickly, and I hoped unobtrusively, along one side wall toward the refreshments. I passed tents of Germany and China. I hoped I wouldn't have to duck into yet another one, but I didn't see Morgan again.

A small, dark girl wearing nothing more unusual than slacks and a shirt stood at the refreshment table, taking more interest in the punch bowl than the dancing crowd. She glanced up quickly and flashed an unsure smile. I had never noticed her before, so perhaps she was new. Or perhaps I just had overlooked her. I'm not the most social of beings, as I think I have already expressed. She reminded me of Mrs. Paudwal: a low, dark brow over huge brown eyes.

I said hello and when she did not respond, I tried again in Hindi. She looked up in surprise and explained in English that she was from Pakistan, but knew some Hindi. She was indeed new to Broadman and would be working with a tutor for a while before joining regular classes. I welcomed her and thought to myself that perhaps she was a creature of intelligence not yet sullied by the cultural idiocy of the American teen. And perhaps she could teach me some Urdu. I explained to her that I had lived in London, found that she had also spent a summer there, and we were off, chatting animatedly as the music blared over us.

Sometime later, we stood outside the French tent together. We had moved on to the long-standing animosity between Pakistan and India. Well, *I* had moved on, at least. Basmah, as her name turned out to be, was listening attentively, only needing to be brought back into the conversation the few times she craned her neck over the dancing crowd, seemingly looking for something. I was very involved in my explanation of the transfer of power from the British when I asked her opinion and I found she had gone from my side. I looked up to see her waving apologetically from the dance floor. Apparently, she had been asked to dance at some point in our discussion.

"I hold a different view," came a voice from my other side. It belonged to a young man, wearing a toga, whose sandy hair hung long over brown eyes. He looked at me very seriously from under his crown of laurel leaves.

"I've been eavesdropping and I have to say that, historically speaking..." and he continued at length, and although I did not agree with him in the least, feeling that the foundations of his argument were sorely lacking in logic, I found myself enjoying his company. After some time, Robert, as I learned his name to be, went to get us refreshments.

The air was close in the ballroom and the doors to the garden had been opened. I went to stand by one to catch my breath. Couples had moved out into the night air. They talked and laughed on the terrace steps.

Robert joined me then, placing a cup of punch in my hand. "Shall we walk?"

I assented and we moved past the terrace and into the garden. It was cool for a September night, but I welcomed the damp grass on the bare soles of my feet. Even as I enjoyed the sensation, I shivered a bit. Robert took that purely physical reflex to be an invitation and draped his arm over my shoulder. I surprised myself by allowing it to remain. I listened to him talk about Middle Eastern politics in a broader sense. His father was in the diplomatic corps, which made Robert believe his points were valid. I drank my punch and framed my rebuttal in my mind.

We walked quite a ways into the garden. The torches that illuminated the terrace were mere points far behind us, but the moon was out. I knew because it suddenly held much more fascination for me than Robert's take on…what was he saying? A haze passed over the moon. Actually, it stayed there. I squinted hard and craned my neck backward to see it more clearly. Robert mumbled on. I stretched upward to see the glowing outline and overbalanced, nearly falling backward. As it was, I only dropped my punch cup. It fell into the yew hedge. I felt it my responsibility to go after it and stuck my head into the interior of the shrubbery.

"Are you feeling okay?" I heard Robert ask.

"Fine, just fine," I answered and was rewarded with a twig in the mouth. I spat it out and pulled my head from the bush, snagging a portion of my carefully wrapped sari, unraveling it from around my head. I struggled with the loops of it for a moment. Robert looked on with a half-smile I didn't quite like. He looked like a bad rendition of the Cheshire Cat. I told him so and took the opportunity to throw a twig I'd removed from my hair at him. He laughed softly and came closer to me.

I moved away as quickly as I could, which seemed awfully slow somehow. In the process, I stubbed my toe on a root and barked out a Russian expletive so sordid that, although I had heard it and filed it away, I had never allowed myself to utter it. But why not? The moon was full, the night air cool; why not swear shockingly in Russian?

"Let me help you," Robert seemed to say from far away, though I felt his hands on me immediately.

I suppose he led me to a bench because that is where I next found myself. My sari was quickly coming unwoven and, try as

22

I might, I could not get the fabric rewrapped just right. Robert tried to help too, or so I thought until I realized the wrapping he was doing was much more like *un*wrapping. I was a bit confused on this point until, in the next moment, all I seemed to be wearing above the waist was the unnecessarily filmy and lacy strapless bra my stepmother had chosen for me.

"Hey!" I found myself complaining, though plenty of other words went through my mind.

Robert responded with a rough, "Hush now," and planted his punch-sweet lips over mine while his hand tried clumsily to unhook the aforementioned brassiere.

There is something to be said for muscle memory. I had practiced some basic aikido self-defense moves over and over after reading some horrifically sensationalized reports of the kidnapping of young women for the sex market. I had not for a moment believed its overblown allegations, but it was better to be prepared for anything, I thought. As foggy as my head felt at the moment when Robert inserted his disgustingly hot and roiling tongue in my mouth, my arms and legs knew exactly what to do. I twisted away from him, landed one elbow expertly on his sternum, and cracked the bone in his nose neatly with the heel of my hand.

I was rewarded for my efforts with a fantastic spray of blood. I stood quickly in alarm, shouting something profane I do not even remember. My torso was polka-dotted with drops of blood, the silk of my sari still more wrenched from me and trailing behind me in the grass.

"You bitch!" he screamed fuzzily through his broken nose, and it was a good thing he did scream or I might not have noticed when he launched at me. I saw him in slow motion, as cliché as that sounds, leaving me plenty of time to react. My foot went out and my elbow found its mark between his shoulder blades as he fell. His face landed in the mulch and he was still.

As I crouched down to check his breathing, I overbalanced again, and this time I did fall. Hard. On my rear. I sent my arms

23

back to catch myself and my hand hit something hard. Pulling myself back up to sitting, I examined my find: the crystal punch cup I had flung in the hedge. Hesitantly, I sniffed it.

And it was thusly that they found me: nose in a punch cup, sitting wide-legged in torn jeans, topless except for a thin wire frame of lace, yards of silk flowing behind me, copper curls sprung free from their wrappings.

Mr. Munston kneeled down to me immediately.

"Suny, are you okay?" He began to scratch at the grass behind me, gathering fabric.

"Samuel, if I may call you that in such a moment of extreme informality–" I began and then… then *he* stepped out away from the hedge into the moonlight. It is not of Mr. Munston I speak. He was still busily reining in my wandering sari. The man by the hedge was dark, his hair black and glinting like enamel in the glow of the moon. His eyes. I had no trouble at all seeing his eyes in the darkness. They were blue, a dark, gleaming blue, deep…

"Like sapphires," I said out loud, gaping plainly at him while Mr. Munston began to try to wrap me in the silk. *Like in the crystal ball…*

"'Clear as a sapphire without flaw or fleck, 'Twas here the siren lay in wait to wreck…'" I quoted from the depths of my foggy brain.

My sapphire-eyed man had begun to crouch down to check on the stirring Robert. He stopped when I spoke and gave me a quizzical look with those blue orbs. Meanwhile, Mr. Munston took the punch cup from my hands and sniffed it. "Doesn't smell like alcohol," he said to my mystery man.

"Probably Valium," Mystery Man answered, his voice soft and a bit deep. He looked at me again, still sprawled on the grass. "Something like that, I'd guess."

"Me too," I intoned ungrammatically, trying to match the lovely baritone. Brown. His voice made me think of the color brown.

I mouthed the word, "Brown," over and over, feeling it on

my tongue. Mystery Man caught me at it and gave a quick, lopsided grin before he took out a handkerchief and began to wipe blood gingerly away from Robert's cheeks. Robert's eyes fluttered.

"Who are you?" I whispered. His sapphire eyes looked up at me again. Mr. Munston continued to wind fabric around me. I realized he had been trying to get me to raise my arms for some time now. I complied and said, perhaps too loudly, "'Gold upon gold, would wrap him o'er and o'er, wrap him, and sing to him and set him mad...'" I grabbed the bundle of silk from him. He supported me as I stood.

Robert was sitting up now, staring blankly at me. I felt his stare deserved some response.

"You..." I began. "You...he..." I turned to Mr. Munston, "...is...you...are not nice," I finished lamely. And then, to punctuate my remarks, I stuck my tongue out at him. Mystery Man let out a snort that could have been a laugh, but my hazy brain could not be sure.

"You..." I began again, "you are an imperialistic, naïve... narrow-minded..." I couldn't think of a noun "...stupid-head," I finished and nodded to accentuate the point. "And your tongue tasted like old Kool-Aid," I said and wiped my own tongue on the silk half-wrapped around my arms.

"Come, Suny," Mr. Munston was cooing.

"What about him?" I asked, unwilling to leave as yet. I pointed vaguely at Robert and the man assisting him. I wasn't sure myself to whom I was referring.

"The young man will be disciplined and banned from mixers here if I have anything to do with it."*****

"Yes, yes, yes," I said, impatiently. "But who is that, Samuel, my dear?"

The man in question rose, leaving his handkerchief for Robert to busy himself with.

"I'm Anthony Scarborough. Your father's assistant. I'm here to take you to your new school."

I barely heard him speak. I took him in, standing again as he now was. He was about my height, and leaned toward stocky. He was well-muscled, but not unnaturally so. He dressed in khakis and a light sweater. He didn't look quite so manly to me now. He could almost have passed for one of the boys at the mixer. A stray wave of a curl had fallen over his eye as he had ministered to Robert. I had an urge to blow it up away from those deep blue eyes. I might even have pursed my lips to do it. He gave me another of those quizzical looks. Then Mr. Anthony Scarborough glanced up at his stray lock of hair and blew it up out of his eyes himself. He looked back at me and gave me a half-smile. It was disarming and I suddenly felt rather sober and blushed.

It was then his words filtered up from the nether regions of my drugged brain and hit me full force.

"New school? I'm not getting kicked out for...for... defending myself against this over-stimulated, psuedo-intellectual war-mongering cretin, am I?" I flung a length of silk at Robert.

Mr. Munston drew it back in and handed the fabric to me, explaining, "Your father emailed instructions to us just now. He's flown Mr. Scarborough in to escort you... We'll explain inside. Come now."

My head spun, along with my body as Mr. Munston turned me back to the building.

"'Then drag him down to no man knoweth where...'" I intoned, trying to get that warm, *brown* baritone just right as Mr. Munston dragged me, walking backward now, toward the terrace.

Mr. Anthony Scarborough must have been a true American teenager at one time because, as he led the hobbling Robert behind us, he gazed at me and rolled his eyes. I tried to mimic that expression as well as his voice, but it must have been too much for my over-taxed system. I think someone carried me from that point.

Chapter 3

I awoke with my cheek plastered to a clammy window that dripped rain. The faint, but acrid odor of car exhaust and damp air assaulted my nostrils. My hair was mushed flat on one side and sprang out on the other. My chin was wet with...well, apparently I had been sleeping heavily with my mouth open. I wiped my face on the sleeve of a shirt in which I did not recall dressing. A seatbelt pinned me uncomfortably to a leather seat. I pushed against it and turned toward the driver.

His face brought back some foggy memories: *the cut crystal pattern of a punch cup, red scattered polka-dots, cold bare feet, and silk on my skin.* My temples throbbed in protest when I tried to think further.

He looked over briefly and indicated a steaming styrofoam cup in a holder.

"Coffee," he informed me and turned his attention back to the road, peering out through fast-moving windshield wipers.

It was bad coffee, but hot and stimulating all the same. I tried not to look at him while I let the caffeine run its course through my system. I hoped it would revitalize my memory as well.

I was wearing sneakers with no socks, the sweatshirt upon which I had wiped my chin, and jeans cut raggedly at waist and cuff...and it all came back at that. I remembered the spat with Morgan, the mixer, the fight with...was his name Robert? And Mr. Munston helping me with my sari, rewrapping me...

I blushed as I recalled the situation.

I had been drugged. I had broken someone's nose. I had reeled half-naked across the terrace, then been carried by...not Samuel; he wouldn't have been able to lift my considerable weight up several flights of stairs.

It was this man, father's new assistant. Anthony, I thought I remembered him saying. I tried to shrivel into the space between the edge of my seat and the door. I tried to stop myself from remembering any more, but in that effort, I was unsuccessful.

Had I really sung Carly Simon loudly in his ear when I "came to" on the stair landing? He'd almost dropped me, if I remembered correctly. A mole. He had an angel kiss right behind his ear, at the base of his jaw. And Morgan. I had challenged her to a duel when, upon returning to our room, she wouldn't let me try on her borrowed coral heels. But that was much later, while Anthony had been packing for me.

Packing? I squinted at a road sign, only visible briefly through the rain as we passed. Delaware River Bridge, it read. Wasn't that beyond Baltimore? Well, wherever we were headed, it was northeast. I couldn't bring myself to look at Anthony, much less ask him for details about our destination.

I took advantage of a toll booth soon after to steal another look at him. My perceptions had not been at their most finely tuned the previous night, to say the least. I remembered his dark hair and his eyes—

Sapphires.

I blushed madly again, grateful he was too busy with the toll attendant to pay me any attention. He was handsome. My memory served me right on that account. But his good looks were earthy, casual. He was not one to primp, one could tell. In fact, he looked like he hadn't managed to drag a comb through his hair this morning.

Morning. I reflexively bent my arm up, looking for the time. My wrist was bare, but I noticed a clock on the dashboard. It was almost noon.

"We'll stop for lunch soon," Anthony offered, noticing my glance.

I nodded. "I'm fine, really, thank you."

My stomach let out an embarrassingly loud growl. I blushed again and felt annoyed. Anthony smiled a half-smile I think I'd seen before.

I fidgeted about. I am not averse, as a rule, to prolonged car trips, but I typically prepare for them very thoroughly. Along

28

with books requiring various degrees of concentration, CDs of music for different moods, a sack of periodicals, and perhaps a project of latch-hooking or beadwork, I invariably included in my provisions a day pack with a change of clothing and sundry toiletries. Feeling the lack of such articles, I endeavored to smooth my head and surreptitiously rubbed my equally hairy teeth with the evermore grimy sleeve of my sweatshirt.

Anthony reached back to the backseat, then dropped my canvas backpack into my lap.

"I grabbed some things I thought you might need. I mean, I packed everything, but I threw some things in there for today. We should be there by this evening." He looked doubtfully out at the rain.

"Thanks," I muttered. "For packing too, I guess. Had I known…"

"Well, as I'm learning, your father can be somewhat spontaneous. He decided on the spot to move you when he heard…well, your advisor contacted him last week. He had me make a slew of phone calls, made arrangements, then I suppose he forgot about it…" He glanced at me. I made my face impassive and watched the rain.

"Anyway, I was finishing up yesterday– God, was it only yesterday? I told him to enjoy his weekend with you. Well, next thing I know, I'm on a flight to Richmond. He had overscheduled and forgotten…So I was recruited as delivery boy to come down and fly us both on an early flight to Hartford. He sends his apologies."

I ignored this last. "Connecticut? A flight?"

"Well, what with having to pack for you, and then this hurricane–"

"Hurricane?"

"Lois, is it? Or Louise…I forget which, but we're ahead of it still. I think…" Anthony stared harder through the glass at the pelting rain. He had slowed the car considerably after the toll booth.

"So, excuse me if I'm a trifle slow to understand this

29

morning. You are saying our flight was cancelled because the storm is so bad, and instead you chose to drive in this?"

If I was not mistaken, Anthony's naturally olive skin deepened in color. Reddened, really.

"We missed the flight. I was up half the night packing for you since you were in no condition to do it yourself. Your father and I were up most of the night Thursday taking readings…I laid down for just a minute before dawn. There was no use going to a hotel. I had already packed your alarm clock. Well, you didn't wake up and I didn't wake up. And then all the later flights were cancelled because of the storm coming… Why am I making excuses? Your father wants you at school before Sunday morning so you can get oriented. How else could I have managed that?"

"You might have called him. I am sure that, while Father would prefer me to be ready to begin a new week of classes, a delay of perhaps a day…"

"You don't understand. I have to get back to work. And we had to pull some strings."

"We?"

But he did not answer and I pushed no further. I still thought it was odd. Anthony must have been an overly devoted assistant, as new as he was. Father did inspire that in people at times. But still. I wondered if Anthony didn't have his own reasons for wanting to get me to school so precipitously.

He had turned his attention back to the road. It was not a poor decision. The rain was beating so hard now that it was impossible to see beyond the hood of the car.

I used the silence to collect my own thoughts while I made a make-shift toilet, or washing-up, or…what do they say here in America? Freshening up helped my thoughts come clearer. Connecticut, he had said. I had never been to the northeast. My previous boarding school had been in Virginia as well, and while we had moved around a bit throughout the States when we were here, we had never alighted in the northeast.

I wondered briefly about my new school, but speculation

would do me little good and Anthony remained intent on the road. The speedometer hovered around thirty miles per hour and the strain of holding the steering wheel steady in the wind made the tendons in his forearms stand out in sharp relief.

Father's assistant. He went through assistants quickly. It was not because he was difficult to work with, but because he was obsessive and driven, forgetful and disorganized. They left because they couldn't keep up, or he forgot to pay them for months at a time. Anthony must have been with him only a short while. Father did inspire dedication in like-minded individuals, as I have related, but family errands on weekends? In a hurricane? He had never pushed an assistant quite so far as this.

I'd left Father this summer in Charleston. He was researching some local ghost legends and taking readings at certain historical sites. Why, I do not know. There was certainly a plethora of books written on the subject of Charleston ghosts. But he had hinted about some treasure legends, and about some little-known tales in the African-American community there. The Gullah women of Charleston wove ghost tales as well as sweet grass baskets.

I looked at Anthony. He didn't seem the type to spend hours typing transcriptions, reading atmospheric meters or developing film. He came across as more down to earth than most of father's assistants. He looked instead like he should be...perhaps chopping wood?

The car slowed, then stopped and idled.

"What do you want?" Anthony asked.

"Excuse me?"

"To eat."

"Oh." I hadn't even been able to tell we'd left the highway, but when I squinted to look past Anthony through his window, I could just make out the lighted menu board of a fast-food restaurant.

It was a fight to be understood through the speaker with the wind howling in the background. The young man who passed

31

us our bags of food obviously thought we were crazy to be out in this mess. Most people agreed with his sentiment, the parking lot showed; it lay empty and gray. The storm was moving more quickly than they had predicted, the burger flipper informed us. Anthony did not seem impressed with the information. As he pulled away from the window, his face was set in grim determination.

I insisted that he pull over into a parking space for us to eat. The rain was so torrential, I informed him, that I feared we would meet disaster if he attempted to chew his ground cow burger while steering. Anthony sighed in undue exasperation and yanked the steering wheel forcefully to pull the car aside. He tore into his meal as if it had once done him a wrong, while rain thumped on the roof with surprising force. I was unsure whether his behavior was due to his desire to throw my comment concerning the meal's animal origin back in my face, or whether it was to dispense with the meal as quickly as possible to get back on the road.

"Ready to go?" Anthony asked, balling up the remains of his burger wrapper.

I had been picking at a wilted salad after finishing a dry baked potato but I set it aside.

"Actually, if there's any way you could pull up closer to the building, I…"

That was enough for Anthony. He got my meaning and moved the car as close to the door as was possible. I was drenched immediately however and sloshed my way into the restaurant to find the facilities.

I ran back out and dove into the car.

" My hair is actually dripping!" I exclaimed as I pulled the door shut against the wind.

A snore was my only answer.

Chapter 4

I sat for quite a while as the rain fell and the wind rocked the car. Anthony was deeply asleep. Having myself suffered sleep deprivation with Father when he was bent on getting night after night of recordings and readings, I didn't have the heart to wake Anthony just yet. I wanted to get a weather report, but the radio was all static. Either we had lost our antenna in the wind, or a tower was affected by the storm as well. I hoped it would pass soon. Still hungry after my paltry meal, I mused irritably about the state of American restaurant offerings for some time.

Although I worked myself into quite a tizzy, I managed to keep from marching through the deluge to register my complaints with the restaurant manager. Such displays of dissatisfaction seldom brought results, I'd found. So, while I composed a letter to the corporate headquarters in my head, I used my time to peruse the map. Once I'd managed to get it out from under Anthony's muscled thigh, that is. He'd charted our route but, much to my surprise, the inked line passed up along the east coast and ended in western Massachusetts, in a small town called Mt. Billington.

Looking up from the map, I thought that perhaps the rain had lightened some. I had sat with Anthony snoring softly for over a half hour. How long, after all, could a storm last? Father and I had left Honduras before hurricane season and I had been only two at the time. I had never experienced such a storm as this. The burger flipper had said it was moving faster than expected. Maybe it was winding down here now.

I gently nudged Anthony to no avail. He was even more deeply asleep now. His oversized lunch of red meat and grease had only added to the depth of his repose. I nudged him a bit harder as I was sure now that the storm was lessening. And frankly, I was bored. He seemed to sit up for a moment and then began to slide toward me.

I scooted forward as quickly as I could, and as a result, he fell across the front bench seat and sprawled against my door. He then began to snore in earnest. Seeing as how the majority of his form now rested in my seat, I found I had no place to sit. I clambered awkwardly over his legs, my own long limbs tangling with the steering wheel and gearshift. I managed to squeeze myself against the driver's side door and, with successively firmer shoves, succeeded in moving the rest of Anthony into the passenger seat. He slept so soundly I thought he might not awaken even if I had stuck his head out of the window into the rain.

The precipitation had definitely fallen off now and, aside from a queer cast of light to the sky, all was calm and seemingly normal.

I looked at the clock. It was nearing two in the afternoon. Anthony had scrawled times on the map. He'd planned a dinner stop at six just outside of New York City, then a continuing trip north into Massachusetts, where he'd penciled, "ETA 10 p.m." and another note, irrelevant to me, I supposed, "Call Kathy."

Well, we were going to need to sally forth, as they say, if we were to get there even by midnight now. I fingered the rental company logo keychain that hung from the ignition, musing. It took me only another minute to wrangle a seatbelt around snoring Anthony and then we were off.

While I hadn't managed to shop much over the summer, I had made a point of acquiring a driver's license. I had been driving for many years, as Father had always been quick to make use of anybody who was around when he needed an errand run or a pick-up made. I was no exception and, though I tried to dissuade him, citing various countries' penalties for unlicensed vehicle operation, he pooh-poohed my concerns and I was made to learn at the age of twelve. Luckily for him, I was taller than average even then and had no trouble reaching the requisite pedals and such.

I had no trouble now as I headed the car back to the

highway. I had not been able to see the road as we'd left it for the restaurant, so it is only to be expected that I made a few wrong turns. The roads were very wet and even flooded in places, but after having driven through cobbled medieval towns in Europe, where a narrow road meant tucking in your side mirrors and praying, U.S. streets of any kind were easily navigated. When we reached the highway again, it was truly smooth sailing.

We passed deeper into Delaware quickly. The storm seemed to be lingering here. The rain began again and continued to increase in intensity. The bridge over the river was subject to heavy cross-winds, or so the posted signs warned, but I had the road almost to myself, so when the car was harder to control than I expected, and I found myself on the left side of the road, it was of little consequence.

I had thought the winds heavy on the bridge, but they seemed to pick up even more after I left it. As I took my ticket from the New Jersey Turnpike's automated machine, a gust almost ripped it from my grasp. It was all I could do to get the window up again before I had a puddle in my lap.

Winds had twice forced me to the shoulder before I voluntarily pulled over. Gusts rocked the car and Anthony stirred. I pulled out the map. We had not gotten far. The turnpike snaked up the state. There were plenty of exits that led inland. That would be the way to avoid the strongest throes of the storm, would it not? I counted up how many exits until the next westbound one, and directed the car back onto the road.

There were surprisingly few cars on the turnpike, which was a major thoroughfare, I had thought. Even taking into account the stormy conditions, I was amazed at my inability to make out the outline of any other vehicle near me. But then, I was unable to see beyond the sheet of water that washed over the windshield despite the hyperactivity of the wipers, so the road could have been bumper to bumper and I wouldn't have been the wiser.

Goodness, I thought. I had driven in sand storms, and even through London's famous fogs, but nothing compared to the combination of wind and torrential rain that had my arms aching as I tried to keep the car on the road. When the third exit finally appeared through the gray, I blindly pulled off. I found the toll gate abandoned, with barrier arm frozen two-thirds of the way up, and squeaked by, hoping Anthony had taken the optional rental insurance against paint damage.

The next two hours were a nightmare. I could not tell how far I had managed to steer the car through the hammering rain and wind. I could barely make out the road, much less any signs alongside it. I forgot everything outside the world of the weak beams my headlights as we advanced against the pummeling water. My whole body was tensed and my mind was focused in its single purpose.

Therefore, I am sure one would have to agree that when Anthony woke up and let out a squawk, I could be expected to do nothing less than run into a tree.

Taking into account my decidedly slow pace, I knew that little damage could have occurred. It took me a moment to figure out that the tree was the least of the reasons why Anthony took to yelling at full volume. I put the car in park and tried to steady my shaking hands.

A large branch from the aforementioned tree stopped Anthony in his tirade. It landed with a mighty thud across the hood of the car and brought with it a sprinkling of smaller branches that scattered across the windshield before being lifted away in the wind. Anthony looked up through the rain, and though I am sure he could not see anything in the gray of pouring water, he must have heard, as I did, the ominous creaking of limbs about to fall.

Anthony leaned over me, fumbled for the latch, then shoved at the door. He pushed me out, scrambled after me, and ran, trailing me behind him from where his hand gripped my arm like a vise. Water streamed off his nose and eyebrows as he turned and watched, as I did, a cascade of branches shower the car. I could not ascertain if they had pierced glass. Anthony did not give me any time. He remained clamped to my arm and threw himself against the onslaught of the wind.

I didn't know we'd reached a house until I tripped up the steps. A storm door slapped loudly against its frame only to be torn open again in the wind.

Anthony tried the door, then cursed forcefully, loudly enough that I heard him over the howling gale. He pulled me stumbling down the steps and through thorny bushes that raked my hands and ankles.

We tripped up another flight of steps, then miraculously, we were through a heavy wood door, which Anthony shut behind us as quickly as the hateful wind would allow.

"Oh, thank goodness for someplace dry!" I exclaimed.

Anthony lost no time. Through his panting breath, he managed to continue his lecture. "What were you thinking? Why didn't you pull over? Were you trying to get us killed? Do you know where we are? Do you even know how to drive? I can't believe this…if you weren't his daughter…" He wound down to mumbling.

Usually I can give back verbal abuse as well or better than I get it, but I seemed to have run dry this weekend. I sat down hard on the bottom step of a wide, polished stair and tried not to cry.

The windows rattled incessantly and once there was a loud crack, which only could have been another tree succumbing to the storm. Aside from that, I immediately felt safe in the big, sturdy old house we had invaded.

I was sure it was unoccupied. If Anthony's first shouted admonitions had not brought tenants running, surely his noisy trampings throughout the ground floor would have. I gathered he was still quite upset as he took no pains to tread softly in his squelching sneakers, nor did he try to close any doors quietly after he concluded his tour. I heard a chair scrape back over tile toward the back of the house. Several minutes of silence ensued. My melancholy self-pity soon gave way to annoyance. I decided to venture forth in my own explorations. In particular, I searched for one particular sort of facility.

Upon washing up, I noted the soaps were inscribed with "Groately's Seaside Inn" and some stylized gulls. I nodded my appreciation for the homeowner's frugality. I always made full use of the complimentary toiletries left for me at way stations of hospitality. My make-up bags never left a vacation establishment empty.

I was soon disabused of the notion that the homeowners shared my parsimony. I followed the sound of Anthony's grumbling and found him in a dining room. It did not hold a typical dining set. Rather he was seated at one of eight small tables. He had a beer bottle in one hand. Another sat empty at his elbow. It seemed he was helping himself to what I'm sure was not normally a complimentary beverage at the Groatley's Seaside Inn. He recognized my presence and put his bottle down on a gull emblazoned coaster.

Funny how gulls kept cropping up.

"Where are we?" I asked.

Anthony snorted unbecomingly in disbelief.

"You drove us here," he stated blandly.

"But I turned inland…"

"Tell that to the seagull," he said flippantly, pointing to yet another of the inescapable birds, this one hanging from the ceiling in a manner I'm sure some unlucky diner beneath it would have found disconcerting.

"But…"

"Did you cross back over the highway? Oh, never mind…"

"But there's no one here…" I went on, voicing thoughts without connecting them.

"Hurricane Evacuation Area, my dear."

And as if to underline his remarks, something large slammed against the side of the building and blew in a blur past the window.

The sound startled me and set me to shivering. I was

drenched to the skin and, though the house was warm enough, wet cotton does not hold heat well.

Anthony stood.

"There's no phone service here for my cell, and the house phone is dead. The inn has no TV, though I bet there's one in the owner's cottage across the way. It's amazing we have electricity. I don't think there's much chance…Let's…" He didn't finish, but led me to the side stairs and propelled me up them and along a dark hallway. He peeked in doors along the way, but ultimately, we went through a double set of heavy doors with "Anemone Suite" engraved on a ceramic - one could guess immediately– gull mounted over the knob.

We found ourselves in a small sitting room. I could see an ensuite bath through another door.

"I'm going to look around," Anthony said and left me.

I ran a bath and drowsed in the warm water. As my shivering subsided, my mind searched back through the horrific series of events since I had driven away from the restaurant in what I now recognized had been the infamous eye of the storm. Again, I had no experience in such matters, so I felt I could hardly be blamed for attempting to make the best of the situation as it had presented itself to me at the time.

How I had managed to leave the turnpike so disastrously was the next negative wondering that crept into my head. I put it down to fate. Direction was not my strong suit. There was that time in Kenya, for instance, as Father was investigating at the Gedi Ruins when, in my puerile naiveté, I had wandered off to do what I thought was an extremely important population count of the Gold-banded Forester, a common butterfly that makes its home in the forests surrounding the ruins. I had been unable to navigate my way back to camp. They had searched for hours.

Thus satisfied that I had done only what could have been expected of me and that landing us in a quaint seaside inn, albeit with accompanying hurricane, was perhaps not the most horrific of all possible blunders, I turned my thoughts to hot

Kenya. These thoughts, along with the warmth of a soothing bath, allowed me to drift off for some time. I woke with the water cold and the house creaking mightily in the wind. I dried myself quickly and made use of the thick robe and slippers the Anemone Suite provided. I hung my dripping articles over the tub and found my way back into the sitting room.

The suite was apparently set up for honeymooners. There was a cellophane-wrapped basket of cheeses and fruit and a bottle of champagne that I managed to pop open after I had chilled it as well as possible in a sink of cold water. I did not want to venture out for ice. I wasn't ready to see Anthony yet. I needed to build up my strength a bit before another encounter.

I needn't have worried. Anthony found me when he was good and ready.

"You're too young to drink."

I made a show of draining my flute and pouring another.

"How very Puritan of you, Anthony. I've been drinking wine– with meals and in moderation– for many years. Americans wouldn't have so much trouble with teens drinking if…"

"Americans? You say it as if you weren't one yourself. And seeing as how you are in America, and how you are in my care as well…" And with that he yanked the flute from my hand. I started indignantly, then seeing the rings around his eyes and his tired frown, I relaxed. He was so easy to fight with but neither of us was really up to the strain.

I moved to the window seat that nestled in a broad bay window and stared at the rain. Anthony came to my side.

"Here," he offered, handing me back the champagne. "I really don't care enough right now."

He watched the rain with me. "We'll never be able to leave tonight."

I turned to him. "Why in the world is it so important for us to get there tonight?" I demanded.

His blue eyes flared, but he did not answer. "We really should go lower in the house," he blurted instead.

"I thought that was for tornadoes."

"You know what? I don't think you've taken in one thing I've said without an argument!"

"I am merely trying to dialogue as to what is the best..."

Anthony stormed out of the room, slamming the door. I had meant to apologize about my judgment and driving, but now I had no intention of doing so. After all, he had been so very asleep.

"I do have a license, by the way!" I screamed at the closed door.

Chapter 5

Anthony soon discovered that the larder at Groatley's Seaside Inn had been abandoned fully stocked. Cooking smells wafted up to me, and I was forced to admit that they were good enough to draw me downstairs. I could not assume that Anthony would cook for me, especially in his present state of annoyance, unjustified though it might be. I walked into the kitchen showing, I hoped, my confidence that I had just as much right to be there as he. Anthony took time from chopping vegetables to scowl at me. I ignored him, found a bag of pasta in the pantry, and was trying to remove a large pot from its perch when I met his angry blue eyes.

"Sit," he commanded. And, quite unlike my usual self, I obeyed. I watched with growing admiration as he sautéed vegetables and seared tuna. When it was finished, in quite good time, Anthony presented it with what approached a smile. I allowed myself to partake of the fish, something I have to admit I had missed in my years as a vegetarian, only in an attempt to further mend the rift. It was startlingly good. Anthony explained, in answer to my appreciative noises, that he had worked his way through college as something of a sous chef.

Anthony did not blink when I opened a bottle of wine from the small, but good cellar I had found while he cooked. As he took a sip, his face relaxed. I think he approved of the selection and we finished the bottle between us.

A good meal often leads one to a state of calm contentment. The rain was still strong, but the wind had died. We sat for a while at the table afterward, saying nothing. Anthony closed his eyes and I followed suit after a moment, listening to the storm.

I opened my eyes and caught Anthony staring at me. He looked away quickly, but there had been something in that look. Something…Well, I was not allowed to dwell on it long, for in his discomfort, Anthony stood and procured a dishrag, which he threw at me unceremoniously.

"Cooks don't clean," he announced and smiled wickedly at me. His sapphire eyes positively danced as he registered my surprise. I stayed, dumbfounded, as he took a pint of ice cream from the freezer, found himself a spoon and left the room.

I had, of course, planned to offer to clear away the dinner leavings, but I sulked as I filled the sink with suds. I would be quite happy to move on in the morning, I thought and violently scrubbed a pan.

When I had left the kitchen sparkling, I found my own pint of ice cream from the decadent array the freezer contained. I found Anthony in the parlor. He had discovered a games closet somewhere and was enthusiastically setting up Scrabble. He challenged me to a game with the same devilish taunt in his eyes. I steeled my own gaze and accepted.

I have always been very good at word games and I often found that opponents suffered poorly at the disillusionment with their own skill that facing me provided. Not so with Anthony. He played with a ferocity that I felt was due in equal parts to his intelligence and to his frustration at our situation. If ever I had played someone who matched my skill, it was now. When it was over, it was not easily apparent who had won. Anthony tallied the points. He had beat me by four.

"No one's ever come that close to beating me," he said with what I thought was genuine appreciation. "Not even… well, no one." He grew quiet again.

It was not disappointment at my loss that led me to seek the comfort of the long parlor couch. I was more tired than I remembered being for a long time. I closed my eyes as Anthony played with the tiles. Their soft clicking lulled me.

"Tell me about my new school," I murmured, determined to stay awake at least a bit longer into the evening.

"Your father asked me not to."

I opened my eyes at that.

"What do you mean?"

"Relax, Suny. It's just not a typical school and your father thought you might have reservations."

"It's not something bizarre like a Druid school, is it?"

Anthony laughed. It was a fabulous laugh, deep and mellow, and it served to distract me momentarily from my protest. Sorry his back was to me as he sat at the table, I wondered if his eyes twinkled when he laughed. Shaking myself out of these thoughts, I explained.

"He sent me to a Druid summer camp once, you know. When we were in England. Talk about a convocation of dopes! I pray he hasn't saddled me with a whole year of idiocy!"

Anthony's shoulders shook.

"It wasn't funny, I can tell you. To belittle the industrious architectural triumphs of a truly spiritual civilization by dancing naked under a solstice moon around monoliths of stone...I don't care what anyone says, the south of England is still quite chilly on a June evening..."

Anthony spun in his chair.

"You danced naked at Stonehenge?"

I closed my eyes again, a half-smile on my own lips this time. It did seem comic in the retelling. The exact details of that long ago midnight I would not share. And I had seen his eyes as he'd continued to laugh. They did truly sparkle like sapphires.

I expected to hear the renewed clicking of Scrabble tiles being arranged, but only the continuing pelting of the rain met my ears. After a moment, the hair on the back of my neck stood up, despite my reclining position. I heartily wished I had an afghan to pull over me. I wouldn't lower myself to check, but I could feel Anthony's eyes on my body, scantily clad as it was in the too-short robe I had belted loosely around me. I cursed my father silently. Why couldn't his assistants be female? But I knew that my present stepmother's influence was the answer. Father was not to be trusted with a female assistant for long.

After a moment, my ears told me Anthony had gone back to his game.

"I promise you, they're not freaks," he said softly. "I know

45

some of them personally. In fact, it's my alma mater."

Aha, I thought. So this was where the 'we pulled some strings' comes in. No wonder Father had sent Anthony to deliver me. Who better than someone familiar with the terrain? And I bet I knew the name of one of the people he knew personally. I wondered how old this Kathy was. She couldn't have been older than eighteen. That would make Anthony a "cradle-robber," a term I had learned last year when I had happened to hear some discussion amongst the girls as to who might be the lucky one to win Mr. Munston's heart. Idiocy rears its ugly head in many a place.

I drowsed, imagining what Anthony had looked like at sixteen. He was not so much older now, I supposed. I thought of asking him his exact age, but I didn't want to let him think I was interested. And, in any case, I wasn't interested in him really. He was pleasing to look upon, but I doubted that any man could hold my attention for long. I speculated that, in matters of the heart, I would be much like my father. Although it was not an exaggeration to call him promiscuous, he was something of a romantic. I suppose I was as well. That tendency was compounded by Mr. Munston's literature classes and my own readings. Love was something to await, something one would recognize immediately and cherish forever. Well, not the forever part, perhaps if I did take after Father in that way, but one never knew. The idea of love at first sight was foolish perhaps, but I was a sixteen-year-old girl, after all. And all I recognized immediately when gazing upon Anthony's handsome face, was that he was infuriatingly condescending and quick to judge other's good intentions. Compounded by the fact that he worked for Father, so he obviously hadn't a brain in that pretty head, as anyone who might believe all that nonsense...

"Damn," I heard him mutter through the fog of my fatigue.

"Forage," I mumbled. "Try forage."

Silence shot through the room like electricity. It was followed by the deliberate clicking of tiles being arranged, then silence again.

"Suny?"

I pretended to be asleep. Therein lay the safest course, I thought. Russian expletives of the most lurid shot through my mind. I had let my guard down and now…

Anthony turned in his chair. Once again this evening, I could feel his eyes on me.

"Suny?"

I mumbled something irrational to do with turnips, but I don't think he was fooled. His chair creaked as he stood. His steps brought him closer.

"Like father, like daughter, huh?" I heard from above me.

I shut my eyes more firmly.

He hovered, then left the room, his footsteps echoing in the empty hall.

I stood quickly and went to the table.

"Hell and damnation," I muttered.

Aligned on the wooden surface was the word– FORAGE. Only a ten pointer, but I had gotten it right.

Suny, Suny, such a *dubiina*! Did I have to be such a *viyebnutsa*?

I suppose it had been the wine. And the champagne. And perhaps even the hurricane. Rarely did I knowingly express anything I had sensed. It was never very fruitful.

I should explain. I do not consider my abilities as abilities, really. They are so mild that I am sure that what I sense at times is simply the same as anyone who bothered to focus their attention might notice. Father had tried to push me, but I absolutely refused to try to "develop" what was obviously only a healthy dose of intuition.

We all know someone who can't take a hint, who needs to be hit over the head with an implication before they respond. Well, that's one end of the spectrum, I believe. The other end is simply a heightened ability to involuntarily pick up on those stimuli. Most likely, Anthony had been muttering as he picked each letter tile and looked at it, and I had simply heard him subconsciously, stored the information, and then processed the mutterings without being conscious that I was doing any of it. It was a kind of hyperactivity of mind. I always tried to keep my mind occupied with something of some actual use so that these unwanted interferences were kept to a minimum.

I was fairly successful at that. The Scrabble incident was the only one in a while. Well, some might try to suggest that my dressing like Morgan's St. Thomas outfit was indicative... and then there was the whole crystal ball phenomenon... No, I wouldn't be drawn into speculating about coincidences that might occur to anyone.

Some have a subconscious that only comes alive in dreaming. Others are cursed with one that actually settles in to work on practical matters, using the information with which it is constantly bombarded every day. Lacking a filter for useless stimuli is not a blessing, as much as Father might have tried to convince me of that in my earlier life. I give no credence to the testing to which he subjected me when I was young. I was immature and suggestible and had not yet realized that anyone who excels in any area other than academics is made to look a monkey on a stage. I hoped Father had burned those studies. He had been more than disappointed when I had allowed my scores to drop off so he would leave me alone.

Over the years, I had become very good at pooh-poohing events of this kind as they unfortunately chose to occur. I quickly closed up the Scrabble game and found a passably intelligent read from the Inn's library. I retired to the ridiculously large bed of the Anemone Suite, shedding my bulky robe and snuggling into the covers.

The wind had died considerably, but the rain pattered on. I had always enjoyed the sound of rain on the roof and I found myself glad of the break the storm and my unfortunate navigation afforded. I was quite used to adjusting quickly to new surroundings, but to be thrown from one school into the next over the course of a harried, not to mention drugged, weekend was not my idea of fun. A peaceful rainy night in an abandoned inn was just what my nerves needed.

I was not halfway through my book when the rhythm of the rain and the fatigue of the day overcame me. I slept soundly until a loud clap of thunder woke me with a start. It was followed by another flash of lightning and accompanying thunder and, in that electric glare, I saw a form perched on the side of my bed.

It was quite the weekend for muscle memory. Instinctively, I sat up and shot the heel of my hand forward, connecting for the second time this weekend with a nose.

"Christ almighty! What the hell....oh, for god's sake, pull up your sheet! Jesus, Mary, and Joseph, Suny! Why'd you...?"

I cut him off.

"Do you have any sense in your head? What did you suppose I might do upon waking in a strange place with a dark form leering from my bedside! Hand me my robe!"

"I wasn't leering at you, for god's sake...hell, this hurts! I was sleeping in the sitting room and the thunder woke me and then the lights went out. I wanted to ... to check on you. I thought you might be..."

"I'm fine. Hand me my robe."

"I think I'm safer with you confined to your bed."

"You are dripping blood and we should look for candles, and I am now fully awake thanks to you!"

Anthony threw my robe at me and then went to moan to himself in the bathroom. I already knew that said chamber did not contain a first aid kit. I inventoried the contents of the bedside table but they contained no candles, only some discreetly packaged prophylactics and a complimentary tube of...well, marital aid.

The room was pitch black and I cautiously made my way around unfamiliar furniture. Anthony had found the sink and was splashing about. I followed the noise and soon found him.

"Suny! That's my foot."

"Sorry."

"You can't help me in here in the dark. If you want to be

49

useful, find some candles."

I left him and stumbled my way back out to the sitting room. Remembering the approximate location of the fireplace, I felt my way there, hoping they had stocked it with supplies even though it was early in the season. Luck was with me and I breathed a sigh of relief as I walked back to the bathroom, my finger on the trigger of a gas-fed firestarter.

Anthony's nose was not broken; it was only bleeding. He cursed quite a bit though and refused to put his head down, though I told him it was the fastest way to stop the flow.

He glared at me in the flame's light, his eyes flashing. I took pains to remain aloof and not succumb to his unspoken, but obvious demand for an apology. I was tempted, though. He did look quite the disheveled hero, with his hair sleep-tousled and his shirt off, face battered as it was. And I looked the part of the heroine worth protecting as well. The bath's mirror showed my hair wreathing my face in a halo of curls, draped down to the white of my throat, robe collar open, breast heaving with my still-startled breath. The pair of us looked straight out of a gothic romance. And to accentuate my observations, lightning flashed again.

The sound seemed to awaken Anthony to action. He brushed by me roughly and stalked out of the circle of light into the sitting room.

"Where are you going in the dark?" I called after him.

"Away from you," he answered, which was neither polite nor specific.

The next morning broke with the sun feebly trying to peek through the still, gray skies. The rain had dropped to a drizzle and, apparently, Anthony had made a run out to the car for some of our things. I found my knapsack and a small suitcase on the dressing stand when I woke.

I dressed quickly and straightened the room the best I could. Anthony had done the same downstairs, including in his courtesy a note of apology and thanks to the owners, along with Father's phone number. I did not find Anthony himself, however, until I made my way out onto the porch. He picked his way through fallen limbs and twigs as he stepped out of the rental car, its dented hood and crumpled fender the only apparent casualties of my driving misadventure.

He wiped his face on a wet sleeve and winced as he brushed his nose.

"The engine's fine, as far as I can see."

"May I?" I inquired, indicating the hood.

Anthony's raised eyebrows were not quite an answer, but I ignored them and lifted the hood anyway.

"So…how's it look in there?" he asked after a moment, condescension dripping from every word.

"Well…" I answered, letting the hood slam shut loudly when really, the poor car had been through enough already. "It is harder to tell anything about the engines in these newer models. One would need a diagnostics machine in order to be sure, but I can see no cracks on the manifold, or the head gaskets, so I concur with your finding."

I looked around for something with which to wipe my hands, but found nothing. Anthony stared at me, drops of rain holding like little balls of silver in his dark hair.

"Why do you stand there, staring?"

Anthony only shook his head and grabbed my suitcase, which he managed to wedge in amongst my other belongings in the back seat.

"Why should you be so surprised? When one is likely to be camped for a good length of time in areas which may be remote, it behooves one to know a little something about…"

"Suny, get in the car."

I obeyed without further comment, which was becoming a bad habit.

His last command was about all I heard from him for the next six hours, other than informing me that Father was unreachable by phone, but he had left word with the research group as to our status. He seemed to be brooding about something. Perhaps he still felt the pain I had inflicted upon him last night. His nose did look a trifle swollen still. Judging by how often he checked his watch, however, I suspected it might be more than that.

It took us a while to weave through the fallen trees and debris of the town but, as we moved down the road that led to the turnpike, we made good time. The radio, which Anthony had managed to get working, told us that Hurricane Louise had not hit quite as hard as they had expected in coastal areas, but had still been one of the biggest storms seen this far north in a long time.

The radio played and Anthony did not speak. I found a small comfort in the fact that we seemed to share the same musical taste. It would have been a trying trip otherwise.

We made our way past New York City and continued northward, making much better time than I would have imagined possible. It seemed that despite our late start and my...uh... directional misadventure, we would arrive soon, with much of the daylight left.

I busied myself with the map, though Anthony did not need my help in navigating at this point. There was no airport closer to Mt. Billington than Hartford, in the next state over. Had we flown, we would still have made more than an hour's drive on back roads to arrive in the Berkshire Hills of Massachusetts. Father seemed to have dumped me in the middle of nowhere this time.

I ran my finger along the penned line of our route. When my finger touched the little dot that read Mt. Billington, my vision blurred and instead of the map, I saw a swirling of leaves driven hard by a harsh wind, swirling up and up toward my face, a black emptiness in their wake, threatening to overtake them, to bring with it...

"Oh!" I pushed the map off my lap and blinked hard.

"Are you okay?" Anthony turned from the road a moment to glance at me.

"Fine. Fine. Whatever do you mean?" I composed myself.

He eyed me again for a moment. Just to reassure him, I retrieved the map and held it firmly across my knees.

As we turned off the northbound parkway, we wound through small town after small town. Anthony did not refer to the map once. It was obvious he was in familiar surroundings.

I was trying to forget the unfortunate imaginings of my road-trip-lulled brain and enjoying the bit of sunshine that peeked through the clouds, when Anthony finally spoke.

"Where did you ever learn Aldrich?"

"Aldrich?"

"Yeah. You were quoting Aldrich…at the mixer. When you were…"

"Oh, God. Was I?"

Sapphires…

Balvan! It had been those eyes. Sapphires piercing through the dark.

"Suny?"

"Aldrich. Well, you see, I was reading the works of Twain this past summer and was interested to learn that he was influenced in the writing of Tom Sawyer by a little known novel…"

"*The Story of a Bad Boy,*" Anthony supplied.

"Yes, quite so. And that, of course, led to my perusal of Aldrich's other works." I shut up quickly, hoping Anthony would let it drop. The quote could only have meaning in reference to the color of his eyes, and I was blushing madly already. But no such luck.

"They made me study Aldrich as part of a regional authors course. Aldrich is from New Hampshire, you know."

"Portsmouth," my brain produced before I could stop my tongue.

Anthony glanced at me quickly.

"Yes, that's right. I analyzed 'The Laurelei' for that class. It was interesting when you started to quote it as soon as I showed up." He looked suggestively at me.

Whether he was trying to get me to say I'd read his mind, or

53

trying to make me admit that his eyes had been inspiration enough, in my drugged state, to move me to quote poetry, I don't know. But I didn't care to find out either. I chose to remain silent. I wished his mind would wander to something else. Like to this Kathy person perhaps. I decided to help him along in that direction.

"Who's Kathy?" I asked and plucked at where her name was written, only a bit wary of touching the map.

It was Anthony's turn to blush. "Just a friend at the college," he muttered and as if to change the subject, he added, "We'll be there soon, by the way. You might want to fix your face or something."

My indignant glare at this unnecessary suggestion was interrupted by the dawning realization that he had not said "school." He had said *college!*

And it was then that I saw the first sign on the side of the road. It read, "Preacher's Ledge College, 7 miles."

Chapter 6

"Preacher's Ledge began as an experiment."

The voice belonged to a fiftyish woman dressed casually on this Sunday afternoon when she might otherwise have been raking leaves. Her hair was pulled back loosely into a bun and she wore no make-up on her smiling face. She had greeted Anthony with a warm embrace and had introduced herself to me only as Sylvia. When she had taken my hand, she had enfolded it, more than shaken it, in welcome. She now perched on the corner of her desk, which I could hardly believe was more comfortable than sitting properly on a chair, seeing as the style in which the desk was constructed left the corners rather sharp.

"A group of graduate students at the state university began to mentor some gifted kids in an after-school program. The program leaders invited the kids on a field trip to campus to sit in on some of the university's undergraduate courses. The professors there were so impressed with the students that some of them came on board and together they hatched a plan for Preacher's Ledge, an undergraduate college for high-school age students where the gifted could pursue higher academics without being thrown into a traditional college setting.

"One of the professors donated this land, a farm called Preacher's Ledge, and we've been teaching students here for over thirty years. Our population is a small, but we feel optimal, 400 students. Our professors are some of the brightest and most innovative teachers in the nation. In fact, one of our professors was a child prodigy of some note himself. Our graduating seniors have already completed graduate caliber theses on topics ranging from rainforest pharmacology to microcredit community building to medieval music and dance.

"Most go on to some of the finest graduate schools in the nation. Like Anthony here. Now, having…uh, rather quickly… reviewed your test scores and records, I believe you'll fit right in. Welcome."

I could do little but nod to acknowledge her sentiment. I had been shocked speechless by Anthony's revelation as to the type of institution I was to attend and I had remained not quite my loquacious self even as he led me through the administrative building, a converted stone and timber barn. Now, having received the orientation spiel from Sylvia, who was apparently some type of administrator, though I had yet to learn her last name, much less her title, I found myself in the rare state of being at a loss for words.

"Well then, do you have any questions before we tour the campus and get you situated?"

Did I have any questions? Here I was, dumped yet again by my father in some out-of-the-way spot, dragged unceremoniously through a hurricane over the course of a single weekend, and then I find out that, without consulting me, he has chosen to stick me this time with a bunch of under-age, overly cerebral misfits?

The dam was breaking. I had to say something.

"So…this is a school for geniuses?"

"Well, we don't like to frame it that way." I could tell I had succeeded in unsettling Sylvia to some extent. "Our students' test scores are above average. Your scores— we are lucky that your last school required testing for preparatory reasons— your scores are actually exceedingly high, even by our standards. You've maxed your verbal—"

"Maxed my verbal? How…how ridiculous to think that phrase has any meaning! That I can read a book and understand it, is that what it means? Do you know how long it took me to fully grasp the workings of an internal combustion engine?"

"Excuse me?" Sylvia was openly flustered at this point, and I didn't dare look over at Anthony.

"Several attempts, I can assure you. And even then I lacked the upper body strength to use the tools required in the manner for which they were designed. Of course, after adopting a course of circuit-weight training, pinpointing the upper body, and some effort in re-engineering–"

"We have a state of the art gymnasium with a full complement of circuit and free weights–"

"I'm sure the facilities here are adequate. I was referring, however, to the inadequacy of standardized testing to fully indicate the many and varied intelligences possessed by the human individual. I don't know if I can enroll in an institution that separates out those with the highest scores on today's standardized tests. I may test high in your estimation, but–"

"Suny, they don't teach auto mechanics here. But they do teach Arabic," Anthony interrupted me to speak for the first time since our arrival.

"Oh."

It was quite unnerving how good Anthony was at getting me to shut up.

"Well then," Sylvia breathed. "Uh, good. So let me just get some of this paperwork finalized. I hear Anthony calling you 'Suny.' Do you prefer that to your full name? Well, I guess you might. Four names all squeezed into the first name spot on the application your father faxed. And that, even with a short surname is quite a mouthful. We weren't sure if you would go by just Simone, or if you expected us to call you Ursula, Nicole, and Yvonne all after that. Oh! Isn't that clever! I didn't notice that: an acronym. Suny. I see."

Sylvia shuffled through some more papers. I tried to ignore Anthony's smirk and to keep from blushing. But, of course, Anthony couldn't let it lie.

"Why the four names, Simone?" he asked softly while Sylvia scrounged for a pen.

I raised my eyebrows quite high at him, an expression I have down pat, as opposed to my as yet amateurish rolling of the eyes.

"If you must know," I hissed, "I was named after my mother."

I hoped to leave it at that and I was only successful due to his distraction by the stack of papers Sylvia foisted upon him to sign on my father's behalf. My four names were the result of my father's lack of imagination and his wish not to dishonor whichever of the four women might actually have been my mother. It had been quickly shortened to Suny, and no one had ever dared to call me Simone.

I glared at Anthony's bent head as he huddled over the desk. I suppose he had forgotten what I'd done to that Robert person back at Broadman. There is only so far I will allow myself to be pushed. Anthony would do well to remember that and forget my unfortunate string of imbecilic names.

Sylvia looked me over and tried to catch my eye. I avoided hers and ended up standing to study the art on the walls as if it really interested me.

So, they taught Arabic here. I supposed Anthony had offered the college as a solution when he heard my father raving about the situation with my Italian. I did not question the propriety of discussing one's daughter's educational difficulties with one's assistant. I considered myself lucky he hadn't held forth with the pool boy, as he was known to find any ear available to let loose his tongue when something bothered him. It was, if I remembered correctly, the doorman at a weekly rental in Quebec who helped him decide he should let Naomi divorce him as she desired.

"What if I want to transfer to another college?" I said loudly, standing and moving away from Sylvia.

"I'm sorry?"

"What if I decide, after a time, that this institution no longer affords me further educational opportunities? Say, in a year or two?" I glanced at Anthony to see his reaction.

Anthony looked up and rolled his eyes. I raised my eyebrows at him. If that was his expression of choice, I would use mine.

"Well," began Sylvia, "we're proud to say that eighty-five percent of our freshmen stay through graduation. But, of course, after a year of successful study, any college or university would see you as an accomplished freshman whom they might consider for transfer. We are fully accredited and well-respected as to the caliber of student we produce."

"Hmm."

Anthony sighed.

"Suny, there is no way you will get bored here. Trust me. You can customize your own major sophomore year–"

"Oh, yes," Sylvia enthused. "In fact, if your advisor will make the journey with you, you can study any subject, even outside our offered curriculum. We have had many creative interdisciplinary majors. Anthony's advisor was John Gilbert, the professor I spoke of before who was himself a prodigy. He teaches biology and physics. And Kathy Larson– wasn't she a friend of yours? She quite successfully structured a major–"

Anthony leapt to standing. "Okay, Sylvia, there's all the paperwork. All i's dotted and t's crossed. Let's get on with that tour, shall we?"

I would have taken the opportunity to rib him about Kathy once again, especially considering his calling me Simone, but he looked genuinely distressed at hearing her name and never let it be said that I am without pity for the lovelorn.

In the doorway of the stone building, I hesitated before following Anthony and Sylvia out onto the campus grounds. I felt a dull ache in my body, and my head wasn't quite clear. The melancholy I had felt during our drive north threatened to descend upon me once again. I had no reason, despite Sylvia's proud exclamations, to think Preacher's Ledge would be any better than any place I'd previously attended or lived. Inside myself, I felt as I often had as a child, felt an unnamed longing, a lack of I did not know what. I still could not name it, but I doubted I would find it satisfied here.

But, as I stepped out and trudged along behind the others, I began to feel a lightening. The campus was breathtaking. September brought crisp air to New England. The calendar may have said it was still summer, but the first touches of color to the leaves and the clear blue sky hung with low clouds nudged one into the recognition that autumn was the truest season to New England.

Gravel paths laced through fields and up small hills. The tops of the latter were dotted with Frisbee players, book readers, and not a few clusters of musicians.

Anthony's gaze kept returning to a cluster of three dormitories. His attention only returned to us as we crested a hill whose valley was bordered by woods.

"What in hell is that?" he exclaimed.

"That, uh…structure is our new, state-of-the-art science building. It is open for the first time this semester."

Lifeless brown leaves swirled around the building in question. It looked like a three-story, post-modern fishing pier with a rather large dog house cantilevered from one side, roofed in greenhouse panels. It screamed in metal and glass, all angles slashed out of the hillside. To top it all off, in both senses of the phrase, an exceedingly large bump jutted from the top of the taller roof. It appeared to be a dog house/pier with a gnawed off chimney. Or a wart. Take your pick of metaphor.

The whole effect unsettled me for some reason.

Sylvia went on, "An alumnus was kind enough to donate the money for outfitting the labs in exchange for the choice of submitted designs. He awarded the project to a young firm of architects in order to help build their business. Very philanthropic, we thought."

"I don't know if it will help their business any…" Anthony grimaced.

"Well, if the architecture doesn't intrigue you, perhaps this will. It seems to be haunted."

Oh, for goodness sake. If ever I asked for a chance to practice my eye-rolling…

Anthony, however, was positively drooling.

"There is already a student planning a study surveying the grounds, searching for any history or tales of unrecorded burials," Sylvia added.

"Violent history, perhaps?"

"Well, violent something. The first week of classes, a

student went in late to work on the beginnings of a project. He was hit over the head before he could reach the labs, knocked out cold for a few hours. We thought– well officially we still do think– that it was kids up from town running through the place after hours, looking for something to steal. All facilities are unlocked and open twenty-four hours a day for freedom in study," Sylvia directed to me. "Then, a few days later, another student was working late and saw an apparition. We would have written it off, but one of the cleaning crew and another student each have had similar sightings over the last few weeks."

"Who's handling all of this?" Anthony asked.

"No one really. As I said, officially the line is that the attack was kids from town and–"

"Now, Sylvia, why would you even think such an uncharitable thing about us lowly townies?" A young man I first took to be Anthony's twin appeared and threw an arm around Sylvia's shoulders. Upon closer inspection, I noted he was a bit shorter, much leaner, and his hair had actual curls rather than waves, though it was the same dark shade. His eyes were lighter too, and when they caught mine after they'd given me a lingering once-over, they twinkled elvishly.

"Of course I didn't mean to indiscriminately lump together–"

"Say no more, Sylvia. You're probably right. Half my cronies are evil to the core. I, on the other hand, only allow evil to penetrate far enough to make life interesting. And speaking of interesting, who may I ask, do you have draped on your arm this time, brother dear?"

Anthony heaved a bigger sigh than I'd heard all weekend. And that was saying a lot.

"Suny Davis, this is my brother, Nicholas–"

"Nick," the brother supplied.

"– who is not a student here, just a wandering wanna-be, making little of his life after high school graduation. This is Suny Davis, my boss's *sixteen year-old* daughter."

The emphasis was not lost on me, nor was the friendly leer

61

on Nicholas's face.

"How do you do?" I said, which garnered me a comically raised eyebrow.

"What an interesting name. Now, don't let my prim brother steer you wrong. While I don't share his academic enthusiasm, or his pathetically early decision as to what he wishes to get from life, I would not class myself as a wanna-be. My affection for this institution derives solely from my interest in helping the student body make full use of the resources of our region. You may not have heard, Tony, but I've become gainfully employed."

"Oh, yes," Sylvia added in quickly, apparently uncomfortable with the brothers' obvious animosity, "Anthony, your brother is indispensable. He found lodging for all the parents at orientation, arranged some tours, set up student bank accounts, even. He's our new Area Liaison."

"A position I'm sure he convinced you was necessary," Anthony muttered, gazing unimpressed at his brother.

Nicholas smirked.

"Oh, he's really a wonderful representative of the college. It is so fabulous to have members of the larger Mt. Billington community connected to us. We have so few students who come from the local area."

"Sylvia, how can he be representative of the college when he chose to skate through high school with no effort?"

"Four-point-oh, big brother."

"My point exactly, when you could have been here, doing meaningful learning–"

"Like Create-A-Major number twenty-six, "Advanced Babblings on Things That Go Bump in the Night?"

"Double major of Oral Traditions and Quantum Physics: Alternative Communications, thank you very much."

"Excuse me, so sorry."

"Boys!"

I couldn't stand it anymore. I silently thanked my father for his non-traditional relationships that at least spared me the burden of a typical sibling. I proceeded to glare at them both, which I thought might guarantee their silence further.

No such luck.

"Did she just call us 'boys'?" Nicholas stirred in mock indignation. "Well, I never." He broke into a truly attractive grin and winked at me, then freed Sylvia and chucked Anthony on the shoulder. "Mom wants you to come see her before you head back down to the cotton fields."

Anthony nodded, looking away from him, away from me as well.

"Suny, it was lovely to meet you. I hope you will allow me to give you a very personal tour of Mt. Billington."

Anthony turned back to us, his eyes locking on his brother.

Nicholas met his stare and smirked. He gave Sylvia a good-bye squeeze and strode off down the hill.

Anthony stared after him with something less than brotherly love.

Anthony and I walked the path back to the car to move it closer to the dorms. I didn't have as many accoutrements as, say, Morgan Virginia Stanfield, but my trunks were too much to haul up a series of gravel pathways. I broke the silence. "That was a pretty impressive course of study."

"Huh?"

"Oral traditions and quantum physics too."

"Oh. Yeah, I guess. They really encourage you to do something interdisciplinary."

"How long did that take you– the double major?"

"Just the four years. I came at fifteen and graduated at nineteen."

"Then grad school..."

"Yeah. Parapsychology. Your father was a guest lecturer my last semester, this past spring. He really drew me. He's also well-funded, as you know, and recognized for allowing independent research."

"You mean he's rich and absent-minded, which means you

can study whatever you want and he may never know."

"That too," he admitted and we both smiled.

Damn, I had to learn not to let those eyes give me tingles.

Anthony looked away quickly. The next moments were a bit awkward, which irritated me tremendously. In such a situation, I tend to get snippy. Case in point:

"It might get bad, though. Working for Father, I mean. He might not even remember your name when you get back, or the fact that you work for him. Unless you telepathically send it to him, of course. He might pay attention to that."

"Why do you scorn him so much?"

"Why do you revere him?"

"I don't revere him."

"I don't scorn him."

Silence followed. I moved a little ahead of him and walked faster. Anthony lengthened his stride effortlessly and caught up with me.

"You know, he really does have a gift. I've witnessed more real communication events with him than with anyone and I know all the tricks, all the ways to trump up "readings" and messages."

"I know that."

"But you have to admit that sounded an awful lot like scorn back there."

"He's a sloppy scholar, Anthony. He doesn't discriminate between good and bad practice. You could send him a potato peeler in the mail with a crayoned note that told him to stick it in his ear to pick up alien sub-ether communications and he'd try it for a week. He makes a fool of himself and his research every time he accepts without thorough questioning and dissection any event that may occur."

"What about you? You have the gift."

That stopped me in my tracks.

"I…I don't. Well, what about you? I can see where quantum physics might lead you to alternate studies, and I suppose ghost stories might hint at some alternate communications, but…

How about it? Do you have a third eye, the sixth sense?" Do you get the heebie jeebies when you walk through a graveyard?"

"Why would you think I had any experiences?"

"Oh, please. What else could draw an apparently intelligent young man to study gobbledy-gook?"

Anthony looked away. I moved to catch his eye, exasperated. He looked up and stared at me intently, those dark blue eyes boring into me, holding me still, willing me to listen. It seemed as though fixing his gaze on me was the only thing that staved off a heady pain.

"I sense…"

I drew my breath in and held it.

"Never mind."

Oh, that wasn't fair. To think I was letting him get me to talk about this in the first place. I never get drawn in. Never.

"I thought you were going to say, 'Oooh, oooh, I see dead people' and then go hide under that bush over there."

Anthony's eyes narrowed, but I couldn't stop. He had brought it up and I couldn't let him drag me into a serious discussion of…Well, I just couldn't get into it. If he didn't know how it felt to be hounded unbidden…

"Sense something, huh? Have you ever followed it up? Documented it? Was there any basis in this reality for your sensations?"

"I don't want to talk about it."

"Come on, Anthony. You're a scientist. You have to share your findings with the scientific community. You have a gift. It's selfish to keep it all to yourself. It's wasteful not to develop it. Your sensations should be verified, validated–"

"I said I don't want to talk about it!"

He stormed off down the last bit of path to the parking lot. I followed at top speed. When he reached the car, Anthony wrenched open his door, got in, and reversed without me. In fact, I had to jump out of the way or I would have been struck by the crooked fender. He steered the car up the drive toward the dorms and left me standing in the parking lot.

Well, I thought, swallowing hard, I wouldn't apologize. He should thank me, actually. He wouldn't last long under the world's scrutiny unless he developed a thicker skin. A good thick skin protected one from an awful lot, I've found.

Chapter 7

The dull ache had returned to my head, and melancholy threatened as I stood before the dorm buildings, wondering which was mine. But I wasn't left long to fend for myself. Nicholas came up behind me.

"Aha, lost and bewildered already, I see. Has my typically responsible brother lapsed in his duties? How lucky for me."

Nicholas came around to face me and beamed. While Anthony was just an inch or so taller than I, Nicholas was my exact height. He stood uncomfortably close, but he did smell awfully nice.

"You, lassie, would be in Blaubury. All freshmen are in Blaubury. Even the men." He waggled his eyebrows at me suggestively. "Separated by floor, I'm afraid, and guarded at each stair landing by an RA's apartment. That's Resident Assistant–"

"I know what an RA is."

"Aha, not your first foray from the nest, I see. Damn, I was hoping to console you in your homesickness."

I ignored this, though it wasn't easy. He was charming despite his exaggerated style of speech. And Mr. Munston thought I was in need of assistance!

"Your brother drove ahead...with my luggage. I...I couldn't stand to be in that car another minute, so I walked up." If this made no sense, Nicholas didn't mention the fact. He was rather occupied, in addition, with the rise and fall of my breast, as I was still panting from my hike back up from the parking lot. He tore his eyes away in response to my silence and gallantly (or so I assume he thought) led the way through the door of Blaubury, past the student lounge and laundry room, and up the first flight of steps.

I didn't know my room number yet, so I supposed the plan was to stumble upon Sylvia or Anthony or both.

As we reached the first rooms, Nicholas pulled me to his

side protectively. "Men! Don't worry. Avert your eyes and I will come to your aid if they should attack!" He laughed at my puzzled face. My, but he did enjoy himself!

We climbed another flight, but as we turned to follow the stair up to the next landing, Nicholas grabbed me again, this time with a finger to his lips.

"Eavesdropping is an especial hobby of mine."

Indeed, I could hear voices just above. Though I'd known him only two days, I thought I recognized Anthony's low voice among them.

Brown, I thought for a reason I could not fathom. The voice that followed his was female, I could tell, but dry. Dry and cold, I thought.

"...postponed until January. So, I didn't leave this morning." She tittered uncomfortably. "What with recent political events— do take time out from ghostbusting to read the paper now and then, don't you? Oh, don't look like that. I know you're working on important stuff too, even if it is all Scooby-Doo to me. It's just hard for me to think of much else when this administration is sitting on its hands while Africa and the Middle East just— here I go again. Sorry. But that's why I haven't called..."

Nicholas snorted softly in my ear. "Yeah, right."

"...situation is so intense. It's hard for me to tear myself away."

"I'm just glad I got to see you. Are you free this evening? I need to stop by and see my mom, but we could go to The Dive, or hike up to the falls..."

"Oh, Tony. Sorry. Professor Kennigan is on campus this weekend. He gave a stellar lecture Friday night. Now we're all going to dinner. If I'd known you were coming...but I've already invited someone..."

"That'll be Roger," Nicholas whispered in my ear. "Senior she's been assisting in some extra-curricular activities. Wink, wink, nudge, nudge. Poor, poor Tony."

So this was Kathy, I thought, listening to the disembodied

voice sputter its way out of a relationship. Anthony didn't seem to catch on, however.

"Maybe afterwards, Kath? We could go for a drive, or I could come here. If you left me your key…"

Oh, it was just too painful to bear. Shaking off Nicholas's restraining hand, I clunked loudly up the remaining steps.

"There you are! At least you didn't completely abandon me!"

Anthony stood with two of my trunks at his feet. The door to the girls' RA apartment was open, a short, willowy blonde taking up barely a quarter of the space on the threshold. Her hair was almost white, it was so pale, as was her skin, a porcelain pink. She was tiny; her bird-like figure and shining, straight hair was dwarfed by Anthony's taller, bulkier form. I could imagine that she would shine in a tennis outfit, a sailing costume, an evening gown. She wore instead, army surplus pants and a shirt with something printed on it in Arabic or Farsi. I gleaned that it was something political, something feminist…

I must have seen the slogan before. Perhaps some pundit had spoken of it. I clamped down on my mind and thought no more of it.

Anthony flushed at the sight of me. I suppose he didn't want me around while he was wooing. Suddenly I felt rather overdone, too fleshy, too much hair, too loud. From the look on Kathy's face, she thought so too. He began, "Suny–"

"There you are!" Sylvia came down the hall toward us. "Oh, I see you've run into your RA. Suny Davis, meet Kathy Larson. And Kathy, I'm so glad you're here for another semester. You can help Suny get off to a solid start. Suny will be studying Arabic, like you. Kathy's spearheading a group that's off to the Sudan– in January now, right? Kathy, Suny has an absolute gift for languages. You two will have to talk."

"Oh, but Sylvia, in what language do you suppose they will converse?" Nicholas took in the gathering from the top step, enjoying himself again, it seemed.

"*Yebn el kelb*," Kathy spat at him.

I laughed despite myself.

Kathy turned to look at me. "*Hall tifhamee elarabee el feeh sheteema um bitifhamee elarabee elfeeh essaa?* How about– *Ezzay elhaal habibtee?*"

"*Haally tamam*," I responded without thinking, and added, "*Atmanaa lik lilla saeeda maa elhabaiib.*"

The look she gave me went from shock, to understanding, to a narrow-eyed speculation.

"Suny! Hell! You didn't tell us you spoke Arabic!" Anthony gaped at me.

Damnation!

"I don't!" I sputtered. "I just…I must have heard it on TV…Lawrence of Arabia, maybe."

But Kathy wasn't buying it. "Gift for languages, huh? Any other gifts I should be made aware of?"

I would never have thought such perfect rosebud lips could twist so sardonically. I could see the gears turning in her mind, putting together the pieces. How much had Anthony told her about my father, about his work? Apparently, enough. I could tell being surrounded by highly intelligent people was going to keep me on my toes.

Having had flighty, spoiled stepmothers did serve a purpose from time to time. Thinking of number two, Caroline, I broke out with, "I simply must get to my room to take these shoes off!" I took Sylvia by the arm and pulled her in the direction whence she had come. "Nice to have met you!" I called over my shoulder in simple English.

I looked back again to see Anthony plant a kiss on Kathy's cheek before she could dodge it. Then he hoisted my trunks and followed, avoiding my eyes. How thick was this man that he couldn't simply *taste* the waves of squirming dishonesty just rolling off of this girl?

The room we entered was too cramped for the two beds it held. One, with bare mattress, was wedged under the sole window. The other bed was in disarray, a tangle of batiked tapestry and commemorative Elvis emblazoned pillows. Every square inch of wall was covered in music posters, bumper stickers, and pictures cut from magazines, recombined with others in amazing, if not mildly crude, ways.

It was overstimulating to say the least.

Anthony dumped my trunks onto the naked bed. Sylvia, after giving me my key and pointing out the bath down the hall, pulled Nicholas away to discuss some fall festival in town.

Anthony questioned me immediately. "Is that how you know so many? Languages, I mean. What did you say? What did she say? How does the meaning come through?"

"Oh, hell! Can you give a girl two seconds? I am not going to discuss this with you. I am not a study subject!" I huffed exasperatedly.

As for what Kathy said, she had called his brother a…a cur, I guess one might say. A son of a dog. And she had asked me if I only knew profane Arabic, and she had greeted me in a style, which felt to me excessively endearing, in a mocking way. I had responded as was expected, and I had added to the greeting what I hoped was a wish for her to have a pleasant evening with…well, a loved one, I think. Even I, with practically no romantic experience, knew that it was cruel to leave Anthony hanging. I hoped she would catch my sarcasm, but being unused to Arabic, I was not sure I had said what I meant nor that she would take the hint. In reference to how it all worked, so to speak, well…it came very fast and I actively attempt to repress any such happenings so, in other words, I don't really know. And I'm quite happy with that, thank you very much.

Anthony had no need to know any of this. He apparently thought otherwise. He was positively sullen as he left the room to retrieve the remaining articles of my luggage from the car.

I chose not to assist him, instead using my time to rest a moment. I hadn't closed my eyes for two minutes when the door flew open.

My new roommate stood in the doorway. She had to be my roommate. Who else could appear through the door in such an

71

abrupt fashion, so dramatically, so... so pink and fuzzily? Let it be known that it was not her abrupt appearance, but rather her *physical* appearance that gave me pause.

I could tell that the young woman who stood framed in the doorway of my new domicile would be...let us say...unusual. She was clad as if from the movie *Grease*, which I had recently reviewed for the purposes of better acquainting myself with the development of the American teen through history. She wore a bright pink poodle skirt and a tight white cashmere sweater, whose short sleeves and peter pan collar virtually glowed off her deep brown skin. I had never seen skin so incredibly dark. She seemed carved of polished ebony. Under a magnificent bosom, which far surpassed my own, her comparatively small waist was cinched by a wide patent leather belt with a rhinestone buckle. Incongruously, she was shod in sadly worn Birkenstock sandals. Her hair was twisted into dreadlocks, except for a close-clipped patch above her right ear. The locks were pulled up into a high ponytail, around which was wrapped a scarf of pale pink chiffon.

Her large brown eyes took me in for as long a spell as I spent digesting her appearance, so I did not consider my lengthy appraisal rude.

"I forgot my– oh, never mind. I'm Petra–" She extended a hand to me. "– which means–"

"Rock," I responded without thinking. I stood and offered my own hand, which was swallowed by long, slender fingers.

"You know Latin. Cool. They said you were into languages."

"It's a lovely name."

"Thanks. My grandfather named me– said after five boys, a girl was going to need to be strong." She moved around the room, tossing pillows off her bed, opening drawers. She smiled at me with beautiful white teeth. "Everyone calls me Rocky."

Well, I did not know if I was to be lumped with everyone and expected to call her Rocky, but I much preferred Petra. At the time, however, I was still stunned by her attire. I had seen the Elvis pillows, I'll grant you, but...

"They told me you'd be in last night."

I shook myself. "Uh, we were waylaid by the storm. Anthony tried to–"

"What did I try?" He struggled into the room with four suitcases, two under each arm like a bellhop.

"I was telling Petra–"

"Rocky!" Anthony exclaimed. "Are you still camping out here?"

"Oh my– Tony!" She turned to me, a gleam in her eye. "You were waylaid with Tony? Yum, yum."

Anthony dropped my suitcases and Petra gave him a hug while he blushed red.

"Look at you in that get-up! Are you still meeting every week?" he asked.

"A sock-hop?" I ventured, already feeling left out and wondering if dances here would be anything like Broadman's mixers.

They both looked at me as if I were from another planet, then burst out laughing.

"At The Ledge? Lord, help me," Petra exclaimed and fanned herself as if she were hot. "Séance, girl. Sock hop? Oh, my."

"Rocky here, and a bunch of other wackos– ow, no need for violence– they get together and try to channel Elvis–"

"And Marilyn, and the Big Bopper. Actually," she said in an aside to me, "it's really just an excuse to get high and have an orgy. Ooh, Tony, look at her eyes!"

"Rocky, don't tease her."

I stood in the midst of this jocose reunion and I didn't quite know how to take it. It was all rather surreal and I was tired and hungry. I sat back down on my bare bed.

"Another virgin, huh?" Petra eyed me speculatively, as if she were cataloguing items and trying to decide exactly where I belonged.

Anthony ducked his head in embarrassment, and nudged Petra in the ribs.

"No, no, that's okay. We can take care of that," Petra

exclaimed loudly. Her eyes never left me, suddenly serious, appraising.

I can tell you candidly that if it had not been for their physical forms blocking the way, I would have bolted for the door at that moment.

"Screw the séance. Tony, let's get ourselves up to the dining hall and scope out the prospects for this neophyte."

With that, I closed my eyes and swallowed hard. I'd only been at Preacher's Ledge for a few hours and so far I'd been broadsided with much more than I thought any sane person could handle, much less one who had been through what I had in the preceding forty-eight hours.

Oh well, I told myself as I opened my eyes again and took in the peculiar sight of my bizarre roommate and the young man with whom I'd survived a hurricane, things couldn't get much stranger, now could they?

Chapter 8

I had underestimated the comfort to be found in solitude. At Broadman, as was the case at the few other institutions to which I had been subjected, the other students avoided me. I ate alone, I studied alone, I was alone. Privately, I sulked a bit about that. There must be someone of my cohort with whom I could have a meaningful conversation. I used to wonder, would I never find one person of substance at Broadman?

No. I would not. They were all at Preacher's Ledge. In the dining hall, to be precise.

Petra had not bothered to change. She strode into the hall easily and, with keen, predatory eyes, took in the room. Her appearance did not raise a single eyebrow. Anthony's, however, caused a stir. He was hailed from all sides, even from a cluster of tables peopled with professors. Anthony raised a hand in greeting to a woman I swore was the doppelganger for silent film star, Gloria Swanson, and another lady who could have passed for a lumberjack. Anthony called out to a Joe, to a Margaret (making it clear to me that professors and students here were on a first name basis). He nodded perfunctorily at a clean-cut professor, who looked up briefly before returning to his meal, then was pulled away by a gaggle of young women in dance outfits.

Meanwhile, Petra gave me a running monologue. She informed me, and in a voice not too low in volume, I might add, as to the sexual status, practice, and skill of nearly every male in the room, including some of the aforementioned professors and a number of young women for good measure. How she gathered the information, I did not care to ask. I made every effort to pull her away, inching toward the stack of trays stationed by the kitchen entrance.

"Carnivore or herbivore?" she inquired abruptly while we gathered our silverware.

"Excuse me?"

Petra did not elaborate, instead calling out toward the back of the kitchen, "Jason, why is it that every day I have off, you're making something African? I think you miss me. Last week it's Ethiopian, then some fish and banana thing– what was that, Caribbean? West African? And now, Morocco? I hate this slop…" Petra raged on, "Give me some butter, some fresh cream…"

"She's not shy, is she?"

Anthony had come up behind me, having made his escape from the ballerinas.

"No, I guess not," I mumbled, though, not being very savvy myself as to what proper teenage etiquette was, I often found myself misinterpreted and thought abrasive.

"Rocky wrote a paper once on how a person should be able to choose their own characteristics, even the ones that are stereotypical of your gender, race, who your parents are, whatever. That no matter what you are told you should or should not be, no matter who is making up those rules, pre-colonial to the present, it's up to you to create yourself."

He was looking at me, and I realized he might be trying to say something, though I wasn't sure what.

"In any case," Anthony began again, "she cooks here four nights a week, and she's always hated grains, hated most of the vegetarian dishes, unlike half the campus. But everyone forgives her. You think the dining hall is full now, you should see it on her nights."

I squinted through the steamed glass panels that protected the night's entrees. To my surprise, there were two vegetarian choices and one tray of lamb and spiced vegetables.

Anthony explained, "Over half the students here are vegetarian by the time they leave. Some say," he added, lowering his voice so Petra was sure not to hear, "the meat is just not worth it. It gets so if you're work study here, you know how to make more vegetarian dishes than not by graduation."

I remembered the meal he'd prepared at the inn, the vegetables in particular. Had he learned it all here, working in this kitchen to pay for his studies? Not that I had a reason to care, mind you. I felt my surmise correct when I noticed the familiarity with which Anthony addressed the staff behind the serving line. He was holding up the queue of hungry students, in fact.

Petra sailed off out the kitchen entrance, and I was about to follow, when I was stopped by a high, nasal voice, which spoke to me from the end of the service line.

"You're eighty-two-oh-one. I've been waiting for you. Eighty-two-oh-one. You'll need to remember that for meals and books, and other necess...necess...necessities. If you ever forget, though, I could tell you. You could find me and I could tell you right off the top of my head. I know everyone's number. I could tell you anyone's, though, actually, they're supposed to be confidential. So, you're eighty-two-oh-one, okay?"

Now I am not an expert on American college life, but I could tell immediately that the young man was...a nerd. Quintessentially. He wore glasses for a start, and although they were not very thick, they were large, owlish even. His skin was...well, let's just say it was bad. His hair was a dark, dull brown, made darker and duller still by his apparent aversion to shampoo. His teeth were equally neglected, a fact made only too clear to me as he smiled broadly in conclusion to his brief oration. I winced, then attempted to return his smile, only to be startled by a loud, sinus-clearing snort I don't believe he was fully aware he executed.

"Thank you," I stammered. If someone had told me there was a college for those underserved by high schools due to their higher-level abilities, I would have assumed it was peopled by those just like–

"Brian! I think you've been glued to that spot for the last four years!"

Anthony and the unfortunate Brian talked physics for a few minutes. When it looked like they would not be soon done, I timidly made my way through the kitchen exit, alone.

A multitude of eyes stared plainly at me.

"Everyone's staring at me."

Petra came up and took my arm, patting it in a motherly way.

"This is a small place, honey. New blood– and especially new blood with your figure– well, it doesn't come often. Everyone's dealing with that instinct to widen the gene pool, you know? Oh, and okay, I know I might be overwhelming you with all of this, or so I'm told." She looked pointedly at her tablemates as we approached. "So, I'm going to stop. But just to let you know, Todd– the one to the left of my tray– he's got real good rhythm. Never been with him, but the boy can dance, and that usually translates, if you know what I mean. Okay, now I'm going to shut up 'cause these guys think you might get a little freaky on us if I keep on. At least until you know me better. Come on, everyone wants to say hi."

We sat, seven of us at a large round table. I was introduced around. I tried hard not to blush when Petra got to the "rhythmic" Todd. The only female was a blond, Frieda, with white-blond hair and sharp blue eyes that shot daggers at Petra, never leaving her face. I wondered if I would be privy to that story someday. Or maybe Petra just inspired strong feelings among most young women. If she was as promiscuous as seemed apparent, one could understand how she might attain multiple adversaries.

Soon, Anthony joined us, taking the last empty seat, which lay across the table from me. He ate methodically and scanned the room. Looking for Kathy, I thought, who had said she was dining with another.

Todd began to ask me questions about where I'd been before Preacher's Ledge. He told me his own background– homeschooled in Nebraska– then filled me in on everyone else present, including Petra. It seems she was raised by her grandparents, two classics professors in a historically black university in Louisiana. She grew up listening to lectures on philosophy, language, the Bible and culture, clinging, it appeared, to a rather narrow view of the hedonistic philosophy of Epicurus. Sexuality was, of course, one of the pleasures of being human, but I seem to remember some cautions on excess, even in the thought of Epicurus and other Greek ethicists in the generation of thinkers following Aristotle.

Petra soon broke in to defend herself, having caught on to our line of discussion, and very soon, I found myself in the middle of a voluble, but amiable and amazingly learned discussion of stoicism and the rise of asceticism. I have to say I enjoyed myself immensely. I felt the unfamiliar glow of being in good, intelligent company, eating food that met my approval on many levels, and generally feeling…well, happy, I guess.

I looked up during an emphatic point of Frieda's to see Anthony staring at me, a little half-smile on his lips. Caught watching me, he quickly made the smile disappear and launched into the argument himself, making several weak points designed solely to stir things up. He so actively attempted to avoid looking in my direction that he missed seeing what I saw out of the corner of my eye. Kathy and someone who could only have been Roger walked arm in arm across the dining hall parking lot, dressed up just a bit, and headed for a little white sports car. I didn't bother to bring it to his attention.

Petra and I returned to the room in fresh, chilled darkness. Anthony had mumbled something about seeing his family and informed me he would be back on Monday to get me started in my classes. I would have felt affronted at his apparent need to baby me so, but the night was too beautiful, my appetite satisfied, and my head full and swirling with bits of stimulating conversation. I smiled at him rather too largely in my satiated state and regretted it immediately when he gave me only a quizzical look that wiped the smile quickly from my face.

Petra lolled luxuriantly in the midst of her many cushions as I unpacked my few cases, their contents. My possessions were rather colorless in comparison to her veritable rainbow of belongings. Seeing me struggle with where exactly to place the few personal tidbits I did possess, Petra shared with me her interpretation of what she called, "The Admin's latest attempt to roust me".

Petra had been accepted late her first year (somewhat like my own situation), after a miserable summer trying to advance beyond her high school curriculum with courses at a Louisiana community college that allowed such students. She had decided she'd had enough of high school, of Louisiana, and "all of that," as she put it. That summer, she had found a brochure inviting her inquiry into Preacher's Ledge buried in the waste can in her grandparents' study, decided to apply, conducted a phone interview without anyone's knowledge, forged a few signatures and was accepted and packed to leave before the elderly professors knew what had hit them. Their hands tied, lest she drop out of school altogether and travel Europe alone to further her education, as she threatened to do if thwarted, her grandparents acquiesced and sent her up the Eastern seaboard. As Nicholas had informed me, Blaubury was a freshmen dorm, and a smallish one at that. Petra had been awarded this room, a largish single often reserved for visiting lecturers, during her freshman year because it was all the college had remaining for housing.

Be that as it may, once here, Petra determined to keep the coveted single no matter what the cost. She managed, through dubious means, threats and cajoling, to maintain possession of her room until now. Realizing she was not going to give it up in this, her senior year, The Admin had finally been clever enough to knock her down a peg by saddling her with a roomie, and a freshman at that.

"I'm sorry," I apologized, feeling a bit awkward as I sat on the edge of my bed, so obviously crammed into a space for which it was not meant.

"Hell, don't apologize, Suny. It's all an adventure, girl. As long as we work out some kind of system so we each know when the other is in need of some...some *privacy*, we'll be okay."

80

I blushed and worried that Petra would launch back in on her quest for…well, her quest. But I needn't have worried. Petra decided to extend my reprieve, choosing instead to examine closely the few articles of clothing I had hung to one side of the small closet, stuffed already with Petra's colorful "costumes," one could only say.

"Suny, we gotta get you some togs, too," she exclaimed, then murmured disapprovingly some more and rooted around in the large pile of fabric at the bottom of the closet.

As I listened to her mumble and dig, my fingers worried the clasp of my dressing case. I still did not feel completely settled, but I was beginning to feel…I don't know…okay. I opened my dressing case and pulled my flokati rug from inside, where I had stuffed it. As I lay it across the bottom of my bed, a piece of stiff paper fluttered from its folds. I picked it up and saw that it was a much creased photo of Father. One that he had kept on his study desk, it showed him in his usual khaki pants, collar of a chambray button-down open to show a tanned throat below his tanned face and pale blue eyes. I had stolen the photo— Father never thought to give me any such bit of memorabilia— and had cut out the stepmother who had been by his side in the shot. I don't recall which one it had been. When I was younger, when I was first sent to school, I had carried it with me in the pocket of a skirt, or tucked in the top of a sock even. I think I regarded it then as a talisman of some kind, or perhaps as a way of keeping close the Father who was, in truth, not ever truly close to me in person. I held it in my hand there on a bed, in yet another new home that was not really a home, not sure really where to put it.

"Wanna wear this tomorrow? My boobs don't fit in it anymore." Petra burst into my thoughts, having emerged from the closet with a lacy bustier and a very short, pleated plaid skirt, a sexy wink at a parochial school uniform.

I would have groaned rather loudly if she had not been so obviously in earnest. As it was, I swallowed hard and tried to smile at the gesture.

"Thank you. I'll...consider it."

Chapter 9

Nights in the Berkshires were darker than in the Shenandoah Valley, or so it seemed to me as I gazed out my window and up at the stars. Petra snored with intensity. I mused and smiled a bit to myself. My opinions as to the benefits of a roommate were slowly shifting. At the very least, she was not going to be dismissive, or boring for that matter.

Petra had laid out six other possible outfits for me before retiring, pulling articles from her rumpled bedclothes, from desk drawers, and, from some girls down the hall, a pearlescent tubetop ringed with black and white feathers, for which she had persistently banged on the door of some girls down the hall, demanding it back. I put off trying any of them on, only getting away with that postponement by agreeing to borrow some nightclothes and allowing her to paint my nails a bright blue-purple.

I sat now, in said nightclothes, a fairly sedate, though still sexily-cut, translucent green silk handkerchief halter and matching French-cut bottoms. The room was over-heated (another strategy of The Admin. to get her to move out) and I was sweating even in my skimpy attire. I tried to no avail to open the window. It seemed, inexplicably, to be stuck.

I had meant to call Father to tell him of my safe arrival and settling, but the evening had gone quickly. Petra had suddenly announced she was "done in," peeled off her cashmere sweater and poodle skirt and fallen into bed, raining oddly-colored stuffed animals and a Richard Nixon pillow over the side as she got comfortable.

Deferring to her, I had put out the light, but I was in no state for sleep. My head pounded with fatigue, but sleep would not come. My mind was awhirl. I felt both an unfamiliar tinge of satisfaction at my school of the moment, and a measured reluctance to give in to any feelings of comfort that might be premature. I had never really felt happy in any one particular

83

place, and anytime I had come close to that state, I was whisked away again to someplace new.

I again thought of calling Father. It was late, but I knew he was likely to be awake still. Somehow, though, the thought of calling him was not comforting, and the call itself, should I make it, would not, in all probability, yield any desirable result. I knew from long experience that Father was apt to forget he was supposed to be conversing and, while the other party spoke, he was likely to think of something, put the phone down, and wander away.

I rolled over and stared at the ceiling. My limbs ached and my head pounded with fatigue, but sleep would not come. The morning of driving carefully around storm-downed tree limbs with Anthony seemed a hundred years ago, the hurricane of the night before, an eon away.

I blushed hotly, alone there in the dark, when I thought of Anthony bare-chested in the candlelight of the storm-darkened inn. The flush of unwanted emotion (and really it was happening all too frequently) did nothing to assuage the uncomfortable level of warmth I felt. The temperature irritated me, as did my thoughts of Anthony when they went beyond those of his admittedly attractive form to his haughty condescension and general ability to annoy me without undue effort.

I sat up, not willing to lie there with unbidden thoughts any longer. I tried not to stumble around in the dark as I made my way past Petra's bed. I could not find my robe. Petra had inadvertently pulled down some of my things from hangers as she'd scouted out my week's wardrobe. I came up from the heap on the closet floor instead with something, which I realized once I got into the dimly-lit hall was a camouflaged Army top, lined absurdly with hot pink satin. Ah well, I thought, at the very least the satin was gratifyingly cool on my skin.

It seemed as though Petra was correct on one point. Her room was inexplicably and measurably hotter than the hallway.

84

All of the twelve or so doors that lined my hallway were closed with no light showing under them. Everyone seemed tucked well into sleep. It was far after midnight. No time to be calling anyone, and yet…

I knew Mr. Munston's phone number from the various times he had needed to speak to me about my…well, about things. He had always told me I could call him at anytime. And I was sure he would be interested in hearing of the discussions that had been held in the dining hall that evening, and about how I thought I might even like this new roommate, and about how…

I found myself standing in front of the hall phone, unable to bring myself to raise the receiver.

He had not even come to say goodbye when I left Broadman. Perhaps my ridiculous behavior (the portions of which I recalled, at least) had taxed our relationship beyond what he could accept. Though he was an important figure in my life, perhaps to Mr. Munston, our relationship had only been part of his job. Perhaps even a part of his job that he had been happy to see concluded.

I walked from one end of the hallway to the other, studying the door-mounted expressions of the individuals with whom I was quartered. There was a good bit of crude humor, many scantily-clad male pin-ups (and some female ones to boot, bringing back to me Petra's quick evaluations of even some of the female population's sexual proclivities) and some fairly high-quality poetry.

All were asleep. I was alone amid many. Again. I felt something well up inside me, but I pushed it down. I had been through worse. This feeling of melancholy would prove fleeting if only I kept myself from dwelling on silliness and on things that could not be changed.

I had reached the back stairwell door, which led onto a blank landing, Kathy's RA apartment being on the opposite landing in a bumped out area at the front of the building. I carefully tried the door but its hinges swung only an inch before emitting an awful, screeching groan, and I let it fall shut. I was about to turn, resigned to sleep in the sauna that was my new room, or to break a wrist trying again to force the window open, when I was stopped by the appearance of a quick arc of light through the stairwell's one wide window. It drew me and I waited, rewarded soon after with another wavering pass of a yellowish glow, which changed suddenly to rose, and then was gone.

A year or two previous, Father and I had managed a few moments alone, a precious few when he was not poring over notes or staring with glazed eyes, a look sure to mean he was sensing, or thinking, or musing privately, but sure not to be aware of anyone nearby. It had been a crisp night out on a stone patio, somewhere in Europe, though the exact locale escaped me at the moment. Father had been smoking a cigarette of cloves mixed with god-knows-what (tarragon perhaps, as I remember the smell reminded me of a soup from one of Naomi's dinner parties). He was testing its hallucinogenic properties, of which I'm sure there were none. He had turned to me and given me a string of terms, something he had tested me with since childhood, asserting that finding a pattern in unspecified communications was an intuition-building exercise (arguing, of course, that intuition was a skill to be honed).

"Digging at Machu Pichu, scuba-diving the Great Reef, ballooning around the globe, trekking the mapped sightings of Sasquatch, replicating at least one Houdini illusion."

I was expected to guess the link, the meaning in this string of activities.

"Lifestyles of the rich and famous?" And slightly demented, I'd added to myself.

"No, Suny. It is my list– well, the beginning of my list– of things I would like to accomplish before I die."

I'd thought about that for a while, struck a bit by the thought that *he* thought about dying. He was so alive, so... well, active, I guess. Always moving, always doing. Even when he read, he was usually taking notes with one hand and eating some sandwich with the other, the desire for whose strange ingredients had hit him with the full force of a pregnant woman's craving. And that was part of it too, I suppose. He always seemed to immediately acquire whatever he wished, be it sandwich ingredients, some new electronic gadget, or someone else's wife. There was no delay in his gratification, or so it seemed to me. To think he had a list of activities he wished to complete before he died, but was not prepared to undertake at this precise second, was a mind-boggling concept.

I had been steeping in these silent thoughts when he had spoken again.

"I suppose a search for your mother would be on your list," he ventured, dragging on the sickly sweet cigarette, and wincing as he held the smoke in his lungs.

"No," I said quickly to head off this line of thinking, one which I was thankful was rarely brought up. And then I rapidly shot off the beginning of my own list, "Spending the night in the Valley of the Kings…in a sarcophagus, I would think. An audience with every recognized monarch still reigning. To see the aurora borealis."

It was really just to quiet him, to lead him away from his probing about my questionable maternity, but the more I thought of it in the later days and months, the more I realized that I did have desires. And it was the last in that budding list that bid me to push through the squeaking door to the stair landing, ignoring its loud protest. Had it been the northern lights I'd seen? My geography is fairly strong, but I was not sure exactly where it was possible to see them. Northern Minnesota, Canada, parts of Scotland, Alaska. Were the Berkshire Hills part of that elite club? I squinted through the window, my hand shielding the glass from the dim landing light that reflected off it otherwise, but saw nothing.

And then, across the campus toward the hilly area of academic buildings, I saw a brief glow. My viewing angle was not the best, however, and without further thought, I sprang down the stairs and pushed open the back door of Blaubury, moving into the chill night.

As I was oriented, the academic area was to my right. I wrapped my cover-up around me and padded quietly through the grass, wet with dew and cool on my bare toes. The stars were brilliant against the blue-black of midnight sky. I wondered at the difference a few degrees of latitude and the absence of city lights could make.

There it was again! As I approached a stone wall that retained the ground from a much steeper fall of land below it, I saw a quick burst of yellow, then rose. Seeing it fully, I immediately knew it was not my sought-after aurora borealis. This light glowed from the ground farther down some distance behind the campus hills, a suffusion of hazy light in the dark sky, and then nothing.

I kicked a twig, and then a stone, in my disappointment. My disruptive impulses did not serve me well, however. Lifting my foot and swinging it with more violence than necessary to dislodge a small twig or stone left me with only one foot on a part of the ground that abutted the stone wall. A shaded part, in other words. Where moss grew. Slippery moss, apparently. My kick unbalancing me, and my supporting leg led inevitably to quite an unfortunate happening. I fell heavily on my backside, and for the second time that weekend, the wind was knocked out of me with a grunt, leaving me to slide down the bank along the stone wall, breathless and gaining speed.

Fortune smiled upon me, however. At least in one small way, as one might optimistically interpret it. Petra's camo/satin shirt caught on a stone that jutted from the wall, slowing my progress.

At least until my arms pulled out of the sleeves, that is.

I slid the rest of the way, still trying to suck air into my lungs, slitting Petra's silk, French-cut bottoms even higher at the leg than they had been before. I came to a stop several feet from where the retaining wall disappeared into the bottom of the slope and sat stunned as my breath came back to me.

"What was that?" A dry, nervous voice came from the other

88

side of the wall, from a sitting area carved into the hill.

"It's nothing. You're hearing things. I thought we were going to talk."

Brown. I knew that voice. My skin tingled in recognition.

"Tony, I would talk if you'd stop trying to paw me."

"You haven't even let me kiss you once!"

Oh, my. What a thick-headed dolt!

"Do you think I want to kiss you after you scared the hell out of me, lurking in the corners as I came up the stairs?"

"Well, I really wanted to see you. If you would've let me come in the apartment with you, we could already..."

"Don't blame me for following the rules! You know I can't have men in the dorm after hours!"

"It never stopped you before," Anthony muttered, almost too low for me to hear.

"Would you stop that! For god's sake, Tony! You could give a girl some warning the next time you come into town. I haven't seen you in– what– three months? And you expect to spend the night with me?"

"It wasn't a problem the last time I surprised you."

"That was...that was...hell, Tony. I just don't like that you didn't let me know you were coming. And...and you show up here with that...that trollop that calls herself your boss's daughter --"

Trollop? My body tensed and my skin burned all over.

"– doing him a favor to get in his good graces, I'll bet. Can the poor girl even read?"

"You're jealous!" Anthony exclaimed.

"What? No! I–"

"You are!" His voice lowered. He teased. "She is quite something to look at, isn't she? All that hair, big, brown eyes with lashes so long they lay on her cheek. And the body! My goodness, and at just sixteen! Legs that go on and on. You know, I can actually look her in the eye without...Ow!"

"You are such a Neanderthal!"

"I think you're jealous."

"Tony, I have a mind. And a nice body, too, or so you used to tell me. Why would I think you'd be attracted to some brainless bimbo you were sent to babysit? So what if she speaks– what? What did you say?"

"Nothing."

But I had heard him. Anthony had moved away from Kathy as he teased her and ended up over near the wall. I was crouched, ready to launch at the skinny little feminazi, and I had heard what he said, softly and only for himself to hear.

He'd said, "Her scores are better than yours."

Now, granted, I did not hold much with the overvaluation of test scores, but frankly, I was bowled over. He'd defended me. Not so loudly that she could have heard, but...

Kathy was going on, a mocking lilt in her own voice now. "Well, if it wasn't to get in your boss's good graces, it must have been to get back on Gilbert's good side. I know how much you love that man and you know he's on the fundraising committee now. Bringing in a rich brat would be just the thing."

"I do not love that man." Anthony strode away again. I could hear his shoes scrape against the gravel that littered the sitting area. "That man– I couldn't care less about being on his good side. If I cared anything about him at all, he would need to be scared. I could have his tenure revoked ..." Anthony moved far enough away from the wall that I could see his face as he lifted it to the moon. Emotion seethed under the skin, then relaxed as he settled his breathing.

"He shouldn't be teaching kids. He should have stayed at that research facility he left in order to bestow his supposed gifts on us. But Gilbert is not worth my time or energy."

"But ghost-busting is? Oh, don't look at me like that. I was just kidding."

"Kathy, I love what I do down there. The people are fabulous. I love Davis too– he's a kook, but he's incredible too– he really is. I would love for you to come down to meet him. Hell, he'd hardly even notice another person in the house.

That's how it is down there, you know. He's great to work with, but there's no one else around. It's been lonely the last few weeks."

Anthony had come back to the wall with this, back to where Kathy was sitting below my hidden perch.

"I miss you," he crooned.

The sound of clothes rustling reached me.

"Tony, for god's sake– cut it out! It's not what I want, okay? It's different now. You're different. I...oh, hell. I have to go now. No, don't– just let me go!"

I ducked down close to the wall's cold stones as Kathy hurried past back to Blaubury. I waited a moment, listening to see if Anthony would follow her. When I heard nothing, I crept on hands and knees away from the wall and towards the dorm. I had no desire to meet with Anthony when he was in an agitated state.

A stone skittered past me, then another. Oh, hell! Anthony was kicking rocks in his frustration. Having found out the hard way myself only minutes before that this activity led to no good, I started to scurry faster. Another rock sailed by.

Then one hit me square on the cheekbone.

"*Gavno*!"

"Who's there? Suny?"

I felt blood through the fingers I held on my cheek. The sound of gravel underfoot gave way to the padding of sneakers on wet grass.

"Suny? Oof!"

I felt his leg connect with my shoulder as I crouched, rolling me a few feet and turning me onto my back. Anthony fell across my body, his hands landing in two unfortunate positions as he threw them out to catch himself.

What he'd caught was by no means himself.

"For god's sake, Suny!" Anthony roared as he rolled off me. "What the hell are you doing out here? Jesus, Mary, and Joseph! This is not even worth it! Does your father have any idea how much trouble you are?"

Why do you think he sent you instead of coming himself, I answered silently. To Anthony, however, I replied, "I...I thought I saw the aurora borealis..."

"What?"

"The Northern Lights? Solar wind interacting with the edge of the Earth's magnetic field..."

"I know what they are! Here?"

"Well...I...it was just some lights from down by the academic buildings...in the valley..."

"And so, disappointed with that, you chose to eavesdrop on me?"

"I...I...You made me bleed!"

Pathetic, I know. But to tell the truth, the pain was intense and I could feel already the skin beginning to swell below my eye.

Anthony pulled me up to standing along with himself.

"Christ, Suny, what are you wearing? Why is it that, since I've met you, every evening you insist on being half-naked?"

He didn't wait for my answer, which would have been more than rude and less than pointless. Instead he walked and pulled me along behind him, in much the same manner as he had when we had gone from house to house in the hurricane. He muttered something as we went. Something about women and emotional vampires, sucking him dry.

Anthony took me around the front of Blaubury and punched a code in at the door of the building, a code I didn't know by heart yet. Perhaps it was a good thing after all that I'd stumbled into Anthony.

He took me to the laundry room and commanded me to sit down even as he flipped on the light. There was no place to sit so I hopped up gingerly onto a washer and waited, trying to keep my hand from stealing up to the cut on my face, though I could feel it still wetly pumping blood.

Anthony turned on the tap in the sink, then turned to me, seeing me for the first time in the light.

"Oh, holy god. Suny...oh, Jesus...you're going to need

stitches."

My whole body stiffened.

"No, I'm sure that won't be necessary."

"Let me clean it so I can tell for sure."

He looked around for something to clean it with. There weren't even any paper towels.

"I can't believe this," he groaned. He pulled off his shirt and began to tear the hem of it off in a strip.

"Anthony, don't do that– I can clean it up myself upstairs."

"Suny, you haven't seen yourself. Just sit still and shut up."

As was typical of the last few days, he got me to do just that. Anthony moved toward me with a wet strip of cloth. It was awkward because I was sitting so high. He had to come up right against the front of the machine, pressing into my legs to see well enough in the dim light of the laundry room. I could feel his heart beating rapidly in his frustration with me, and taking notice of it for the first time, my breath was coming a bit quickly as well. He daubed at my wound a couple of times, his body shifting uncomfortably so he would not press me so. Suddenly, he pulled quickly away and grabbed the rest of his torn T-shirt.

"Here, for god's sake, put this on." Anthony demanded gruffly. "How in hell am I supposed to …"

I began to pull the shirt over my head to cover the translucent silk top. "It's Petra's," I mumbled, though he had not requested an explanation. I winced as I tried to pull the ribbing of the collar down my face.

"Wait," Anthony said. He pulled the shirt back off my head, took it in his teeth, and ripped the collar so it would go over my head more readily.

Thus clad more modestly, I sat while Anthony tried as gently as possible to clean my wound. To give him credit, he *was* gentle and he winced just as frequently as I did, in sympathy, I suppose.

"Suny, the skin is split apart. I must have got you just perfectly with the point of a stone. You're going to need stitches, or at the very least, a few butterfly bandages. And those–" he broke off and took a deep breath, rolling his eyes heavenward, "– those are only available at this hour in your RA's apartment."

I do, on occasion, know when to keep quiet without being told. As the bare-chested Anthony led me up the stairs at some time after midnight, my cold, tired and bleeding body clad only in his torn T-shirt and Petra's ripped silk pajamas, I did not say a word. And as I stood by while he knocked on Kathy's door, knowing by the look on his face that he was dreading her response, I shut my eyes for good measure.

Chapter 10

I had often wondered what it would feel like to be in a classroom where I found the lessons more stimulating than the state of my cuticles. My first week at Preacher's Ledge showed that it was possible.

My Arabic class met three times a week, and once a week for a conversation class. Mahmet, who joyfully celebrated our attempts to master his "most beautiful and lyrical" language, was available to throw in suggestions and fill in vocabulary gaps. I found the new alphabet a challenge, and an enticing one at that.

Kathy appeared during the last classroom meeting of the week. Apparently, Mahmet had been her advisor. She smiled coolly at me, then remained for the duration, watching me, I felt– perhaps looking for signs that I was taking the language in by osmosis, or some other diabolically psychic way. This I pointedly did not allow myself to even attempt, so if that was what she was truly after, she surely left dissatisfied.

Of course, she could have been present as part of my "action plan."

After Kathy got over her initial shock at my and Anthony's appearance on her doorstep (enough to let us in, at least) she proceeded to watch with narrowed eyes as Anthony doctored my wound. What exactly her suspicious mind filled in as the details of my harrowing experience, I could not say. She would not let Anthony get more than a few words in before she shuffled us both out the door, slamming it so loudly that I am sure she would have been reprimanded if she were not herself the floor's RA.

At breakfast the next morning, Anthony did manage to corner her and sputter a few remarks animatedly before she pushed past him and found me at my seat, alone for the moment while Petra went back for seconds of French toast. Kathy had faced me, and with a motherly tone, explained to me that, as my RA, she was noting the disturbing incident of last night as such, and would be instituting an "action plan" whereby she would be responsible for "checking in" on my "adjustment" to The Ledge, and, most importantly, she stressed, my "nocturnal activities." Before I had a chance to speak, much less explain, she had pushed her chair back abruptly and sauntered off, pausing only briefly to glare at Anthony, who in turn, took the opportunity to give me a withering look.

Petra took my injury in stride. She launched into a story of how she had broken her arm crawling into a boyfriend's window back in Louisiana. My protestations of innocence as to romantic intent where Anthony was concerned fell on deaf ears.

Others in the dining hall either politely ignored my bandaged cheek or wished me quick healing.

Brian, however, had plenty of advice for me. Before letting me carry my breakfast tray out the door, he subjected me to a veritable pharmacopoeia of remedies for lacerations, abrasions, contusions, etc. Apparently, he was himself very familiar with such lamentable injuries, having been ill-treated at the high school he had attended prior to his arrival at Preacher's Ledge. I thanked him for his interest and made a hasty retreat, afraid he might offer to nurse me himself before too long.

Anthony walked me to class that morning. I tried to shake him, I believe one might say, as soon as we neared the academic building that housed my first course of the day, but he followed me in, chatted with the professor, and did not leave before he found me where I had attempted to hide in the back of the classroom.

It was not that I wasn't politely appreciative of his efforts in settling me. I did feel appreciative, I did feel…well, I wasn't quite sure what I felt, and that was an uncertainty I was willing to foster. I did not want to be forced to think of him any longer than was necessary.

"Bye," I rapidly, and rudely I admit, exclaimed as he

approached. "Thanks for everything."

He ignored my dismissal and crouched down to be at eye level with me. He peeled back the gauze covering my three butterfly bandages for inspection. I attempted to roll my eyes at this patronizing display but apparently that act required, however minutely, some of the muscles in the cheek. I winced instead and was surprised to see genuine concern in Anthony's blue eyes.

"I wish you had let me take you in for stitches. You may end up with a scar." He said this all with clinical detachment, never looking right at me after that brief glimpse of his distress at my pain.

"No matter," I chirped. "Thanks again." I heartily wished to be rid of him, if only now, as a few students arrived, to quell the rapidly-spreading boyfriend rumors of which Petra had informed me.

He did look at me then, pressing his lips together in displeasure. His eyes were still magical, but I looked swiftly away and toward the classroom door, where a steady stream of students filed in.

"Okay, Suny. That's that, then." There was a note of something in his voice. Surely not hurt? Disappointment, perhaps? Maybe just fatigue. I felt chagrined, but remained silent. He turned once as he reached the doorway and then was gone.

Well, enough of that.

As the week sped by, I found my days more than filled by classes.

In addition to the previously described course in Arabic, I had an unstructured arts class with a flamboyantly dressed young woman of perhaps thirty. She energetically encouraged me to choose a discipline that "spoke to me." I indulged her, as I had been told she was very talented as both an artist and a teacher, but in the end, I stayed safely in an area in which I felt I could do little damage: landscape painting. The campus was sprawling, encompassing much more than the few acres the core of buildings utilized. Jacqui, the aforementioned arts teacher, bade me to spend the next week or two wandering to find a "mystical" spot that, again, "spoke to me." I promptly found a picturesque stream tucked in the woods, steps from the academic buildings, and set to painting, hoping the choice would be of sufficiently loud voice to "speak" to Jacqui when she hiked out in the coming weeks to give me instruction on technique. I found the activity surprisingly engrossing. In fact, I learned quickly to set the alarm on my watch so I wouldn't get lost in the pursuit of the perfect shade of gray for a jutting rock, or some such absorbing task.

Literature, as it was entitled simply, was similarly flexible. We were asked to provide book suggestions, then to divide our time and energy equally between pursuing pieces of our own choice, a selection from others' choices (including Marshall's, our professor), and from the traditional collegiate canon. It was up to us to link the works as to theme, style, or some other element. Marshall, a painfully prim man in his late forties delighted in the requirement that he read all the works in question in order to properly evaluate our progress. This meant dozens of books per semester, there being fifteen students in the class. This was not undoable for Marshall, however. He insisted he could read as well as drive on his way to and from campus each day, and was therefore famous for his many car accidents. Luckily for all, he lived only two miles from the college on a lightly traveled lane.

I had yet to be assigned a math class. Instead, I met twice with the math chair, an elderly woman, Natasha, of quite large proportions who thrust complicated equations at me to finish as quickly as possible, if possible. I was to be placed according to who wished to work with me based on my performance. That I had met traditional college-level math requirements was made clear by my test scores, I was told. But I was further required by Preacher's Ledge to continue my mathematical pursuit "until such time as the Department and Student in question concurred in the decision" that I had had enough.

98

My professors each gave me a schedule for making up the work I had missed during the first weeks of the semester, though Marshall needed to be reminded twice that such a thing was necessary. Each gave me what I believed to be sufficient time.

All but one, that is.

My fifth course, Freshman Thought, was a seminar course, its curriculum full of readings from all disciplines. A rotated course, it was taught by different professors each term, each of whom, of course, had their own areas of expertise. This meant that some years a professor of physics would be expected to moderate a seminar that included readings in the arts, psychology, mathematics, history– what have you.

Such was the case in the section to which I was assigned. Gilbert, the one and same who had rankled Anthony so, was a professor of physics and biology. Gilbert was not a professor of psychology, as he made it quite clear to us on the first day of class that week. Gilbert would not give me special consideration and expected me to turn in a paper on each: the impact of NASA and the space program on consumer product development, the trends in American political strategy of the last fifty years, and comparative economic theories of Adam Smith and Karl Marx. By next Tuesday. In addition to staying "on track" with the topic of the week– the criminal mind.

At this admittedly hefty assignment, I gave a genuine smile. Gilbert (who eschewed Ledge convention and went by Gilbert rather than his first name, which appeared to be an innocuous John, according to my course schedule) had thrown down the gauntlet. I enjoyed a challenge, always had, and as I had already read two of the prescribed texts, both literate, but popular books available at any library, I felt more than equal to the task. If Gilbert was taken aback by this easy acceptance of an unreasonable workload, he did not let on. Frankly, he did not let on about much of anything, leaving the discussion of Dr. Emile Anderson's tome, 'A Sociopath Dissected' to the students and his senior moderator, who happened in this class to be Brian, Keeper of the Numbers.

In an effort to instill in departing seniors the value of giving back to the community their intellectual gifts and wisdom, each senior had to moderate a seminar or lead some kind of workshop at the local library or community center. Brian chose this seminar, to be sure, simply because he liked to hear himself talk.

"...and so I much prefer the thought of Kowalski, who is sadly neglected in Dr. Anderson's work. The truly dangerous criminal is unaware of his own wrong-doing, not because of a neuropsychiatric underdevelopment, but because he has so thoroughly intellectualized and justified his wrong-doing that he could honestly, in his own evaluation, declare he was committing no wrong. Not to say that there are not those who..."

And so on in much the same vein. I made an effort to contribute, but as I noticed Gilbert's evident distaste for those of great verbosity, glaring as he did at Brian throughout the entire period, I tamed my opinions and interpretations, keeping the majority of them to myself.

At least for the time being.

Seeing as the seminar was only one of five courses, I did not dwell on it overmuch. My other courses made up for anything the seminar lacked, in that they were stimulating, well-taught, and flexible, yet attentive to content.

As I said earlier, I believed myself in a sort of academic heaven.

I told Father as much during a mid-week phone call. Whether he remembered any of my tales, or the event of the call itself, I cannot be sure. He raved on and on about a new member of his staff, a statistician named Bianca whose utility appeared to be in her skill at crunching the numbers related to the probability theory of psi events. Between the lines of Father's telling, however, I could tell Bianca's utility extended to being female and "delightfully redheaded" as well.

My sympathies to Magdalene, my stepmother of the

moment, were soon to be warranted, I suspected.

I briefly asked after Anthony, to be polite only, I assure you, but Father merely murmured something about transcription and left it at that. With Father's new interest in Bianca's work, I felt sure Anthony would be the only one transcribing the Gullah histories from this point on.

The end of the week arrived swiftly. Although I had just a mite of reading to conquer, I allowed Petra to "kidnap" me, as she called it, at the end of my last class. During the week, I had begged off donning any of her wardrobe, save an overly-bright T-shirt or two, but she was determined to take me to the next town for shopping as soon as could be arranged. As I left my Literature class (Marshall had to be told several times that class was over and that, no, he would not see us tomorrow, as it was the weekend. I missed Mr. Munston terribly) Petra accosted me and insisted we leave immediately.

This we planned to do, but as we strolled in that lazy way that comes after last classes on Fridays, we spied Frieda and Brian hurrying our way. They paused on spotting us.

"Off to town to pick up gigolos?" Frieda spat with a saccharine smile.

Petra flashed her bold, white teeth, suddenly predatory, but ignored the remark.

Brian snorted loudly and spoke, "We worked out a buddy system. Frieda had some work to catch up on. Incredibly effective. Increased our lab time exponentially. Well, at least about twenty percent. We go up together. Then we're sure to resist alternate activities, right Frieda? You ladies want in?"

"Thanks Brian," Petra began, "but we've got a hot date with Suny's credit card. Oh, shit on a stick– I do need to head that way first. I've got some cultures to check. What say you, Suny? Want to tag along with us science dweebs?"

I shrugged and followed them, trying to bring Frieda into conversation. I did not want her obvious dislike of Petra to sour the possibility of another friend. And her points in our philosophy discussion at the dining hall had been intriguing, though a bit off-target. Further discourse could show her the light, I was sure.

We walked a bit ahead of the others, Frieda deliberately setting the pace a notch above Petra's easy gait. We talked lightly, mainly about my first week, until we crested the hill from whose summit the slope led down to the valley that cradled the horrid monolith that was the science building.

I shuddered at the sight.

"You don't like post-modern architecture?" Frieda asked. It was apparent that she held the structure in high regard.

"I suppose one might learn to appreciate it."

"It's a fabulous facility. Really it is. We lobbied hard for the greenhouse. They're only a half dozen of us in plant science, but I think the bonus of costs-savings for the grounds crew helped sell the idea. They grow all the campus's landscaping annuals from seed and overwinter some things as well."

I nodded but the glass and steel gnawed at my eyes.

"Each bit is just so...stuck on, I guess."

"They've segregated each science physically. The architecture serves the needs of each discipline. Plant science has the greenhouse. Physics is on the top floor–"

"Is that bump on top an observatory? Astronomy perhaps?"

"No, actually, that's chemistry. Right next to physics. The bump is an industrial exhaust fan. That way, the rest of the building can maintain its air quality. Especially important for the greenhouse, you see. Each bit serves a purpose."

A third voice chimed in, "It's completely inconvenient for those of us doing interdisciplinary science study. Biology labs are on the second floor, but if you're working with plants too... Used to be this institution valued interdisciplinary study. It is a liberal arts college, you know."

Petra had caught up with us and could not resist putting in her two pennies, so to speak.

"There are those of us who know themselves well enough to know where they'd like to specialize already." Frieda shot back.

"Find themselves narrow enough is more like it." Petra gave another sweet, but scary, smile.

Frieda stomped off down the hill. Brian seemed at a loss, then scampered after her, loyal to his lab "buddy."

Petra broke out in uproarious laughter so loud it sailed down the hill after Frieda like a hunting harpy. She answered my questioning, and more than slightly disapproving, gaze with a simple shrug.

"What can I say? I inspire strong emotions." Petra waggled her eyebrows at me and skipped down the hill.

Chapter 11

Squeaks and scurryings reached my ears as we pushed through double doors reading *Biology*.

"Ugh! Heebie jeebies," Petra whispered as we passed row upon row of rodent cages. She crossed herself and spat into her closed fist, then shivered.

"I hate walking through here. Why they had to put all these guys on display when they claim to discourage animal experimentation, I don't know. It's the damned professors who are doing all the animal study anyhow. Do you know they charge us a $400 lab fee? Hell, they spend it all on gerbil food and I can't say there's one of us who has any interest in the dirty little things."

"You don't like them?" I paused and poked a finger through the wire towards a writhing heap of baby white mice.

"When I was six, my cousin–" Petra began.

"Oh yes, the hamster thing." I interjected, a vision of a miniature Petra, face screwed up in disgust, flashing through my mind.

"Did I tell you about that?"

Gavno! What a *dubiina* I am!

"Sure…sure," I stuttered, "Your cousin…Xavier. You were playing pirate and he tied you to the porch post like it was a mast. And then he put your other cousin, Salome's hamster in your jumpsuit."

Petra swung around and looked at me hard.

"Suny, girl, I have never told anyone that story."

"I'm sure you did. On Wednesday…when we were talking about…about…"

"About hamsters?"

Oh, hell.

"I'm sure of it. How else would I know? Perhaps you were sleepy at the time and forgot," I offered pathetically.

Petra did not know anything about my father. After all,

105

there were millions of Davises in the world, weren't there? I wanted to keep her, and everyone else on campus, in a state of ignorance, if that was at all possible. Kathy might already have figured it out but…

When Petra opened her mouth again, I was no longer certain that it would be an easy undertaking.

"Perhaps I was sleepy, or perhaps you've got the sight." She opened a door and continued in as if she had not just said something momentous.

I followed her.

"And…and what if I did, Petra?" I asked, deciding impetuously to be bold. "Ha, ha," I laughed tonelessly in an attempt to appear nonchalant.

"What if you did what?" she muttered, already busy with Petrie dishes she pulled from a glass-fronted refrigerator.

"What if I were…well…"

"Touched? Hmmm…" she said, distracted for the moment by her specimens. "Lady up the road from our place, big ole Creole lady– dressed in old silk gowns and had to have her maid help her dress, she had the sight. Told me when Toby Soileau fell off an overpass and was in the hospital that he would be just fine. She said she knew because he was due to drown the summer he was eighteen, and sure enough, he did. She knew that, she knew when a baby wasn't going to come out right, knew when a girl was pregnant before she even skipped her time…"

Petra turned to me, something bright blue and crystalline growing over the edge of the glass dish she held.

"She told me I would die young too. Die violently at the hands of an evil and greedy man."

Her words hung in the air and it was my turn to shiver.

Then Petra let out a cackle so loud and high I was surprised it didn't break every specimen bottle in the lab.

"Of course, telepathy's a bit different than clairvoyance. If you can read my mind any time you call it up–"

"Oh no, I never call it up. It just comes without–"

Suny Davis! What a *balvan* you are!

But Petra had her head back in the refrigerator, my words unheard.

"Someone's been fooling with my molds," she muttered.

I surveyed the rest of this inner lab area. There was actually a gurney of some sort over by the window. I didn't want to think about the possibility that they dissected anything larger than a frog or pig here. However, some anatomy work was done for sure, as there was a full human skeleton hanging on a metal stand in the corner. Was he plastic or the "real deal," to use a colloquialism? I went closer to determine the material.

Petra emerged from the refrigerator and noticed my interest in the skeleton. "Say hey to Suny, Ambrose."

"His name is Ambrose? Was that his name when he was living?" For I had ascertained that he was a true skeleton.

"Naw, that's just what I call him— it means, 'belonging to the immortals.' Pretty appropriate, I thought. He keeps me company late at night— not that I'm coming too often after dark anymore. Those ghost sightings even have me a little spooked. Want to hear his favorite song?" She launched into a jazzy rendition of "Dead Man's Party" by Oingo Boingo. Really, I much preferred their version.

Petra happily sang away and scraped blue bits onto microscope slides. I made use of this opportunity to slip out, calling behind me, "Back in a moment."

The stairs that connected the three floors of the science building were a loose, multi-colored spiral, suspiciously similar to a double helix. I took the downward path and, as I stepped off onto the first floor, I heard birdsong at a volume that told me at once it was not heard simply through an open window. I followed the chirping and squeaking until I found myself in front of a glass door, steamed opaque.

This was Frieda's prized greenhouse, I deduced. Through the fogged door I could just make out movement. I pushed through, the birdsong hitting me almost physically with its volume. It was a tape apparently, though why it was unnaturally loud, I could not see.

"Oh - you startled me." Frieda turned from a tray of leggy plants.

"I'm sorry. Is it okay to come in?"

"As long as you're not Brian, it's okay with me. But if you wouldn't mind, could you stay in the taped area?"

I looked down to find myself contained by a rectangle of black and yellow caution striping adhered to the floor.

Frieda continued, "You'd be surprised how much damage pollen or spores can do to a controlled experiment. Bacteria even. All of it can be brought in on your shoes and clothing. This can't be exactly a clean room environment, but we do the best we can. That Brian ruined my last batch earlier this month. God knows what he's carrying around on any given day. I'm not taking chances anymore. Half the reason I come down here with him is so I can make sure he doesn't touch anything in here. Mr. Nosy."

Frieda ducked behind a curtain of plastic sheeting strips. I noted the lab coat and plastic shoe coverings she wore. The space behind was filled floor to ceiling with trays containing various shades and shapes of greenery.

"I really don't have much to do today, but I did promise Brian and, like I said, he should not be left unsupervised, if you know what I mean. And it doesn't hurt to check on everything. The grounds department has their own section–" I gathered she spoke of the area on the opposite side from where I stood; chrysanthemums sat in trays, an earthy rainbow of sorts. "– but even this week someone tramped through and disturbed things. It's hard for people to understand just how delicate life is– plant life, I mean. The difference made by a slight adjustment to temperature, to exposure. Any of it can spell disaster."

"What is it you're testing?" I asked politely, but loudly. Really, the birdsong was a bit over the top. Immediately, I regretted my question. I fear Frieda was the type to ramble on

108

interminably, including irrelevancies in every sentence.

"I myself am really interested in herbology but we've received a grant from the state's agricultural extension service to test plants for the home gardener and market farmer. Seems they're looking for the best of the more southern crops for our agricultural zone." She indicated the curtained area. "Watermelon, tomatoes, eggplant– heat lovers. So we're testing greenhouse environments on dwarf varieties, trying different hybrids, different conditions. There's drip irrigation, southern species birdsong, sunlight filters…"

I let her go on, wondering if Petra would conclude her culture "checking" soon.

"…red plastic mulch for boosting yields, but as I said, so much has to be greenhouse grown here in the north, so we paneled the glass in one section with red plastic to act as a filter. It keeps falling off though because of the humidity. And that's another variable. The humidity in the northeast can be just as high as the south, but our nights are cooler…"

"You'll have to let me know how it all comes out," I remarked quickly, and moved toward the door. But Frieda's voice stopped me, its tone changed from lecturing to timid.

"Are you…are you and Rocky…you're shopping , huh?"

"Yes. That is, I find myself lacking the proper attire…" Mr. Munston's admonitions about my diction came to mind and I amended my response. "We're clothes shopping."

"I don't know if Rocky is the person I would choose to help me pick out clothes. She dresses like a whore." This last was said with such venom that I had to turn.

Frieda was trying to control her face, but her eyes burned and her mouth was pinched shut. To keep from growling, it seemed to me. I would have to tread carefully with this one.

"You and Petra are not the best of friends…"

"You can say that again. She's a bitch."

"Well then," I began, hoping to hold off a tirade, but to no avail. It seemed plants were not the only subject on which Frieda could expound at length.

"I never should have told her Willie and I were having problems. That was my stupidity. But did she have to speed things along by seducing him? To hear her tell it, she would never touch someone in a strong, solid relationship, but did she give us a chance to get stronger? No. She steals him away for a casual fling and then discards him. He won't even talk to me now. I can't believe I ever confided in her. I thought, with her experience, maybe she'd have had some advice, you know? We were working together all that time here in the greenhouse those first weeks and I thought she was well, not a friend, but… someone to talk to. Hell, I'm glad Gilbert wouldn't approve her thesis. At least it got her out of the greenhouse. And I believe in karmic retribution. I think it serves her right, having to scramble to find something new. I hope he bats her next choice down too. Though I'd be happier still if she would graduate and just leave. Suny, I feel sorry for you that you got saddled with her as a roommate."

"Oh, I don't find…that is, I'm sure…Well, I don't have a boyfriend, you see. And with the courseload…"

"I thought you and Tony Scarborough…"

"Anthony? No. No, I can assure you…Anthony is five years my senior and… no, no, definitely not."

"So, he didn't hit you?" she asked, indicating my bandaged cheek.

"He did…that is to say, he didn't mean to…"

"I heard you snuck out to meet him. I used to do that with Willie."

Zacroy roat, will you? I wanted to shout at her, but I held my tongue. Better to just end the conversation.

"I believe I hear Petra calling me," I stated brightly and went though the door before Frieda could shuffle after me in her plastic-covered shoes. I couldn't bear it if she continued to fill me in on the rest of the distorted story that was circulating about my run-in with Anthony.

My, the drama life affords some people!

After a peek into the rodent-ridden biology lab confirmed my suspicion that Petra was still consumed with her molds, I continued up to the third floor to see what there was yet to see. I didn't have an official science class this term, but I planned to do some reading to make up for the fact and it didn't hurt to be familiar with the facilities.

I nodded at a huddle of students "gaming" with an intricate map and playing cards in the student sitting area. They were oblivious to my passing, though one emerged from the hood of his velveteen character cloak to look past me to the clock on the wall. Most of the doors along the hallway leading to the chemistry labs were closed. There didn't seem to be anyone about and, though the labs appeared well-equipped and I had been known to putter with a Bunsen burner myself, I had no set task or interest and did not even know if I had the proper clearances to do more than walk down the hallway.

I was just about to turn when a great humming sounded through the corridor. Now, up until that point, I had forgotten the tales of the building being haunted. The stories brought to mind by the sound (it was almost a moaning really) did not scare me, of course. My sudden intake of breath and abruptly frozen limbs were...er, simply a reflex, a reaction to the unanticipated noise. I was simply trying to remain still to be better able to ascertain the disturbance's origin.

It took me a moment to figure that the humming was fed into the hallway through a series of air ducts, exchanges really, and that the noise was only an indication of the cycling of a fan. The humming subsided to a loud whisper as the air of the chemistry wing began to move.

My heart rate returned to normal. The result of the puzzling out of the unknown was always a return to equilibrium, I've found. I spun on my heel to retrace my steps.

This last I did too quickly. A door swung open and smacked me right on the cheekbone. My bandaged cheekbone, I might add.

Poor Brian, the person who had opened said offending

111

door, was treated to a most indelicate introduction to the Russian language.

When I'd finished cursing and had gingerly determined that if my wound had been reopened it had not yet soaked my bandage with blood, I assured Brian that I was not seriously harmed.

But Brian was not hovering solicitously nearby as might be expected. With a distracted apology he had retreated down the corridor, walking as if in a dream.

My concern for myself quickly diminished, only to be supplanted by worry for Brian. He appeared positively dazed. I caught up with him quickly.

"Brian, are you alright?"

He turned to me as a drunk might toward a cautioning bleat of a horn.

"Oh, Suny. I thought you were shopping," he mumbled, already moving away as he spoke.

"Brian?" I called as he reached the stairs and began to descend. But he was soon gone.

I stood perplexed at the top of the stair a moment. My hand stole up and felt a wet patch on the gauze there.

"Ouch," was all I could think to say.

Petra brushed off my run-in with Brian, relating how he had once inadvertently locked himself in a chemical supply closet, yet hadn't called out for help until several classes beyond his own. Apparently, he'd hit on some theory while trying the knob and wanted some time without distraction to think through his hypothesis.

"He was probably on the verge of some breakthrough. Hopefully, sticking your face in his business didn't confuse him. Get it? Sticking your face in... Oh, you're no fun. Let's get you cleaned up and out of here."

I followed Petra obediently, my new habit of acquiescing to demands apparently passed from Anthony to her, but Brian's unfocused eyes and furrowed brow remained with me.

The rest of the afternoon and evening flew past. We ate at a succulent restaurant where Petra was known, if not loved. She too was able to tempt me into eating seafood, but just a heavenly morsel or two from the plates of her well-chosen dishes. Satiated, we moved on to shopping.

At a largish mall in the next town, Petra made some outrageous suggestions for my wardrobe, but it soon became apparent that our respective tastes in clothing were too wide a chasm to be easily crossed. Petra suggested we split up and do our shopping separately, then meet up again in a couple of hours. It was thus that I managed to weasel out of buying anything uselessly filmy or ridiculously skimpy. I ended up with quite a satisfactory set of outfits, not to mention some bras that fit. After we met up again, I even convinced Petra to try on a sedate frock or two. The fact that she chose to purchase one satisfied me immensely. Never mind that she thought it made her look "like a spinster schoolmarm...in a good, kinky kinda way."

Try as I might to be engulfed completely in the newly-discovered pleasures of shopping with someone other than a stepmother, something tugged at my mind as if I should be somewhere else. There was an urgency to this distraction, a pressing need of some kind. I attempted to push it aside, thinking it might only be resistance to the ease with which I enjoyed Petra's company, unaccustomed as I was to that circumstance.

In this surmise, I was horribly wrong.

When we returned to campus that evening, we were stopped at the gate by uniformed police. The officer was professional but reticent. Still ignorant as to the disturbance causing the police presence, we made our way up the hill after he'd checked our identification cards. One would have expected us to speculate aloud, but Petra and I remained silent despite our wonder at the swarm of officers and news vans that had descended upon the academic buildings.

We were drawn to the revolving lights of police cruisers like moths and soon stood among the gathered throng of what must have constituted the whole of the student body, collectively watching the doors of the science building.

As they finally opened, ejecting a cluster of emergency personnel and a gurney, low voices buzzed. And though I already knew whose face was covered by the glowing white sheeting on the gurney, the sound of his name met my ears and echoed through my reeling mind.

Brian.

When Petra leaned on me and quickly soaked my shoulder with her tears, two innocuous thoughts passed through my head. The first was that it appeared the group of students pressing me at all sides was not the entire student body after all, and that the particular missing someone was in no position to join us. The second was that it was a good thing I had found that dress for Petra.

She would need it for the funeral.

And some waterproof mascara too.

Chapter 12

Dead. Brian was dead.

I let my arm fall, hairbrush dangling from my hand, and peered closer into my mirror. Some day, I too, would pass from this earth. And Father– though I could hardly believe that could ever happen. And my mother…perhaps already…

This last thought spurred a pang in my heart. The thought had crossed my mind before. Perhaps she was dead, perhaps that is why she has never once, not once, tried to… I attempted to shake myself from my musing, but the thoughts would not go. It did not help that I could see, from the corner of my eye, the canvas that I carted back and forth to the Ledge with me, the painted scene that was the site of a mother's grief at separation from her child so deep, so incessant, so fierce…

I suppose it was a good thing that Petra chose to burst back into our room at that moment, with utter, gossipy nonsense spewing from her lips. Soon, I thought nothing of death, of fathers or mothers, so ridiculous were her words. I could not hold back my objections.

"A ghost? You can't believe them! Someone's just trying… trying *veshut lapshu na ushi*! They must all be *p'yan v stel'ku*!"

Petra plopped down amongst her cushions and regarded me, "Okay, Suny, I don't know what the hell you just said, but I'm telling you, from what I hear, that chem lab was like a scene from Poltergeist. Flasks, bottles, 'scopes flew all over the place– it's lucky the whole building didn't blow up. As it is, they're not quite sure if it was fumes from the chemicals mixing, or the cabinet that fell on him."

I winced at this last. Either death could not have been pleasant. I had not known Brian for long, but still, the thought of toxic asphyxiation or of dying crushed under a stainless steel storage cabinet, with no hope of moving it, with no hope of anyone coming… Well, one must simply console oneself with the conjecture that surely the blow had been sufficient to

115

render poor Brian unconscious, no matter what the ultimate cause of death.

But such surmises could not replace the intellectual outrage I felt. What a bunch of stuff and nonsense. I'm sure Petra's informants had not been truly drunk, as I'd accused in my exasperated Russian, but I did hold that they were trying to - how would that translate? Literally, hanging spaghetti on someone's ears, but in English, I guess one would be more likely to say, pulling the wool over someone's eyes.

A poltergeist? Was this not an institution that purported to value critical thinking? One could only hope that the police were of sound enough mind not to be taken in.

I sighed.

Petra's eyes were still a bit raw from crying and fatigue. "I'm just telling you what I overheard at breakfast. And this was from one of the teacher's tables too."

Surely this last did not bode well. Professors of higher education, to be seduced by such drivel?

"Anyhow, Suny, why are you getting all dressed up? The memorial service isn't until tomorrow morning. Hell, you haven't even had chow."

"One must appear credible as well as sound credible in one's statement if one is to be believed by law enforcement officials."

"You going to tell them they're a bunch of wackos for believing in ghosts?"

"That may constitute a portion of our conversation. But no, you see Petra, I have reason to believe that I was one of the last to see Brian alive. I can only infer from that truth that I shall quickly be called to aid the police—"

A peremptory knocking sounded.

"I'll be right with you, officer!" I called and gave one last glance at the mirror, frowning only a moment at the bandage that marred my cheek.

Petra cocked one eyebrow in surprise. Apparently, she was too overwrought with grief to have deduced what I had. I opened the door and brushed past the blue-clad young officer. He remained standing in the doorway, a puzzled expression on his face, until I beckoned for him to follow with as much patience as I could muster.

Police officers amaze me. When all else is in total chaos, they appear preternaturally calm. They never forget their jargon, their stoic countenance, or their detached courtesy.

Just such an automaton asked me to wait outside Sylvia's office (a temporary base camp, as it were) to speak with "the Chief." I only got a glimpse of this figure as he poked out the door and sent the officer scurrying for some "damned coffee, for chrissakes."

Mt. Billington was large enough, with the college, a private school for boys, a sprinkling of businesses, and an annual deluge of summer people to have a respectable police department with a handful of officers and, at their head, Chief Vernon. In his late forties, I surmised, and of good form with a still thick crop of curls, the Chief was apparently a heavy coffee drinker. At least, that was my deduction as to why he did not find Sylvia's collection of herbal teas adequate libation at eleven in the morning.

If I were to list my weaknesses– well, the weaknesses I saw in myself– I would be forced to admit to inexorable impatience. Here I was, making myself readily and uncomplainingly available to the authorities when I had a prodigious amount of reading to do, and I was made to wait.

And wait.

My only consolation was in the admittedly wicked thought that the Chief too was made to wait. For his coffee. Apparently, the officer was experiencing difficulties in procurement; he had yet to return.

I gave myself up to constructing a letter to the editor of whatever paper serviced the Mt. Billington area, observing one credo: never complain without offering a possible solution. This presented no problem, however, as I was quite assured

117

my developing plan to improve police efficiency would be received as an intelligent, thoughtful resolution to the situation in which I found myself.

A loud bark brought my musings to an abrupt end. The Chief was displeased and I was sure his waning level of caffeine was not helping.

The door flew open. But it was not the Chief who stood in the doorway, indignation in every tensed muscle. A plump, graying woman started through, then turned to face the Chief yet again. She attempted to calm herself, breathing in raggedly, but her limbs twitched at her sides, aching to throw something, I'm sure.

"That's not the only thing you'll find in my report. I intend to add a scathing evaluation of your illogical–"

"When I want your report, I'll ask for it!" the Chief bellowed, his voice disembodied, yet powerful enough to make me flinch in my chair. "I'm not ruling out a damn thing yet, so don't come in here telling me I'm crazy for keeping an open mind!"

The woman took this last and turned on her heel. She stomped past me, oblivious, then spun and made a show of returning to slam the door. With that she marched out.

Well. Sounded like a woman after my own heart. Provided I figured correctly, this flustered person was the medical examiner. If the Chief was falling prey to the circulating notion of a poltergeist, I too would take issue with his "open mind."

I shot a look at the door. The Chief did not know I was here, apparently. With the officer still absent, I supposed it would be within the parameters of proper protocol to simply knock.

He had been awfully angered, though. Perhaps it would be better to allow him some time to cool down.

And perhaps the medical examiner knew something he should know, the relevant nature of which he would only see if he had her knowledge to add to my observations of Brian's odd behavior. I could find out what she knew and relay the information in a much more diplomatic fashion. After all, as much as I admired passionate conviction, poor Brian deserved an investigation unsullied by petty quarreling. And there was something tugging at me, something that demanded my attention...

I had no time to waste, however. I dashed out to find the medical examiner.

Outside the building, the September sun blinded me temporarily. I looked left and right. Then I saw her, moving toward the parking lot.

I didn't understand why just then, but I felt that same tugging and I was hit with a sense of urgency. She couldn't simply drive off. Somehow, if she did, if I were to shrug and head back up to see the Chief, if...

Brian would want me to go after her.

I bolted out into the road. Brakes screeched. A bumper nearly collided with my hip. The shock unbalanced me and I fell solidly on my rump.

"Oh, shit!" I heard through the open car window.

I struggled to stand. I hoped I had not done serious damage to my skirt.

"No, no, don't try to move. I'll get a doctor."

"Todd! I'm fine. No, really. Help me up, then follow that car!"

"Suny, you need a doctor!" Todd paced back and forth ineffectually, wringing his hands.

"Don't be ridiculous! You didn't actually *hit* me, you just— don't stand there, you big *durak*! There's a doctor in that car! Now follow the damned thing!"

I threw myself into his vehicle. Todd clambered in after me and put the car in gear, hands shaking. We sped off.

"Gosh, Suny, I'm so sorry. I didn't see you at all. Are you going to be okay? Does it hurt anywhere?"

"Todd, pay attention," I snapped my fingers in front of his face, which may not have been the best idea. It jolted him and he swerved sharply. I grabbed the wheel and righted us.

"I am fine, and will continue to be so if you will concentrate

119

on driving the car. You did not hit me. And if you had, you would not have been at fault seeing as I am the one who darted off the curb without looking."

"Are you sure?"

I attempted to roll my eyes, then grimaced at the pain from behind my gauze bandage.

"See, you are hurt!"

"Todd, it is only my cheek that hurts. I was trying to catch that car before it drove off. I believe it was kismet that you nearly crashed into me. How else would I have been able to catch the medical examiner?"

Thankfully, Todd was too busy worrying over my health to wonder why we were stalking the medical examiner. He was a good driver, despite his earlier deviation from the road. He kept the blue car in sight. We headed down through trees toward town.

Ultimately, the blue car pulled off and up a winding drive, and stopped in a vast parking lot. A bulky white monster of a house, sober and crisp, was the apparent destination. A discreet sign near the front steps read, "Kennedy Funeral Services."

I had expected to follow her to the courthouse, the police station, or a clinic perhaps.

"You can drop me here, Todd." I watched the plump woman walk around to a side entrance.

"Suny, I've been thinking…we've only just met but… well, maybe it was fate, me running you down and all… Do you think… would you like to meet me at The Dive later for a soda?"

The heavy door closed after the medical examiner. I craned my head back and forth, trying to see her through the windows facing us.

"Uh, Suny?"

"What? Oh, sure…The Dive…in town? Then you can drive me back up to campus."

"Awesome," Todd exclaimed.

I almost forgot to wave my thanks as he drove off.

I made my way up the steps. The front door was double-wide. Inside was quiet. The carpet was quiet. The colors on the walls, quiet. Even the hinges that closed the door behind me were quiet.

There was no one around.

A reception desk sat unmanned in the lobby. Above it hung a bad studio portrait, a grouping of an older man, an even older woman, the plump medical examiner much younger, and a man so close to her in features and age, he could only have been a brother. A brass plate captioned, "The Kennedy Family of Undertakers, Your Family in This Time of Sorrow."

A clanging racket pulled my attention down the corridor to a descending staircase. Ignoring the attached "Private" sign, I pushed through the door and ran down. Perhaps it was the sound's harsh similarity to that which I imagined would be made by a stainless-steel cabinet that produced my alacrity.

"Test Two," I heard echoing ahead. Then a reverberating din. The door from behind which these sounds emanated was locked, I discovered as I tried the knob.

There is, at times, a benefit to being nearly six-feet tall. A small, square window in the door allowed me to see through into the room.

Dr. Kennedy (I presumed) stood high on a stepladder. Below her perch, an eight-foot tall metal cabinet lay flat out on the tile floor. Loudly, to no one I could see, she said, "Only great force applied to the uppermost portion of the cabinet, casters locked–"

"Suny!"

"*Zaebis*! *Chyort*, Anthony! What are you doing here?"

When he had hissed my name there in the corridor, I thought my heart would stop.

"Me? I've been looking all over for you. If I hadn't run into Todd–"

An earthy grunting rumbled through the door. Dr. Kennedy squatted like a weight-lifter, strain in her limbs as she heaved the cabinet upright. She had removed the glass panels from the door fronts, but it remained a difficult task.

I raised my hand to knock. I simply had to speak with this woman.

Anthony caught my arm. "Oh no, the police are looking for you and Sylvia has campus security scrambling too."

"For what reason? I merely desired to speak with the medical examiner–"

"You can't just leave when summoned by the police as a potential witness!"

"Anthony, while I am not familiar with the Massachusetts Penal Code in particular, I am sure– Hey, what are you doing here anyway?"

"I told you. I came to find you, ran into Todd–"

"But you had returned to South Carolina."

"Suny, Brian was my friend."

I looked up at the change in his voice. Those eyes caught mine and I couldn't look away. In them, I was sure I saw more pain than would be expected by the death of an old classmate. And wasn't he here a bit quickly? Brian's name had not been released until this morning's reports, and even if someone had called him from campus last night...

Ha! Anthony thought *I* resisted sharing *my* perceptions? My own eyes narrowed as they held his. Anthony blinked quickly, then looked away.

"Come on, Suny. The Chief wants you."

Though still reluctant to go just yet, I allowed Anthony to pull me up the stairs.

From behind us, the clatter of yet another fall of the cabinet sounded. I would definitely have to pick Dr. Kennedy's brain.

We drove in an old station wagon, presumably borrowed from his mother. The campus was a few miles up the hill from town and I could stand the silence no longer.

"What do you know about the medical examiner?"

"The what?"

"Come now, Anthony, don't be dense. We only just left

her."

"Lillian Kennedy?"

"Is that her name? She is the medical examiner, isn't she?"

"Well, I guess so. I never really thought about it. She's the undertaker; her family's been doing it for years. I don't suppose we have much call for a medical examiner of our own here but I guess she could be it. She went off to medical school, at least. My mom always admired her for that, them being classmates and all, and everyone else in their class getting married and nothing more. She won a scholarship, I think."

I understood that desire. Mt. Billington was a charming town, but I'm sure it had not been a well-spring of opportunity for a bright young woman of Dr. Kennedy's generation.

"Then she came back?" This discrepancy bothered me.

"Her father died, and her brother too, in an accident on the Taconic– the parkway. There was no one to run the business. Her aunt Henrietta was the only one left. She'd always done the make-up and taken care of the families, but I don't think she ever did the– well, the other stuff. My mom thinks she's an angel from heaven because she handled all my dad's arrangements."

"Oh, Anthony. I'm sorry. I didn't know. My sympathies."

Anthony avoided my eyes, easy enough as he had the steep curves to navigate.

"Yeah, well, thanks. Lillian had to come back or they would have had to sell. But see, it's also their home. Her aunt still lives there, and now Lillian."

I stared out the window. We were nearing the campus grounds.

"She doesn't seem a happy woman, Anthony. It must be quite unfulfilling to be subjugated to the family business, to be forced into abject servitude at the whim of others. To suffer the idiocy of a gullible police Chief–"

"What are you talking about? How melodramatic can you get?"

123

"It is *not* melodrama, Anthony, merely an honest portrait of a modern woman besieged with the age-old duties of hearth and home. An intellect insulted by the dulled senses of those around her, a police force duped–"

"Chief Vernon's senses couldn't be sharper, Suny."

"Ha! Not according to Dr. Kennedy. While I awaited my interview with the Chief, Dr. Kennedy stormed out in a rage. Apparently the Chief's being drawn in–"

"Suny! Why don't you just mind your own business? Dr. Kennedy and the Chief– oh hell, just stop sticking your nose in. For a psychic, you sure can be blind to what's really going on–"

"For a– what? Anthony, I'll have you know–"

But Anthony jerked the car into a parking space at the administration building and got out.

I sat, my heart pounding against my seatbelt. Damn him.

Anthony rapped on my window.

I gave him a steely glare.

He was unbothered. Through the glass, he mouthed, "Out."

I ignored him.

He rapped again.

"Now!" This I heard, even through the glass.

I slung my seatbelt aside and shoved the door open. I strode past him. I wouldn't have him lead me in like captured prey.

Chapter 13

The Chief waited for me by the office door, a mug of coffee in his hand.

I passed him, entered Sylvia's office, and plopped myself down in the same chair I'd occupied the previous weekend.

"I assume you will be interested in my last encounter with the deceased," I began, not waiting for the Chief to be fully in the room.

He walked to the desk. In slow motion, it seemed.

"Well, Miss Davis–"

"Ms., if you please."

The Chief sat down and rested his elbows on Sylvia's desk.

"*Ms.* Davis. If you would care to start there."

I did care to start there, and succinctly related my "run-in" with Brian in the science building.

The Chief leaned forward further still to better inspect my bandaged cheek.

"Boyfriend gave that to you?"

"Excuse me?"

"I got here," he indicated his notebook, "from several students that you were in the science building, that you chased after Mr. Nelson, calling his name and that you seemed to be bleeding."

"Who said...I mean, I never...That is, I assure you, Chief Vernon, that not only did I not *chase* Bri– Mr. Nelson, but I do not have a boyfriend and..." I held in my exasperation with difficulty. "As I *said*, Mr. Nelson came out of a door, a door which hit me and re-opened my wound, and more importantly, I am sure, he seemed very distracted, out-of-sorts, very..."

"And you were concerned about him, why exactly?"

"I'm sorry?"

"Why did you care that he wasn't paying attention to you?"

"It was not his behavior toward me that was of concern.

125

The mere fact of Bri– Mr. Nelson's aphonia–"

The Chief gave me only a blank stare.

"Chief, Mr. Nelson was typically quite loquacious."

But the Chief was no longer listening to me. He was flipping through papers.

I reassessed my awe of the police. Here I was, trying to tell what I knew about the unfortunate incident as any good citizen might and–

"You're excused, Ms. Davis."

"I'm…what?"

"Excused. We have what we need here and we know how to contact you should we need anything further."

"But–"

The Chief rubbed his brow with a meaty hand. When he looked up again, he looked near exploding.

"I'll be going then, shall I?"

He waved me away and resumed shuffling papers.

Well, that was unsatisfying. I squinted back at the Chief, then closed the door. I truly wondered what he had in those notes. If only I could…

I shook myself. Whatever could I be thinking?

Anthony and Sylvia were arranged in a lounge area, deep in conversation. I was sure I would have my fill of Mr. Scarborough at the memorial service the college had hastily scheduled. I did not want to subject myself to more of Anthony's presence than was absolutely unavoidable, so I tiptoed past the two of them. My reading had been sadly, but necessarily, postponed. Now I looked forward to the escape it offered.

"Suny!"

Gavno! Sylvia had spotted me.

"Suny, join us. Anthony and I were just discussing the… the tragedy. It looks like Brian was the victim of some pretty negative energy."

"Is that your assessment too, Anthony?"

126

"No need to be snide, Suny. There are some things that should be looked into. It's possible Brian was generating a self-injuring poltergeist. I don't know what he had to be guilty about—"

"Generating?" Sylvia was riveted.

"Suny, do you want to fill Sylvia in on what we know about poltergeists?" Anthony leaned back, hands behind his head.

A challenge. I would not fall prey— But damn his eyes! They mocked me, teased, taunted...

"Anthony, last I checked we don't truly know anything about so-called poltergeists. There are several theories floating around, if you'll excuse the pun, and each is near as ridiculous as the next. The one to which you are referring, I believe, is that a disturbed individual, usually in the throes of adolescence, releases stress psychokinetically, often without being conscious of the fact, and in cases of self-loathing or guilt, has been known to hurt his or her self."

Sylvia looked from Anthony to me and back again.

"Psychokinetically. That's using the mind to move things? But there's the ghost, the apparition that was seen in the science building. Everyone's assuming it was the ghost who attacked Brian."

She looked to Anthony for explanation.

"Sometimes an apparition is witnessed in a poltergeist case. A projection from the mind of the afflicted person, usually a monstrous form, not quite human—"

I couldn't stand it any longer. I turned on Sylvia.

"What do you mean, everyone's assuming? You can't tell me people really believe..."

Sylvia gazed at me blankly.

Oh, for goodness sake. And I thought I'd found an intellectual haven.

I sank to a sofa in despair.

"Suny," Anthony said. "Every possibility is being investigated, including— yes, including— a paranormal one. Chief Vernon's invited the New England Society for Psi

Investigation and…AND the local skeptics' organization for their take on the case. Don't get yourself all bent out of shape. Do you think I'd let this opportunity get warped by anything less than a scientific probe?"

"What do you mean, you would let— *Ne puri mne mozgi*— are you investigating this, I mean truly investigating this?"

Anthony smiled at me.

I couldn't believe it. Try to get away and it follows…

"If Father shows up–"

"He won't show up. I talked to him by phone while you were with the Chief. Had to tell him we found you and when I let him know what was going on up here–"

"He assigned you here? Just pulled you from your work and plunked you down here! Typical! And now I have to live with one of his employees lurking around, observing everything I do…I suppose he put you on duty in that way too!"

Anthony looked away. Too quickly.

My stomach flipped. "I was kidding. Anthony, please tell me he didn't designate you my keeper."

"Suny, I didn't say that."

"No, I suppose he wouldn't want me to know."

I sighed.

Sylvia bit her lip and glanced over at me.

"You did have us worried for a bit there, running off and all. And Kathy Larson did think it best that you continue to have a monitored action plan…"

"*Cuchka derganaya* that she is!" I hollered and stood, then caught my breath, surprised at myself even. After all, Kathy meant absolutely nothing to me.

"I'm sorry. I apologize for my outburst. I don't know what came over me. This whole unfortunate business doesn't concern me in the least. I gave my information to Chief Vernon. That is all that can be expected of me. And now, I shall return to my room and finish catching up on my schoolwork." I straightened my skirt. "I expect to be cloistered the entire evening; I have much to accomplish. If

128

anything should be required of me…"

"You could help when the police let me into the chem lab. If you sensed—"

"The only thing I will sense for you, Mr. Anthony Scarborough, is…is…well, nothing. I won't sense a *damned* thing for you!"

I ignored both Sylvia's puzzled expression and Anthony's eyes, glittering as they were in such a condescendingly amused manner. I spun on my heel.

I had made myself perfectly clear, I was sure. That would certainly be the end of the matter.

I read nearly all of my assignments before dinner and scribbled notes for later expansion. I brought a book with me to the dining hall, attempted to feel nothing as I checked off my own number on the sheet at the end of the serving line, and ate alone in a corner. The students who remained on campus for Saturday dinner were buzzing with gossip. I would not be distracted by the inane speculation of those around me.

Later, with Petra at one of her infamous séances (this time "decked out" like Nancy Sinatra and determined to seek contact with the newly departed Brian), I located my stationery and composed a letter to Mr. Munston:

Dear Mr. Munston,

I never thought I'd think the thought, but I daresay I miss Broadman. However is that possible, you wonder? I find myself surrounded by intellectuals of the finest caliber, and yet, their curiosity knows no bounds, their speculation cannot be reigned in, their eyes, despite their indelible shade of blue…

What? I crumpled the paper and began again, clamping down on my wandering mind.

I managed a sensible epistle after all, lamenting in the end only my lack of science instruction. I stamped an envelope and addressed it, hoping it would find him well. I finished up the last of my reading, typed up my papers for Tuesday, and leaned back against my pillows.

Boredom swiftly overtook me. I had nothing left to study. Perhaps Petra could relay to me what she learned in her science classes or in her experiments. Perhaps I could persuade the administration to allow me to take an additional course once I'd caught up with my work.

With nothing else to do, I went to post my letter.

The mailroom was officially closed, but it was easy enough to pop the envelope in the mail slot. That task accomplished, I wandered.

The campus was abandoned. I supposed my fellow students were out on the town, at the three-screen cinema, the bookstore-coffeeshop, or The Dive…

The Dive. I had forgotten about Todd. I daresay he understood Anthony meant to take me back to campus when he ran into him, but I owed him an apology.

I would find him, I decided.

Frankly, I needed to get off campus to rid myself of the strange melancholy that had settled over me. Granted, an acquaintance had been killed, my incisive observations had been ignored, the student and teacher population seemed to have gone mad and lost all hold on reason. To add insult to injury, Father, in his infinite lack of wisdom and discriminating thought had yet again burdened me with the effects of his inglorious occupation. Not only was Anthony to evaluate Brian's death for hocus-pocus, but he was to keep tabs on me all the while.

A babysitter. That was just what I needed.

As I returned to my room for my purse, I tried to regain the calm detachment I had fostered this afternoon when leaving Sylvia and Anthony.

I failed.

If only I could prove it, show them all that they were wrong. That Sylvia was wrong, all the campus drama-seekers were wrong, Chief Vernon, my father…

Anthony. If only I could prove Anthony wrong.

I would leave it for now, but the beginnings of a plan

swirled in my brain. As I smoothed my hair in the mirror, I do believe I was actually smiling.

A shuttle bus runs from campus to town every half hour on the weekend. It drops its passengers at the library. I alighted from it and took a moment to get my bearings. To my left was the town hall, which housed the police station. There was also a bank or two, the elementary school, and a couple of steepled churches. The commercial district lay to my right.

I walked briskly toward the lighted shops and restaurants. It was nearing nine o'clock, but a sprinkling of shops remained open. I tried on some rings in a jewelry shop, though most were too tight for my mannish hands. I also picked up a few paperbacks at the bookstore and nodded to the gang of Ledge students waiting for a guitarist to begin playing in the back. Nicholas Scarborough was there, looking rather handsome and surrounded by several pretty Ledge girls. He struggled free of them and offered to buy me a latte, but I begged off and continued on my way as Todd wasn't among them.

He had said The Dive, hadn't he? I saw its sign across the road up a ways. I was about to jaywalk (its prohibition one of those in America I thought superfluous) when I passed a pub called The Hangar. I didn't expect to see any Ledge students there, yet inexplicably, I felt the need to turn to the window.

There, at the bar, looking a bit worse for wear, was Dr. Lillian Kennedy.

Before I knew what was happening, my feet had directed me through the pub door.

Here again I saw the occasional advantage of my height and my other…well… endowments. I was still dressed neatly as I had been for my interview with Chief Vernon, but I don't believe it was only my skirt and pumps that garnered me a stool at the bar with no questions asked.

I even ordered a glass of wine so as not to appear suspicious as I observed Dr. Kennedy.

She was alone. In and of itself, that could mean nothing, or it could mean a lot. She alternated staring into the mirror behind the bar with staring at a mass of papers under her beer mug and shot glass. She didn't look through the sheaf however. The pages appeared rumpled, as if she had perused them many times before and no longer needed to actually read them to be reminded of their contents.

Whatever they contained, the information assuredly did not make her happy.

I wracked my brain for a conversation starter. But Dr. Kennedy spoke first.

"Hey Benny, whaddya think about ghosts?"

Dr. Kennedy's unsteady gaze pulled the bartender over. He regarded her indulgently.

"I don't know, Lil. Why don't you ask your aunt? She's the one belongs to the society and all, along with Vernon's aunts, and that new librarian."

"But whaddya think yourself, Benny? If Vernon told you that Ledge boy was killed by a ghost, wouldja b'lieve him? Would everyone think he was nuts?"

"Lil, this town loves its ghosts. You kidding? They'd be pleased as punch to have another one to talk about on the summer tours."

"That's what I figured. Still... Hell, what's the use? What's the use, ya know, Benny? No one's gonna b'lieve anything I've got to say 'bout it."

"Against Charlie Vernon? You're right about that one, Lil. Everyone'll think you're just saying stuff 'cuz you and he—"

"Me and him nothing, Benny Brewster! I'll settle up my tab and you won't see me ever 'gin if you say 'nuther word 'bout me and him."

Benny shook his head and went back to slicing lemons.

Dr. Kennedy took to muttering in her beer. She lifted the mug and when some sloshed on the stack of pages beneath, she didn't bother to mop it up. I watched it soak in through the scrawled words.

...multiple contusions...particularly strong...skin of the calcaneus

...page 9... falling cabinet...greatest impact...acid...

My vision blurred. I reached out my hand to grasp something, anything. I knocked over my glass, then my stool.

"*Kakogo chyorta!*" Never had I received something so strong, so unwarranted...

"Suny!"

Both Benny and Dr. Kennedy had sprung to my aid, but it was neither of the two who called out my name.

From around an opening in the wall leading to a back room of booths and pool tables came the wide-eyed face of Anthony Scarborough.

This was bad. Very bad.

I closed my eyes and grimaced. When I opened them, things had gone from bad to worse.

Hands on hips, square in the doorway next to Anthony, was Kathy Larson.

Chapter 14

Some things are simply not meant to be tolerated. The ensuing scene was unworthy of all involved. Kathy insisted that she be the one to escort me back to campus and "march" me into Sylvia's office for an emergency disciplinary council. Anthony maintained that his appointment as my father's agent in charge of my care superseded her claim as my RA. Benny grumbled and cussed about getting his license revoked for serving a minor. Dr. Kennedy ordered another shot, and when that request was ignored, she climbed up and rolled over to the other side of the bar to serve herself.

Somewhere in the midst of all this, I just walked out. I found Mrs. Scarborough's station wagon parked around the side of the building and sat heavily on the hood. I had had only a sip or so of the heinous chardonnay Benny served, but I felt as hungover as I might have had I drunk the whole bottle.

It was the sensing that did it, I suppose.

As I have related, I keep an active shield up at all times, though I am hardly aware of the fact anymore. When I'd decided at an early age to eschew further development of my...talents, as it were, I cultivated the block that I sustained to this day, rarely experiencing a breach. When a breach did occur, it was usually at times of great stress or fatigue, as at the Inn, or - as on one memorable occasion in Germany where I'd mistaken Asbach and cola for mere cola - when my inhibitions were down.

Such had not been the case in The Hangar.

And I had never experienced the force, the intrusive force of these last... communications, I could only call them. My brain was left fogged. I would put off further speculation until my mind was clear. Right now, I conjectured fatalistically, I would await Anthony, and somehow live through the inevitable lecturing and restrictions incumbent upon me.

I closed my eyes and leaned back on the windshield. My, but my head did pound.

Soon, I heard soft footfalls.

"You're getting pretty good at disappearing."

I didn't respond.

"It's not lost on me, you know. The fact that Dr. Kennedy was there."

He paused, looking for my response. He would have none.

"The amount of wine spilled on the bar was almost a full glass. I know you weren't in there to get blotto."

How insightful.

"Look, Suny. You have to understand. The Ledge is in a really sensitive position. They've got kids there with all the freedoms of college students, but they're babies...not you...well, you too, but I mean babies in a relative sense. Hell, you know what I mean. It's a balancing act. They can't have teenagers in town trying to get served."

He sighed.

"Though I have to admit, if I'd been Benny, I doubt I would have carded you either."

Perhaps it was an undue inference on my part, but I suddenly felt self-conscious stretched out across the car hood in my skirt and heels.

I straightened abruptly. Anthony regarded me from the curb, bringing back the hazy memory of the weekend before, his dark hair glinting in the moonlight. My first sight of him. But even then, he had been there in the same capacity: a disinterested guardian.

"I assume that I will be castigated," I huffed.

"Castigated? Where in hell do you get this stuff? No, you won't be castigated." He looked away as he said the next. "Kathy and I struck a deal. And Benny's not in any position to go tattling."

"You...you struck a deal?"

"Yes, and you don't need to know the details."

"I wasn't going to ask."

"Yes, you were."

Hmph.

"Well…thank you, Anthony. Never let it be said that I am one to be unappreciative of a favor. Though, truth be told, I did nothing wrong–"

"Suny, you're not even allowed to step through the door of The Hangar–"

"How arcane! Am I supposed to subjugate myself to the fatuous ordinances of a puritanical locale–"

"Yes, Suny! Yes, and yes again! You must subjugate yourself. You will subjugate yourself. Or else you'll be facing some pretty harsh penalties. Get used to it." He steadied his breathing. "Now, Kathy's not going to give me any more freebies. She's not going to… Would you just get in the car!"

I obeyed.

Anthony stayed on the curb a moment, collecting himself. When he got in behind the wheel, I made an effort to remain silent.

Well, something of an effort.

"Anthony, I'm sorry for interrupting your date with Kathy. I know you don't often get a chance to see her. Maybe now that you'll be in town–"

"It wasn't a date, Suny. And no…" He gazed through the windshield at nothing. "No, I won't get to see her more often."

At this, I did remain silent. Anthony stared through the glass a moment longer, then turned the key.

We sat outside Blaubury, the engine rather louder than it might have been if the station wagon had been a younger vehicle.

"Thank you for the ride, Anthony. And for…well, thanks. I suppose I will see you tomorrow. At the service?"

"Suny, after the service, Chief Vernon is allowing me full access–"

"I won't go with you."

"Why not?"

"Anthony, I don't see how I could add anything to your search for revelatory gobbledegook. You know by now I don't share–"

"But yet you're down there pumping Lillian Kennedy for info."

"I didn't even have time…Dr. Kennedy was in no state… ooh, I need not explain myself to you."

"I beg to differ."

He smirked at me. That *mudak*. He sat there, leaning back against the car door and smirked at me. I fell silent, flabbergasted at his effrontery.

He continued. "Suny, why else would you have gone in there? You're up to something. Now, I'm only asking you to come with me and let me know if you have any insight. And if you won't…"

He let the last dangle impudently.

"Well, Anthony, I believe you have me over a cask–"

"A barrel."

"Whatever! But don't you assume that I will have any experience different than your own. If you want to waste your time and mine…"

"Thank you. I think."

"And don't think that you can pig-tie–"

"Hog-tie."

"Oh, you are simply maddening! Just know that I will not be intimidated again. Telling Father I had half a glass of wine would not allot me much grief–"

"But it could get you in big trouble at The Ledge. Expelled even. They take their relationship with the town quite seriously. If they thought you would continue to jeopardize it…"

"Empty threats."

"Try me."

I crossed my arms over my chest and refused to look at him. I could see my dorm window alight. Petra's dred-locked head bobbed by in silhouette. She was dancing. Happily, from

138

the look of things. As happy as I had been this last week at Preacher's Ledge. I took a deep breath.

"I said I would accompany you– this time. Isn't that enough?"

"For now."

I did look at him then. How I could ever have found those taunting eyes more than infuriating, I don't know.

"Good night, Mr. Scarborough," I said in my coldest voice.

"Tomorrow, Suny."

When I thought about it all a little later, I was not quite as incensed. Anthony's insistence on my help only served to make me all the more determined to demonstrate the fallacious nature of the poltergeist theory and giving in to his very demands would allow me the access to prove it was all a ridiculous charade. Still, I was miffed.

I had hoped to ask him for details as to the animosity between Dr. Kennedy and Chief Vernon; there was more there than met the eye. I was sure now that I would have a difficult time securing the medical examiner's assistance unless I knew what was holding her back. Somehow, Anthony had managed to distract me. I was not pleased with myself. Very few things ever served to distract me from a purpose once set.

That displeasure was apparent in my countenance. Petra sensed it right away.

"What's wrong with you?" Petra asked, looking me over.

"Nothing," I replied, not wanting to detail my evening just yet.

Petra took that easily and resumed dancing. I had expected Bob Marley or even some Motown, but she was dancing to an ancient cassette of Fred Rogers inviting one and all to be his neighbor. I was only vaguely familiar with the man but felt at the moment like being neighbor to none.

I crawled under my covers. My head still ached and was beginning to do so even more, thanks to Mr. Rogers. I heard Petra approach, her huffing breath coming closer.

"Brian says hello, Suny."

"What?" I bolted upright.

"Yeah, your name kept coming up on the Ouija board, you know. Nothing much else to be honest, but we were trying to get Brian. Maybe it was him."

"Petra, you are a scientist. How can you..." Oh, I was not going to get into this again.

"Hell, Suny, don't be such a stick in the mud." She switched off the tape. "There's a lot we don't know. That's what makes science fun. A scientist has to be open to all things, all phenomena, knowing that there is a rational explanation for everything."

Petra sat on my bed to peel off her thigh-high boots.

"Say you've got a group of folks who believe all sickness can be healed by mixing together some precious herbs and offering them to the gods. You can poo-poo that right off; most scientists would. Until you see the success rate. Then you take a closer look. You see that they leave this offering out on a stone altar for three days, the stone gets hot, the mixture ferments. Part of the ritual is then feeding a miniscule portion of the glop to the person suffering, a sign of acceptance of the will of the gods. Well hell, they've just made their own penicillin, or some equivalent, and we can maybe learn something from that."

"Is that true, Petra?"

"Sure it's true. That dumbass Gilbert wouldn't let me go any further with it all, just 'cause I couldn't get the fermentation down right– But that's not the point. The point is, we play with that Ouija board and it doesn't matter if it's really spirits, or if it's someone's subconscious chiming in, pushing the thing. Point is, you're learning something, and just 'cause the source may be a little off-base, doesn't mean you shouldn't pay attention to it. 'Sides, it's fun. You should've seen Frieda's face when we started getting something. I can't believe she wanted to be there in the first place, but she sure as hell got her money's worth for a first-timer..."

"Petra, will you come with me tomorrow? After the service. Anthony's here and he's going to be investigating this supposed poltergeist. He wants me to...assist him, I guess. We could use a scientific mind."

"Tony's got one helluva scientific mind himself, Suny. Don't be fooled by it all looking like hocus-pocus. If there's anything to find, he'll find it."

She stood and stripped off the rest of her skimpy outfit. It seemed I was doomed to forever have roommates who preferred to be nude.

I laid back on my pillows and thought about what she had said.

"New penicillin, huh?"

"Well, it's more than that. Seems to act on the nervous system too. It's got potential to help with MS, Lyme disease, all kinds of stuff."

Petra slid under her satin sheets, and wriggled down, a smile of pleasure on her face.

"I would've thought you'd be more interested in the next Viagra."

Petra sat upright and fixed me with a stare. "That's part of life, sure. A damned fine part of life. But that's not all I'm about. Suny, hon, you've got to live first in order to find any joy in life. And you've got to live well, free of disease, if at all possible. How full of pleasure the world would be without disease, right? That's what I'm all about, right?"

"Right," I could only murmur, ashamed.

Petra nodded, point made. She slid back under her covers. "I'll go with you though. I have to check my molds anyway. Lord only knows what's happened since I didn't get in there today."

Petra promptly began snoring. I stared at her sleeping head a while. Then, before I could force myself to get up and change into proper sleeping attire, I gave in to the rhythm of my pulsating temples, and fell asleep myself.

Chapter 15

The morning broke with incongruously cheerful sunshine. I half-expected the day to be chill and dark. The foggy remnants of headache I felt and the agenda for the morning seemed to demand bad weather.

Petra was tying her dreds back in a black lace scarf. Her newly-purchased "school-marm" dress clung to her in a decidedly un-spinster-like way.

She threw a green rubber thing she called Gumby at me to rouse me further and told me she wouldn't wait long. I dressed hurriedly and followed her to breakfast.

Brian's body would soon be shipped home to Ohio, I gleaned from dining hall conversation. The college was holding the memorial service hastily to make use of the weekend time and to try to return the campus to relative normalcy by the start of classes Monday. One thing would not return to normal so easily, however. None of the students would dare to go alone to work in the science building after dark now, or so they spewed dramatically. The deleterious effect on their studies would soon show them the error of their judgment. But I would not discuss it with them. I was not in any state of mind to listen to any more of the speculative discussion that spilled over from the day before, so I ate quickly and made my way to the chapel.

The non-denominational chapel at Preacher's Ledge was small. More weddings of alumni were held there than any regular services. Most students who observed the Sabbath did so in town. The stone building was little more than one room, a room today crammed to the rafters.

Brian had not been what one would describe as popular. He was well-known, though. Not a student at The Ledge could say he or she had not seen Brian each day, everpresent as he had been at the end of the serving line in the dining hall. The students at The Ledge were also a philosophic bunch.

Brian's death was a momentous occasion; they eagerly utilized the opportunity to examine their own mortality.

"There'll be more than a couple of theses out of this," Petra mumbled, eyeing her cohorts, some of whom were scribbling in notebooks, likely capturing mood and reflection as they hit.

We were not early, and were made to stand along one wall just as the preacher, dressed in rough linen and denim, began to speak. With one ear on the sermon, I allowed the rest of my attentions to wander.

Todd sat near the front with some of the gang of debaters from my first meal at The Ledge. I had yet to apologize to Todd. Perhaps I would get the chance after the service. He was a pleasant enough fellow and he had acquiesced easily to my hijacking of his vehicle. And his person, for that matter.

Frieda stood as we did, but on the opposite side of the chapel. Though the sizable placard of photographs memorializing Brian was stationed nearby, she never once glanced at it, but kept her strained gaze on the hewn wood altar. She did not notice, as I did, the young man who regarded her hastily from time to time, bearing a worried expression. In fact, I sensed Frieda was unaware of her surroundings completely. It seemed she was feeling the oppressive nature of organized religion. Hadn't she been adamant in her defense of Comte's view of humanism in our debate? In any case, she did not want to be here.

I scanned the remaining walls.

I spotted Kathy. Roger stood at her side, a comforting arm around her shoulders. They did make a pretty pair. Trim, blonde Kathy and a lean, not-too-tall Roger, with just a hint of strawberry to his blonde. Kathy reached up and stroked the hand that lay on her shoulder. They were not terribly subtle. Maybe the college did not look askance at RA/student relationships, though I found that hard to believe. Perhaps all the secrecy had been for Anthony's benefit. Now that it seemed Kathy had released him, in no uncertain terms, from whatever the parameters of their relationship had been…

Which made me wonder where...

Aha. Anthony was seated on the dais, somewhat hidden behind a hanging banner, a book in hand. He looked uncomfortable in the extreme. Surely he was not timid, not even about public speaking. Anyone who willingly chose to work with Father had to have nerves of steel. I wondered what it was– his collar too tight, his shoes? He didn't seem to be taking particular notice of Kathy and Roger, but perhaps his inattention to them was a ruse.

And then I saw who sat beside him.

Gilbert. He held nothing but it was obvious he too was meant to eulogize Brian.

Did Anthony hate him so much that just sitting at his side discomfited him?

"What exactly is the nature of...that is, what is "the deal" with Anthony and Gilbert?" I whispered to Petra.

"Anthony and–? Oh, well, that's the same old shi– stuff. Gilbert didn't like the direction Tony was going with his senior thesis and he made him change it completely mid-year. Tony almost couldn't finish his new thesis before graduation. Had to go with something in traditional physics instead of some quantum stuff on the cutting edge..."

She broke off as Anthony stood and began to read. He chose "In Silence" by Thomas Wolfe, an appropriate choice that misted my eyes. He made no personal statement, just read the piece in his warm,

brown

voice, moving me completely with its sonorous tones, so appropriate to the sad occasion.

It was then that Gilbert stole the show, so to speak.

Gone was the taciturn, apathetic professor I had suffered for a week of seminars. This Gilbert was alive, reverent but optimistic. His message was spontaneous but well-spoken. He summarized Brian's study in physics, his accomplishments. He touted his curiosity, his dedication, his love of the college. Gilbert spouted forth from the pulpit, and all attention was on him. Eyes grew damp. He spoke of Brian, but he made it seem as if he were honoring every student present, holding them up along with Brian, and praising all the qualities, ambitions, and character that made them an integral part of the community that was Preacher's Ledge.

"We all will grieve for Brian. In a moment I will ask you to take a minute to remember him in your own private way. But first, let us strengthen our resolve, here in the witnessing of others, to strive for excellence, for new frontiers, for the attainment of new levels of knowledge. All in his memory. All to our collective good."

I daresay I expected the gathering to break into applause as he finished. The students were a bit more sensible than that, but I heard scattered sobbing.

Petra leaned into me. "What is he doing, running for office?"

Gilbert sat again solemnly, but I could tell he was pleased with the effect achieved. Even Frieda had been brought to tears. The same young man who had fixed his eyes on her before did so now again and looked pained. Everyone beamed gratitude up at Gilbert, even as dreary, bass-heavy music erupted from speakers.

Anthony didn't beam. He glowered. Petra too, bristled at my side. They seemed the only mourners who disliked Gilbert enough to be unappreciative of his sentiments.

The service was soon over. I made my way up front, moving against the tide of people leaving. Frieda pushed brusquely past me. Willie– for I had deduced that the attentive young man could only be he– struggled past me as well, tailing her, but not bold enough to call her to a stop.

I found my way to Todd. In fact, I was jostled right into him and caught him around the shoulders so he would not fall. I wasted no time getting to the point, even though I was a little breathless from having been shoved.

"I'm sorry we didn't have the chance for our little rendezvous, but I was called away. It was wonderful of you, sweeping me away when I needed you. I would like to show

146

you my appreciation. Maybe later I can get away and we can—"

I was rudely jolted again and this time Todd had to hold me up. Some friends of his snickered unaccountably and left us, throwing sidelong glances and smirks as they went.

I tried to regain my balance, but Todd was still concerned for my well-being and held on. He grew flushed. It was warm and circumstances made it so our bodies were pressed rather close. I was about to assure him that I was alright to stand on my own now that the crowd was thinning out, when Anthony poked me pointedly in the shoulder.

"Suny, it's time to go."

At the sound of his voice, Todd let me loose with alacrity. To be honest, he nearly threw me at Anthony.

I composed myself as best I could, and said, "I will be with you in a moment, Anthony. When I have finished my conversation with Todd..."

Apparently, my conversation was finished. Todd was nowhere to be seen, he had left so quickly.

"Well, that was uncalled for. I didn't even have a chance to set up—"

"You can meet your boyfriend later." Anthony took hold of my arm now and tugged.

"Boyfriend? Why is everyone trying to saddle me with a boyfriend? I only meant to— hey, we have to wait for Petra."

Anthony had no objections to this arrangement. In fact, after having towed me out into the sunshine, he cast me off and matched Petra's stride, settling into a scientific discussion on the way.

Lagging behind, I tried to remind myself of the positives inherent in the coming investigation. I did not feel in the least like pursuing a study of the evidence left in the chemistry lab. But, I thought as I stared hard at Anthony's arrogant back, I was now being given the chance to assert my superior view of the situation.

I wrinkled my nose at the back of Anthony's misguided head, something I shouldn't have done. It only served to pull the skin of my cheek and cause me pain.

I would go to the science building. I would gather evidence, bring it to Dr. Kennedy, convince her of the righteousness of disseminating the knowledge we shared, relate our findings to a reluctantly grateful Chief Vernon, assist in the unmasking of the culprit, the criminal responsible...

I hadn't thought of that before. So wholly focused on establishing the mistaken nature of Anthony's conjecture was I that I hadn't followed through with the implications of my own hypothesis. If Brian had not been killed by a self-injuring poltergeist, then someone, some living person here at The Ledge, had killed him. The weight of that realization stopped me in my tracks.

Brain had been murdered. How utterly horrible. How unthinkable. Who could have killed such a mouse of a young man? Why? And how could...

A flicker of movement caught my eye. In the browning clumps of towering grasses that surrounded the science building, something moved.

Or did it?

Anthony and Petra were already traversing the pier-like walkway that led up to the entrance. Evidently, they saw nothing. It was all that glass and chrome. The exterior reflected every migrating bird and foraging squirrel for miles.

After we had checked in with the officer on guard duty, Petra made off to check her molds. The building was to be reopened in the morning, but she could wait no longer. Anthony and I climbed to the third floor.

I have never been one to take anything at face value. I was sorely tempted, however, when I entered the chemistry lab. If any scene had ever appeared as one would imagine the aftermath of a poltergeist appeared, this was it.

The police had left almost everything as it had been. There were piles of broken glass, tangles of rubber tubing, reference books, heaps of equipment where pieces had fallen from shelves, and cases that had tipped and were left standing askew. One area of the floor was horribly pitted from an acid spill. The residue of fingerprint powder gave everything a ghostly cast.

Anthony produced a camera and began to snap pictures, following a pattern I recognized as Father's– stationed at the landing point of a particular object, one took photos and measurements radiating backward out from various degrees along a 360' circumference. The aim was to ascertain the origination of each object and to rule out the possibility of the item having been placed by a prankster. I had told Father that he could get the same information much more efficiently by using the common forensic method of...well, that is an issue of contention for another time.

Anthony had not assigned me a task, so I wandered gingerly through the debris.

The cabinet under which the body had been found had been righted. I stood at the foot of it and observed the pattern of broken glass that gave a crude outline of where– well, while I have no qualms about the immutably tenuous nature of a body's hold on life, I did not need to subject myself to morbid consideration of the outline of where Brian had lain. I looked quickly away.

The autopsy report wouldn't be ready for a few days, if I knew anything about such matters. I wondered what Dr. Kennedy would put in the final report. Would she avoid drawing attention to details that didn't fit simply because she thought Chief Vernon was biased toward the poltergeist theory? What exactly had she found?

I eyed the cabinet. She'd not been satisfied that the cabinet had moved of its own accord. What had she said? Pushed from the top with casters locked?

I approached the stainless-steel hulk and gave it a gentle nudge. It moved easily, rolling a few inches, crunching glass under its heavy-duty casters. I drew a quick breath. I hadn't meant to move it.

"Suny! You, of all people, should know not to move

anything until we've taken all our measurements!"

"I didn't mean to–"

"I don't even know if the other investigators have been in. The last thing we need is a skeptic crying foul because we've moved things around."

"Moved what around?"

The voice was as sour as the pinched face from which it had emanated. A short– to be fair, everyone seemed short to me– brunette was in the doorway. She grasped her hair, a shiny sheet of black, and twisted it into a hasty bun, tying it into a knot on itself.

"Uh– nothing. And you are…" Anthony approached from the other side of the room.

"Diana Kowalski, NESsie investigator."

"The skeptics org?"

"Yeah. Don't I know you? You look familiar. No? Maybe it's just that you're NESOPsI." She said it 'Nuh-so-sigh' and it took me a minute to decode it.

"New England Society– no, I'm a researcher for Eugene Davis," Anthony said, with an amazingly straight face.

"Davis? Figures you'd be moving things around. I should have gotten here this morning, but I had a class. I'll just have to hope the police report has adequate measurements I can compare to…" Diana muttered to herself as she readied her own camera.

Anthony let the comment slide. He must be used to it by now. He had worked for Father for more than a day, after all.

Diana ignored me completely at first. I could not be sure if it was this slight that rankled me, but I found something vexing in her slim form, crouching, snapping photos, and whipping out tape measure again and again. She was older than I, perhaps Anthony's age or a bit older and she wasn't intimidated by our presence. Smug even, the way she brushed past me, scribbling in a notebook. Therefore, I pegged her for a doctoral candidate. I had met many and that impending accolade boosted egos far.

I went to the window and brooded. I don't know exactly what Anthony expected of me. Out of the corner of my eye, I caught him glancing up now and then, checking in on my reaction to the room, I suppose. He, being a professional of sorts, should have been the first to realize that, contrary to popular assumption, most psychics did not get slammed with information simply from walking into a room.

And even if they had, I am, I reiterate, most certainly not "most psychics."

I must say, however, I was still reeling from the jolt of the unsolicited communiqué to which I had been subjected at The Hangar.

Father had, at times, attempted to make merry by reading the minds of rather inebriated habitués of his notorious "weekender" parties. These were held sporadically at whichever sprawling domicile he had leased at the moment. He had theorized that an inebriated mind was a much more open mind; less inhibited, as it were. Whether his "sensings" on such occasions were truly that or simply comic conjectures meant to arouse, I could not say. I could, however, testify to the fact that they were ribald in the extreme. I had found it necessary more than once to remove myself from the room so as not to be exposed to matters that should have been beyond my ken.

Speaking of matters beyond my ken, I was completely bemused as to the origin of the forceful transmissions I had received. Had they come from Dr. Kennedy's sodden mind, or from the draft of Brian's autopsy report she had with her? Were they telepathic in nature or was I dealing with more of a clairvoyant situation, picking up on something radiating from the papers on the bar?

To look at it one way, it didn't much matter. Any information to be had could be gotten by traditional investigative techniques. I would just go to Dr. Kennedy and ask. And I knew exactly what to ask about. The force of the communication had burned the words into my mind. Some things about bruising, about the cabinet, about the calcaneus. Well, I didn't know what was so note-worthy about the bone of Brian's heel and I might never know if I couldn't get Dr. Kennedy to talk to me. I insisted to myself that would not be a problem.

But it was somewhat intriguing. To know whence the messages had come that gave me such a hangover. As an intellectual exercise only, of course. I hadn't often intuited anything from an object, without a mind. I had touched a fingertip to the cabinet before and had felt nothing.

Yet that was only a fingertip.

I moved away from the window. Anthony and Diana worked around each other, surreptitiously observing the other's progress as they went. I hopped over a pile of textbooks.

As I had noted, the glass of the cabinet front had shattered and was left in an icy outline around where Brian had fallen. I treaded as lightly as I could on the scattered bits and stood in front of the towering piece.

Before, I had only brushed a fingertip on the side of its mass. This time, I spread myself, arms and legs akimbo, and clasped the metal in a veritable embrace. I clung to its smooth coolness, opening my pores, opening my mind…

Nothing.

It was completely irrational for me to feel disappointed. I had expected no sensation. Shame swept over me. Standing there clutching the metal form, I resolved not be drawn into ridiculous speculation again. And also to remove myself hastily from this farcical position before Anthony got the idea that I was buying into his program.

That was a mistake, to put it mildly. Removing myself hastily, I mean.

The cabinet sailed away from me and slammed into a lab table. It bounced off said table and redirected itself toward Diana, whose unfortunate back was turned as she measured the height of a stain on the wall.

"Jesus, Mary, and Joseph!"

Anthony vaulted over a counter just in time for the cabinet to smack him instead of Diana, who had turned now at the clamor. The metal reverberated off Anthony and shuddered to a stand-still. Surprisingly, he remained perpendicular. But then again, the cabinet was now empty and glass-less, weighing much less than it had when it had assumedly attacked Brian.

"Suny!"

I was becoming accustomed to that particular roaring of my name.

"Anthony, I was merely attempting—"

"To kill Diana? To kill me? To wantonly destroy every bit of evidence—"

"Compose yourself! For goodness sake. If you will look objectively at the circumstances, you will see that the cabinet rolled in one of the only clear paths. It didn't destroy anything. And, more interestingly, even when acted upon with some force, it did not tip, but dissipated the additional energy by—"

"Did you say Suny?"

Anthony rubbed his shoulder and grimaced but Diana had recovered neatly and scrutinized me.

"Suny Davis?" she continued incredulously. "The daughter of Eugene Davis himself. Oh, this is too much." Diana scratched something in her notebook. Something of which I'm sure I would not have approved.

I attempted to roll my eyes, forgetting my healing wound. I regretted it. The pain made my eyes water and served to ignite my temper even further.

"Anthony, you were the one who asked for my assistance in the first place. And, as for you, Ms...Ms...Self-Righteous Skeptic, what do you know of my father? Or, of this field in general? I could surely claim an exponentially greater amount of experience in such matters, so I do not appreciate your dismissive—"

"Prancing around after your daddy, carrying his ectoplasm meter doesn't count for much in my book."

"Prancing? Ectoplasm?" Well, one could hardly expect me to know what more to say in response to such belittling, such denigrating, such–

"What's all the commotion?"

The voice was commanding, to say the very least. We all three stopped cold and gazed in utter wonder at its owner. She was large, ney colossal. A leviathan who spilled through the doorway like risen dough in a pan.

For the life of me, I could have sworn it was Chief Vernon in calico.

"I'm Felicity Maxwell, from NESOPsI." She extended a club of a hand from the tent of flowered cotton that was her dress. The woman had at her throat a brooch the size of a bagel.

"Who's in charge here? I see. No one. Where in hell is Charles? He doesn't even have an officer downstairs anymore. Well, folks, I've got my EMF meter here, so I'm going to need to do a residue check. You all will have to clear out for at least a half an hour."

Mine was the only voice that did not raise a cry at this last. I wished nothing more than to have an excuse to recuse myself from this fiasco. Ms. Maxwell could have the lab all to herself and her outdated, ineffective contraption. I would go in search of the absent officer and see if he could be persuaded to tell a few tales out of school, so to speak. In his current state of agitation, Anthony would not note my absence and I would return before he could have any need of my assistance.

The hallway was quiet. I tried to make my steps likewise. There was no need to call attention to my leave-taking, after all.

A moaning broke into the silence. I froze. And then that metaphor for my immobile state came to be more literal than I'd meant it. A chill ran up my spine. Goosebumps sprouted along my arms. The moaning softened to a hum, and a part of my brain worked to remember the air ducts that had caused the noise previously. But the chill, and with it a sense of foreboding, crept up on me. I turned, though my increasing dread willed me to run.

A haze met my eyes. A cloudy shape, formed but floating, hung in the hallway before me. It vibrated, glowed...

One could not expect me to stay to observe it further without, well without confirmation from others, so I turned and...ran, one might say, in the opposite direction.

A door swung open. It smacked me. Yet again on the cheekbone. This time I did not have the chance to bark in unrefined Russian. The blow was much harder. As my consciousness failed me and I fell to the ground, a figure emerged from behind the offensive door and moved off down the hall.

Just as Brian had done the day he died.

Chapter 16

The room in which I awoke was dim. Actually, one could not rightly call it a room. It was a curtained section of a room and, at the time of my return to consciousness, I could see nothing beyond the crisp shield of fabric that surrounded the bed.

Before I could discover anything more about my surroundings, the curtain was whisked aside unceremoniously, the clicking of the rings along their pole the only warning my privacy was to be invaded.

"Oh, you're awake." The elderly nurse said nothing further, but grabbed my arm and proceeded to take my pulse. Her grasp was cold and firm.

"I realize there is no way to knock when confronted with a curtain, but in the future, I would appreciate–"

She dropped my wrist abruptly.

"Look, you want me to call your boyfriend and tell him you're awake or not? The only way I could keep the sad sack from coming in every day this week too was to promise to call him right away. But if you're going to get uppity with me, I'll just let him stew."

She wrinkled up her nose at me and crossed her arms, waiting for my response.

Well, I didn't know of whom she spoke (again, with the boyfriends!) but I doubted from her demeanor that the nurse would be a fountain of information as to my circumstances. I thought it best to appease her. She took my apology and plodded out.

I felt groggy. I rubbed my tongue across my teeth. My mouth tasted like– well, I needn't go into details. I closed my eyes just a minute and then I must have dozed off again, for the next thing I knew, Anthony's face swam above me, a sweet smile in his eyes.

But they were not the blue I remembered, not the intense

sapphire– I struggled to sit up and failed.

"You're not Anthony. You're Nicholas," I said thickly, my tongue not quite working.

"Ah, so perceptive. The question remains, had I been my deep, sensitive brother, would you have continued to smile up at me in such an adoring manner?"

"Bah!" was all I could muster.

"Tut, tut. That's no way to treat a visitor. But then again, I too would be grumpy on day nine of my convalescence and–"

"What!" My head was suddenly much clearer. "Day nine? Nicholas, I fear you are the one who was hit on the head."

"But it's true. The Nazi Nurse here has kept you confined for over a week. She's liberal with the sedatives. It seems that last year a student flipped over and slammed into the ground during a hackey-sack tournament. Everyone thought he was okay but he developed a subdemerol– subdermal–"

"Subdural hematoma?"

"Exactly. Small leak in a vessel in his brain and the poor bloke almost died. Brain surgery and the whole nine yards and the school got blamed and had to foot the bill. Almost got sued for more too. They're more careful now."

"Well, surely I cannot have been unconscious for a week."

"Not exactly. The first time you came to, you commenced screaming in Russian and tearing at your IV. Elevated mood disturbance, I think she called it. Sign of..." Nicholas broke off and picked up a folder from a cart. "Here it is... 'sign of a severe grade three concussion.'" He flipped through the papers some more. "'Expect symptoms to abate within four weeks, suggest close supervision for fourteen days at minimum.'"

"Fourteen days!"

"'Reported second impact syndrome...' Did you get hit twice?"

"Only on the cheekbone! Oh, for goodness sake!" I made to get out of bed.

"Uh, uh, uh. If you want to get out of here, you can't

continue to berate the nursing staff. She'll only note it down that you continue to...where is it...here, 'exhibits extreme emotional lability, irrational anger. Easily frustrated by staff efforts at assistance–'"

"I tried to tell her that was normal for you."

This was a voice I could not mistake. Anthony appeared around the corner of the wall.

"She keeps doping you to make you more compliant. I was starting to think it might be a good strategy for all time." His eyes twinkled at me, but he didn't seem at his best. In fact, he looked like he had just awakened, or hadn't slept at all.

"Anthony, I don't understand how I can be made to stay here. Now, I refuse to be sedated any further. If you allow that woman– Have I even been seen by a doctor? Who brought me in here in the first place?"

"I did." Nicholas beamed at me proudly. "I found you sprawled flat, out like a light."

"Don't worry, Suny. You'll be out of here in a couple of days," Anthony said, after he shot a withering look at his brother.

"Surely I won't be forced to be bedridden!"

"That kid last year almost died, Suny. They're not taking any chances."

"And I am expected to bear the consequences?"

"Yes," Anthony said firmly.

Well, I had nothing to say to that.

Nicholas hastily returned my chart to its place. "Looks like Nurse is coming."

Indeed, she did come. I will not describe the indecencies I suffered after the "menfolk" had cleared out. When all was said and done, however, I was freshly bathed and unencumbered by tubes and IVs. My compliant behavior had awarded me a drug-free status, although I was tightly tucked back in bed.

Anthony returned to me soon after. I did not speak to him, however. My guardian, indeed. I could not believe that he had

159

allowed such overzealous precautions to lose me a week of school. And to think, I had just caught up. Anthony knew me well enough to know that would be a concern. He attempted to entice me into conversation.

"Your schoolwork will be brought to you. And if you play nice, you'll be out of here soon. At least you have the place to yourself."

I did not respond. Anthony's eyes remained upon me.

"You obviously remember you were hit. You really don't remember anything else? Do you remember the circumstances? Anything?"

I would not allow myself to forgive him just yet. Withholding information seemed to disquiet him. And that was exactly what I felt like doing.

I did remember what had happened. To recall the hazy apparition that had caused my hasty retreat still served to send shivers down my spine. I didn't quite know what to make of it. It was unlike anything I'd ever experienced.

"Suny– uh, this would be a great opportunity to see if concussion has any effect on psi ability. I could do some tests, write them up–"

"No."

"Just the simplest tests–"

"No."

"Your father asked me to run them."

"As I told Father when I was eight, you needn't ask ever again because my answer will always be unequivocally *no*."

"The nurse won't release you until I say I'm comfortable your behavior has returned to normal. Now, exactly what normal is, I'm not sure, but I don't feel comfortable giving my consent until I know that even your psi talents are back to normal."

"Outrageous and sinful blackmail!"

Anthony shrugged. "If that's the way you want it. I won't be back until the weekend, and then maybe the weekend nurse can get a hold of whoever makes these decisions…"

"I could have you fired for this."

"Your father's the one who wants the data."

I stewed. Father. I had already checked amongst the small stack of get well cards and did not find one from him. Yet he was aware enough of my situation to see it as a research opportunity. A monkey on a stage. That was all I was to him. And Anthony just blindly did his bidding, no questions asked. I eyed him blackly.

Anthony took my silence as acquiescence to his request and started setting up a view shield. He brought out a pack of cards, fancier than the simpler ones I knew Father to use in his testing.

Baby games.

It would only take a little to convince him I was alright, but I really couldn't believe Father was forcing the issue. It was all Anthony's fault, I am sure. If he had shown even the slightest enthusiasm for my abilities, it could only have reignited Father's intense desire to have a boldly gifted child. As I've said, Father was disheartened when my aptitude "disappeared."

The more I thought of it, the more irate I became.

Anthony searched for pen and paper. Having found said items, he produced a mini recorder and clicked it on. "Today's date is—"

"Triangle: blue, star: green, purple circle, pink square, blue octagon…" I continued in the same vein rapid fire, not even looking at the view shield that hid the stack of cards. After a moment of shock, Anthony began to flip the cards, attempting to keep apace.

When I finished with the deck, I started in on Anthony. I let myself relax - something I never did - and for the first time since I was a very small child, I actively sought sensation.

A barrage of images, sounds, smells flew past me as if I were speeding through a tunnel. I willed everything to slow. It wasn't easy. Anthony must have been unusually open. Either that or my abilities had strengthened rather than atrophied despite years of unremitting suppression.

"A dog. Black. Yippy thing. Some kind of shaved patch near his tail. And...what is that? Rootbeer? Never liked the stuff. Peanut butter. But I could have gleaned that from residue on your clothes or breath. Doesn't count. But the rootbeer's not from today and it's pretty strong. Something about your mother. And she doesn't speak English. Or rather, she does, but she speaks to you in– no, wait. Nicholas Eduardo– Eduardo? And there's something else, someone else small, a girl– no, I lost her. But, oh–"

A wave of sorrow swept over me. The little girl I saw had dark curls cropped short, wide brown eyes and lips as red as if she had been eating a Popsicle. The emotion that came with the sight of her was as if she had been torn from me bodily. Before I could pull back, tears sprung from my eyes. And then I did pull back, as quickly and as hard as I could. I couldn't tell the details from that brief connection, but I had no desire to learn more. It was gut-wrenchingly painful.

Anthony shook his head slowly, his eyes never leaving me. The whirring of the tape recorder and my own quick breath were the only sounds.

"How can you be a skeptic when you've got all that inside you?"

He stared at me long enough to make me uncomfortable. What am I saying? He always made me uncomfortable. This was just another case in point. I shouldn't have given in to him. At least, I shouldn't have bombarded him with all of it. But now that he had his information, maybe he would leave me alone.

I wiped my face on my hospital gown, suddenly tired.

"Anthony. I...There's a difference. A big difference between... I mean, I believe..."

What did I believe?

He leaned forward in his chair. "You have to believe that it's possible that Brian generated a poltergeist. If you accept telepathy, if you accept–"

"I don't accept anything, Anthony!"

"But your father—"

"My father what? My father is such a gallimaufry of the paranormal it's no wonder I don't know what to believe. He seems to have inexplicable abilities, but he is also an illusionist of the first order. How can anyone look at him and see anything but a charlatan? The small percentage of sterling episodes are so completely enshrouded in obfuscation that one could not be blamed if one were to rashly throw the baby out with the dishwater—"

"Bathwater."

"Anthony!"

"Suny! I can't believe you still won't admit it! I have it here on tape! You are a wildly gifted telepath. You made fifty hits! And you weren't even getting it through me; I could hardly keep up, much less see the cards in time to project anything. That's…that's remote sensation. You picked it up either from the cards themselves, or through some clairvoyance, read what I would see in the future—"

"Enough!"

"And then you gave me stuff straight from my own head. You—"

"Enough, I said!"

Silence ensued. Anthony stood up, shoving his chair out of the way, and paced the room. I examined the edge of my blanket.

"Anthony, I can never be sure of the accuracy—"

"Fifty hits, Suny. Fifty out of fifty. I've never seen anything like it."

I said nothing.

Anthony stopped at the window and looked out across the lawn rolling away from the health services building. From where I sat, I could just make out the wart-like bump of the science building. I took a deep breath. A change of subject was in order.

"So…tell me about your findings in the chemistry lab."

"Nothing much to tell." He wouldn't look at me.

163

"Really. Then I was right all along."

This was too much for him. "No, Suny, you were not right. We found nothing to contraindicate a poltergeist. You saw the damage. Pretty extensive for a hoax. Even that Diana person couldn't come up with a finding either way."

"What about that behemoth– Vernon's aunt?"

"How did you know Mrs. Maxwell was Vernon's aunt?" He eyed me suspiciously.

"Oh, *ya tebia dostal* The woman could be his twin, number one. Number two, Benny the bartender said Vernon's aunts were members of NESOPsI. I simply used my little gray cells, *vrubatsa?*"

All the screaming made my head ache. The wound on my cheek was still tender and began to radiate pain as well.

"I think I should go. Chief Vernon's going to give a briefing to all the investigators, along with the school officials, at five."

"But it's not even noon."

He grabbed his jacket from the foot of my bed.

At the door, he turned.

"Suny–"

I looked up.

"Nothing. Never mind."

And he was gone.

I sat for a long time and thought about Anthony's words. It may as well have been Father standing there, begging me to let him test me, observe me, write me up as a case report, anything but...just...I don't know...be a father to me?

I didn't wipe away these tears as they fell. Rarely did I let myself just go, but I had been through a lot, and the infirmary room was lonely, and boring, and no one seemed to care that I was stuck here, trapped. Eventually, I did wipe my face, settled my breathing, and felt more normal. I suppose a good cry now and then was cleansing. I tried not to feel too silly as I set my mental defenses back in place.

Some time later, I was close to dozing when the entire bank

of ceiling lights glared to life and brought me upright. A metal pail and wringer appeared around the corner of wall, and with it, the scrawniest chicken of a woman I've ever seen.

"Sitting in the dark won't help you heal no faster, you know. Get up and get moving, I'd say."

She slopped steaming water onto the floor.

"Yes, well, to that sentiment I would have no objection."

The cleaning woman fixed me with a sharp eye. "You the one been walloped by that spirit in the science building?"

"Spirit?"

"Got me too, it did. Not walloped, mind you– Don't be thinking I'd ever put up with that– but I know a ghostie when I see one. Plenty of them around these parts. Something about the hills that traps them."

"You saw something?"

"Twas a lady in white floating down the hall at me, plain as day. Fixed me with her cold spirit breath too. Made me close my eyes and shiver the whole length of me, and then when I opened my eyes, she was gone."

"This…lady, you say…"

"A misty sorrow, she was. Probably buried there in the valley. Disturbed souls don't rest easy."

"But it was a woman you saw."

"Sure twasn't a man of no sort. Bent on getting us out, sure as I stand here. Lots of energy in that one. Set my mop a-rattling in the pail. Doom, she brought. If she'd stayed longer, I don't think I could've fought the feeling too long. Fear like I never felt. And now, look see, I told my George, that poor boy paid no heed and she made him sorry."

"Did you ever see it again? Her, I mean. Or, well I suppose it may have been too disturbing to return."

"Oh, I went back alright. No ghostie's going to keep me away from a paycheck, not with my George on nothing but disability. But I never seen her again. Another child though, she saw her too. Come and found me, asking did I see her the same, and feel the fear and trembling. The same words came

165

out of her mouth as did out of mine. Now if that don't make you a believer…"

She wrung the mop hard, her sinewy arms stronger than they looked, then nodded curtly at me and made to leave, the sting of antiseptic in her wake. She turned for a moment.

"I can take care of myself, but mind you stay out of that building. She got herself a taste for death now."

When she was gone, I attempted to roll my eyes. Ghosties. I ignored the ache it started in my face and ignored too the shudder I could not suppress when left with those ominous words. They rung in my ears, much as I tried to dismiss them.

Chapter 17

I awoke the next morning after fitful sleep, fitful only, I am sure, due to my unfamiliar surroundings, and not, by any stretch of the imagination, due to the ramblings of the cleaning woman. The new day brought no promise of relief from my imprisonment. The nurse changed my bandage and, though I felt very much like telling her exactly what I thought of her unsettlingly chilly hands, which reeked of the tobacco that stained her fingertips, I persevered in my quest to be released.

In other words, I kept my mouth shut, smiled sweetly, and complied with whatever was asked of me.

About mid-morning, she served a devastating blow.

"The doctor is off to a conference until Sunday, but he will check you on Monday morning and, barring any return to your concussive lability or other complications, you can expect to return to classes Tuesday. Now, don't look so horrified. Feel lucky that you've gotten out of two weeks of classes. You can't expect to get away with playing hooky much longer than that." She laughed at her own words.

I wanted to strangle her.

"But it's only…it's Wednesday," I croaked.

"You'll just have to get used to the idea. We must return to normal activity some day, right?"

"But…isn't there another doctor? On call? I cannot believe that the student population would be made to suffer medical negligence… that is, uh, the college is so wonderfully attuned to the needs of its student population. I am sure a plan has been made for every contingency."

"Well, yes, there is Dr. Kennedy. She fills in for a lot of the local doctors when they're away." She eyed me. "You can't fool her though. You seem to be improving. She's not going to extend your time."

"It's just that I haven't seen a doctor yet. Whilst conscious, that is, though I've told everyone that I feel quite confident in

167

your care. However, there are a few questions I'd like to ask and I'd be more at ease…"

She looked startled and backed away from me just a bit. "Well, we don't want you not at ease, do we? The last week hasn't been a picnic for either of us. And if you might panic otherwise…slip back into the unmanageable beast…let's call Dr. Kennedy, shall we?"

I tried to look cordial and on the verge of nervous hysteria at the same time.

The nurse hurried out.

Well now. Fate had smiled upon me. Not only would I convince Dr. Kennedy that she must release me instantly, but I would also have her available for questioning. It promised to be a productive day after all.

At noon, my professors descended upon me. Jacqui arranged a still life for me on a rolling cart. Natasha gave me a biography of a mathematician. Marshall insisted on staying to read aloud to me from the works of Robert Lowell so long that I daresay I would never get dolphins and skunks out of my mind.

I was sketching the bizarre arrangement of old socks and discarded hairbrushes, meant to evoke, according to Jacqui, 'the rolling dunes and bristly cacti of the desert," when Dr. Kennedy entered.

She didn't say much, but examined me thoroughly, commenting only that my heartbeat was a bit rapid. At this I allowed myself to let her know I was excited to think she might give me a clean bill of health and allow me to resume my studies.

"Hmm," was her only response.

She led me through the same list of questions the Nazi Nurse read me morning, noon, and night. It was becoming a litany in my head, but I tried to answer in a spritely, positive fashion. I desperately wanted to assure her of my complete recovery.

"Dr. Benslow wanted you under observation for a full

fourteen days. I can see the thought does not make you a happy camper. Sometimes a slow leak of a vessel in the brain doesn't show up for many days, in scans even. It is a wise precaution." She flipped through my chart and made a few notations. "However, I'm not finding any reason to keep you— *But*, I would have to be sure you would check in here, say, three times a day?"

I nodded fiercely enough to give myself another concussion.

"Now, it'll take me a few hours to get this run up through the administration. They do have a stake in your continued recovery. That probably means one more overnight stay. But you should expect to return to classes in the morning."

I felt I could manage one more night if it meant freedom.

Dr. Kennedy gathered up her things.

"Uh, thank you so much, Dr. Kennedy. I knew when the nurse mentioned you were on call that I would be sensibly cared for. I was so very happy to hear that you would be the medical examiner in the case of my friend, Brian Nelson."

She stopped at this and came closer.

"I'm not the medical examiner. I'm just the coroner. Elected. But I am a physician and I do some fill-in work for the district ME from the state, just like I fill in for Dr. Benslow. I only did the preliminary examination of the body until he came back after his weekend off. What…what do you know about Brian Nelson?"

"He was a dear friend of mine—"

Her intelligent eyes were disconcerting. I amended my statement.

"—That is, we had only just met, but we were friendly, and I was one of the last to see him before he died."

"Where was this?"

"In the science building, right outside the chemistry lab where he was killed. The same place, in fact, where I received my concussion."

She raised her eyebrows at this. I explained all that had led up to my stay in the infirmary, leaving out, of course,

169

Anthony's true reason for wanting me to accompany him.

"So, someone knocked you out while you were investigating the chemistry lab?"

"Well, I'm not sure if it was intended, but the person did not stay to assist me, or so I'm told."

"I wonder…" Dr. Kennedy tapped her lip with her pen.

I started in with my surmises. "I thought the cabinet that fell on him– when I examined it with Anthony, I mean– I thought it was unlikely that it would have tipped over, without the casters locked, that is. Without pressure from the very top. It did seem to roll easily otherwise, rather than tip."

"Yes!" Kennedy lit up. "I noticed that too! I have the same equipment in one of my prep rooms. I tested it even. There's no question that the cabinet would have to have been pushed from the top with its casters locked in order to tip. Even if he did it to himself like they're saying. The physics just…never mind that. The important point is that someone had to roll it over the floor from its original position, lock the casters, tip it, then unlock them to make it look like it rolled over of its own accord."

"A horrible way to kill someone," I mused.

"Oh, but he didn't die from the fractures and contusions caused by the weight of the cabinet." Dr. Kennedy sat on the edge of my bed and leaned into me, her eyes keen. "He died from asphyxiation. Hydrochloric acid, I'd say. Spilled in all the mayhem, or so it is believed. Hard to tell for sure the concentration since the fumes had cleared before anyone found him. There may have been a lot spilled, but judging by the burns on the body, death occurred from a much higher concentration in greater proximity to the subject. And on his left side. That is, I think someone spilled the acid, but also put it right up to his face, from the left side while he was pinned under the cabinet. Feeding the fumes to him."

"How wonderful! Uh, I mean, of course, how wonderful that you've figured this all out and put it in your report for the ME and Chief Vernon. They're sure to find it to be murder and not this ridiculous poltergeist now!"

Dr. Kennedy looked as if I had punched her. "I didn't exactly...I mean, there wasn't sufficient ...The ME will surely do a more thorough exam and draw the same conclusions."

She tried to stand but I grabbed her arm. "Dr. Kennedy, what if they don't? What if the school pressures them to get the body home and they figure you examined it well enough? And I have heard that Chief Vernon is quite the believer in this paranormal nonsense. What if he is prejudiced in this case and the murderer goes free? You must tell them."

"Oh, he...they can handle it. That's not my job."

"But it should be. How very astute you've been. You should consider becoming an ME yourself."

"Do you think? No, no, they will do just fine."

"Maybe they won't. There could be dozens of clues they would miss, not used to dealing with homicide out here in the hills. Was there anything else they might miss?"

"Well, there were the extreme contusions surrounding the calcaneous..."

"And what did you make of that?"

"It didn't fit, you see. He was found with shoes on, but the bruising was recent; the blood had yet to diffuse through the surrounding skin much. But it was much more pronounced than the other bruising. The back of each heel much the same and it seemed to be from repetitive abuse." She stared at the wall, thinking aloud.

"And the rest of the bruising was different? Normal bruising, as if things had flown at him?"

"Yes, well, not normal, exactly. The pattern was odd. It was extensive, but none of it along his sides. It was as if his arms had stayed hanging at his sides. And none on his hands and forearms. One would think he would have curled in a protective crouch, but the evidence shows otherwise." She tapped her pen against her lips again.

"Oh, Dr. Kennedy, you are so very perceptive. What an acumen! You simply must relate every last detail to Chief

171

Vernon. Or maybe the ME can convince him."

"I don't know. I never had the stomach really for all of this."

Who was she kidding? She was an undertaker, for heaven's sake.

"Oh no, I beg to differ. I think you've found your calling. And why would I be surprised? A woman whose lab partners called her "The Cutter" in med school."

"How do you know about that?"

How *did* I know about that?

"Uh, um, I'm just guessing, of course. What else would they call you? What else could they call a pathologist of such perspicacity?"

She still regarded me with doubt.

"Hey, hey, hey." Around the corner of the wall came Petra's dred-locked head. Her wildly-clad body followed.

"Company's here!" Nicholas announced, following Petra with a bouquet of red roses in his hand.

Dr. Kennedy stood. "I'll leave you youngsters. Miss Davis, I expect you'll be fine. *Everything* will be fine."

"But–"

She held up a hand to stop my protest and went through the door.

"Well, you don't have to look so happy to see us. Geez, I thought you might miss me just a little bit."

"It's not that, Petra. I am happy to see you. Please sit down."

Nicholas thrust the roses under my nose.

"Mmm, yes, lovely, thank you. Are you sure you shouldn't save red roses for a more appropriate occasion?"

"We could kick Rocky out and try to make them appropriate." He waggled his eyebrows at me.

Incorrigible.

"I thought after I saved you and all, you might be feeling like thanking me in a manner of my choosing."

Petra snorted.

"And where were you, Petra? Nicholas was looking for Anthony, but you were supposed to be the one helping me."

Petra turned as red as she could through her jet skin. "I...I just got caught up with my work. And some of the animals had died, the nasty little rats. I couldn't just leave them in there to sicken all the others. I'm sorry, sweetie, but hey, looks like you had spirits watching out for you."

I blanched. "Spirits?"

"Angels. You know, guardian spirits? Nick found you right away, judging by what the others said when he hollered out for help."

"And you saw no one, none of you?"

"No. As far as we can tell, it was Brian's ghost who sauntered out that doorway and smacked your pretty little cranium," Nick said.

Petra had some assignments for me from Mahmet and also a note from Kathy that my action plan was to be reinstated upon my release. While I was frowning about this, Professor Gilbert came in, bearing an ominously thick folder. When I looked up from it, I noted that Petra was near exploding. Gilbert had taken the opportunity of finding her here to grill her about her experiments. Her progress didn't appear to satisfy him. I wondered if anything ever did.

"Well, come to me whenever you need to be set back on track. I even have an extra free period this semester, so there's plenty of time," Gilbert said.

Petra stomped out, barely waving goodbye.

Gilbert scrutinized my bandaged face. "I'll give you through the weekend to catch up. Rocky gave me your work from before and it was satisfactory. I expect you'll have no trouble with this material either."

I couldn't tell if it was a compliment or not.

He continued, "I hope they're finished cleaning up that chem lab soon. All those students are down taking up space in my biology rooms. Damned inconvenient and you'd think they'd be finished by now."

"What do you think, Dr. Gilbert? About all of that? A poltergeist?"

Gilbert looked tired. "Miss Davis, I am a biologist and a physicist. There are more mysterious things we discover every day."

"It's sad for the boy, of course…"

"Yes, well. I think I covered those bases in my eulogy."

With that, Gilbert left. Nicholas, however, had himself affixed to my bedside.

"Nicholas, please go. It has been a long day and, as you can see—" I indicated my stack of work. "— I have so much to do."

He was forlorn, but followed the professor out.

I heaved a tired sigh. My mind swirled with the information from Dr. Kennedy. It mixed with occasional stabs of anger at Anthony, though one would expect the passage of a day could have assuaged my resentment at his intrusion. I had expected him to come see me again. To give me an update, maybe? I had thought his threat to come back only on the weekend had been just that, a threat. My brain was a bit fogged. I yawned hugely and stretched out under my covers. I was soon heavily asleep.

Something awakened me later. Twilight had settled in and it had again begun to rain. I sat still, with my eyes wide, trying to adjust and see beyond my bed.

A scuffing sound. From across the room by the window.

I snapped on my bedside lamp.

A man crouched in the far corner, his face screwed up in a grimace.

I threw my water bottle at him and screamed at the top of my lungs.

"Hey! It's okay. Calm down. I'm sorry I startled you." He came out of his defensive posture, still blinking with his face screwed up at the sudden glare of my lamp.

He was Willie, Frieda's renounced amour.

"What in all of creation do you mean by creeping around

my room! Did you crawl in the window? Are you crazed?"

"No, no. I'm work-study. Someone's always on duty during the nurse's dinner hour, in case anything happens. It was my turn in the rotation." He looked chagrined. "I was hoping you were okay. On my last duty, you were still knocked out."

"They had me drugged for some time."

"Oh." He kicked an imaginary something on the floor.

"While I appreciate your concern, I don't quite understand…"

Willie worked his mouth around, unwilling to let the words come out. "It's because of Frieda. She didn't mean it, I'm sure. I tried to talk to her about it, but she still won't speak to me. Those damn filters. If it weren't for them…"

"Whoa. Back up, if you please. What is this to do with Frieda?"

"She's the one who hit you. She was up on the roof fixing the red filters. They keep falling off on the inside with the humidity is so high. She must've thought to put them on the outside. Because they fell, you see."

"They fell."

"Yeah. She went in, snuck in really, to check on her plants. If anything dies, Gilbert'll have her head, just like he does with everyone. So she snuck in and there they were, the filter panels all on top the overwintering annuals."

"So you went with her to help?"

Willie flushed red. "Not exactly. I was kind of, well, sort of…"

"You were spying on her."

He nodded quickly and looked up, sheepish.

"Through the glass, in the tall grasses. She didn't mean to whack you, and then leave you. She just couldn't get caught. Gilbert is really unforgiving about pretty much everything."

"She told you this?"

"No. I just figured it out. I saw her up on the roof, and then I heard where you were when you got smacked. Anyway, I'm glad you're okay." He skulked towards the door.

"Wait!"

Everyone kept dropping in and unloading tremendous amounts of information on me. If they would just give me a minute to work through it all...

"What is it about you and Frieda? I never did ask Petra, but it seems to me you want Frieda, not Petra. Or are you spying on them both?"

"Rocky? No." This time he really blushed. Beetroot. "I don't know. Do you know any of the story? See, Rocky came up to me and said she wanted to help, help me and Frieda, because I was, you know, just a little inexperienced... as a lover?"

I nodded as if I knew exactly. "A bit but not all."

"Frieda'd been...well, complaining to Rocky when they were working together in the greenhouse. Because I was, you know, just a little inexperienced...as a lover. So, I asked Rocky to teach me. Like a therapist? A *sex* therapist, you know? She thought Frieda okayed it, because I told Rocky she had. I knew Frieda wouldn't go for it, but I wanted to... to learn, I guess. And, well, after? I got a little carried away. I thought I was in love with her, with Rocky, and Frieda found out. And for a while, I didn't know what I wanted. But Rocky's made it pretty clear she was just...helping, right? Now Frieda won't talk to me." He slumped there in the doorway.

"Does Frieda know Rocky was only trying to help?"

"She won't let me close enough to tell her."

"Hmm. Let me talk to her. To both of them. Maybe I can work it out."

"Would you?" He lit up like a Christmas tree, or some such overly-bright ornamentation.

"Of course. Misunderstandings of this sort happen all the time."

"You can say that again. For a while there, I thought Frieda had moved on to Brian Nelson. They were always at the science building together. Even sometimes when he went alone, she followed him and popped in. Half the time I was following her, trying to get up the courage to talk to her, she was sneaking around watching him."

He let out an abrupt bark of laughter. It caught me by surprise and made me jump.

"She was following him around right up until he died. But then I knew it wasn't an affair. You see, she wasn't upset at all that he was dead. Not upset one little bit."

Chapter 18

I hardly slept a wink that night. Where were the sedatives when I needed them? Finally, well past midnight, I snapped on my lamp and sat up. The only way I would get any sleep was if I tried to sort out the muddle in my head.

I began with Frieda. Willie had inculcated me with the theory that perhaps she had more to do with Brian than simply acting as his lab partner. But, whereas the lovelorn Willie had suspected her of amatory trysts, I was coming to be of the opinion that she was guilty of something far more damning than what Willie had been worried about.

I knew she did not care for Brian. He had ruined her first round of experimental plants. She was worried Gilbert would proscribe her project in its totality. Had Brian returned to the greenhouse and inadvertently set Frieda's project back again, perhaps destroyed her latest specimens? Could he have despoiled her study on purpose?

I was sure Frieda knew enough chemistry, seeing as how she was a science major, to recognize the toxicity of hydrochloric acid. Could she have orchestrated his murder, carried off such an elaborate scheme? She had exhibited a great passion for her work. And she, of all people, would have had no problem luring Brian to the science building. They were "lab buddies" after all.

The details assailed me. The cabinet, the poltergeist, the acid, Brian's bruised heels, his other bruises.

I was convinced it was murder. My own deductions and rejection of the poltergeist theory had brought me to that conclusion. Dr. Kennedy's conversation only reinforced that finding. I even knew now how it was done, the acid fumes being the fatal factor.

As I saw it, there were only two questions. One, who had the motive to kill Brian and two, who knew enough about poltergeists to create a convincing scenario?

Oh, and three, who knew Chief Vernon well enough to know he'd fall for a poltergeist?

Yes, and four, who knew Dr. Kennedy would be hesitant to bring her contradictory evidence to his attention because of …some as yet unknown reason?

Well, then actually, there was five. What had consumed Brian so greatly that he was not of the here and now when he came out of that door and hit me?

Okay, six. Why were his heels bruised? And…and…why were the rest of the bruises in such an odd pattern? And why did he go to the chemistry lab in the first place? And did he tell anyone what was bothering him? Did he tell Anthony? And why did Anthony have to be here, baby-sitting me? And why did I let him blackmail me? And how could anyone have hair that curled just so, and eyes so deeply blue…

The next thing I knew, the Nazi Nurse was shaking me awake, none too gently, admonishing me for leaving my light burning all night long. It was morning. I had fallen asleep finally amidst a cloud of questions. None of them seemed as important now compared to the fact that I was to be released!

Petra had brought me a bag of clothes. I was almost scared to open it, but when I did, I found a fairly innocuous outfit, the only potent item a bandana of hers for my hair, which upon closer inspection proved to be covered with interwoven vines that only half-covered naked fat men in various positions of…well, I wouldn't have it covering my tresses, I can assure you. I stuffed it in a pocket instead.

I was pulling a brush through my hair when Anthony knocked on the wall.

"Hey."

"Good morning, Anthony."

"You ready to go?"

"If you are asking, am I ready to take myself off to resume my course schedule, the answer is yes."

"Suny, I've got to sign you out. I may as well walk you to

your first class."

"Thank you, no. If you must sign me out, then scurry off and do so. I avouch that I will not fall down on my way to Arabic."

"You're making this harder than it has to be."

"I don't know how I can be doing so as I have no idea as to what you are referring."

"For chrissakes..." He left.

If I were to establish the boundaries as to our mutual conduct from here on out, I felt I needed to start now. I hoped that Anthony's taste for exposing my abilities had been satisfied, not whetted, by our recent endeavor, and I, therefore, thought it best to firmly settle in Anthony's mind that I would brook no further forays into the matter. His abidance of my request to do without an escort was a positive first step in separating myself from his interference.

He was waiting for me under a tree.

I walked right past him and made my way down the hill. I glanced back once to see Anthony get up slowly and saunter behind me. I quickened my pace.

I had with me all my notebooks, also provided to me by Petra, and I had partaken of a cold tray provided to me by the soon-to-be-happily-forgotten Nazi Nurse. I headed directly towards the academic buildings. I had just one more hill to climb and descend when Anthony's low voice carried across the space of grass and smote me.

"They're ruling it a poltergeist. Chief Vernon's closing the case."

"What!" I stopped dead. He ambled toward me at a maddeningly slow pace. I strode back the way I'd come and met him.

"Please don't tell me that words of such inestimable idiocy really just passed your lips."

"Passed them, they did," he answered and then pulled those lips into a smirk. "But, to be fair, that's not exactly what the Chief said."

"Well? Tell me!"

"You want me to walk you to class and fill you in?" The smirk traveled up his cheeks and lit his eyes.

"Oh, fine. Have it your way."

We continued on.

"They're ruling it accidental–"

"Acci– What a *kon' pedal'nii!* How could it possibly be ruled an accident?"

"Suny, there's no evidence of foul play. All they've got to go on is a room full of stuff hurled around, a body obviously hit by a bunch of it–"

"But that's not what killed him!"

"How did you know that?" Again with the suspicious looks.

"Never mind, but it was the hydro-"

"Hydrochloric acid, I know. It was spilled all over the place, enough to create a cloud of fumes, enough to kill him. Or anyone. How do you rig that? And more importantly, why? No one had any reason to kill him. They checked the work he was doing, checked his notebooks– nothing sinister there. And they discovered some of his writings, not a diary really but– Suny, he wasn't a happy kid. All he had was his physics. No friends, not real friends, definitely no girlfriend. It must have become just too much."

"Surely the family cannot be satisfied with this finding, Anthony."

"His family's not…well, from what I remember, his family thought he was something of a freak. They're real simple people. I think his dad drives a truck. He was an embarrassment to them, pretty much. Always getting beat up. Wouldn't defend himself. Wouldn't play sports. Brian told me once that he never got mail, never went home for breaks. They were happy he went away to school."

"But they can't be happy he's been killed!"

"I'm sure they're not, but it's not like they've seen much of him in the last three years."

"That's ridiculous. What kind of parents would ship their

child off and not care if they existed, not care if they were hurt…"

Anthony studied the ground, then looked up at me silently.

I met his eyes, then looked away. I stomped off. When I reached my classroom, I put my head down on my desk and steadied my breathing. When I was quite calm again, I sat up and looked out the window.

He was still there. Then, having seen me safely enter the class, he turned and walked away.

At the end of my classes for the day, after I made my prescribed check-in with Nazi Nurse, I went up to the…well, to the mailroom. After all, I had not been in to collect my deliveries for a full week. Surely there would be something.

Nothing.

A student manned the desk that sold stamps and envelopes.

"Has the mail been delivered today?"

"Yeah, I think it's all out. Let me check." He turned to a mail bin packed with larger parcels and boxes. "What's your name?"

"Suny. Suny Davis. I'm new, so there may have been some confusion?" I craned my neck to see his progress.

"Naw. No confusion. I put your name label on the box myself. But wait— here's something. Must've got stuck between two packages."

He held out an envelope.

I grabbed it, thanked him, and hurried out. Once away and in solitude, I checked the return address.

Good, faithful Mr. Munston.

I tore into the envelope.

Dear Suny,

I can't tell you how pleased I was to get your note. You sound very settled. I'm happy for you.

Broadman is much the same, though my literature classes may never be so alive as when you were there to catch the innuendo and subtlety that the majority of the girls miss. It has become rather boring to teach students of a normal cadre. I realize how much I enjoyed teaching you and I want to thank you for that.

Ah, well. Now the joy of teaching you has fallen to others. I suggest to you, in response to your question about science instruction, that you ask to be allowed to take on one more class, hoping of course that you've had no trouble getting up to speed with your other classes. Barring that, perhaps one of the professors could be enticed to tutor you, or a senior student, even. If all else fails, you and I could correspond. Although I was your literature teacher, it was only my minor at school. I am also trained to teach the sciences.

I didn't know where your new school was when you left. Surprise, surprise, you are only a half hour or so from my hometown. If you need any advice on recreation or outings, I would be happy to be of service. And if I end up visiting family over the holidays, perhaps we can meet— unless, of course, your father sends for you.

Speaking of family, and fathers, for that matter, you will never guess who has enrolled at Broadman. In fact, I believe she has taken your room because I see her everywhere with Morgan Stanfield. Your very own sister, Rebecca. She is quite an interesting young lady, and while I don't think she shares all of your attributes, she does look remarkably like you! But I suppose sisters never want to hear that. I never liked being compared to my sister either.

All my best, your teacher,
Samuel Munston

I was pleased it seemed Mr. Munston actually missed me. But that pleasure was soured by the news his epistle brought. He was speaking of my supposed half-sister, Rebecca. I say supposed because she has not been recognized by my father, much to the consternation of her mother, Charlie Anne Monroe, a self-proclaimed channeller from Austin, Texas. Charlie Anne swears my father ravished her in the ladies' lounge during a parapsychology convention in Dallas. Granted, my father was a keynote speaker there, a year before I was delivered to him, but Charlie Anne was decidedly not his type. I'd overheard Father say once that he could not recall "every lovely who'd caught my fancy," but still the family's attorneys wondered why she did not come forward until Rebecca was nearly four, so they balked at her claim initially. Eventually they settled the case. After Charlie Anne refused to subject Rebecca to DNA testing, they agreed only to provide for Rebecca's education while maintaining the stance that she was no blood relation, simply to ensure that Charlie Anne would not sell television rights to her story. Charlie Anne pounced on this resolution as the next best thing and took full advantage of the situation, sending Rebecca to exactly the same schools I went to wherever they might be.

Rebecca was a year younger than I and looked nothing like me, other than when artificially made to do so. It was sickeningly apparent that her mother still wished Rebecca were me. Rebecca had shown up at my last school with hair bleached and permed to approximate my naturally honey-colored curls. My own hair was now hennaed as a result.

Hmm. So Rebecca Davis (yes, she claimed that surname on top of all else) had attached herself to Broadman. The little leach. She would fit right in with all the other phonies there, like Morgan, who seemed to have gotten over her distaste for bastard daughters of charlatan freaks. It looked as though I had gotten out of there just in time…

"Hey, Suny!" Petra hailed me. I pocketed my note. "You've been sprung!"

"Yes. Thank you for the outfit."

"I'm going down to the lab. Wanna be my lab buddy?" she added comically.

"No, I– well actually, sure. I'll accompany you, I mean." I gathered my books again. "Have you heard that they're ruling Brian's death an accident?"

"All of everything's an accident, Suny hon."

I pondered that cryptic response. Petra didn't say much else until we reached the biology lab. She held the door for me.

"You coming in?"

"No. I think I'll go up and revisit the site of my own little

185

accident." I touched my bandage lightly.

Petra let the door close without walking through. "You may want to leave that all alone, Suny. I don't know a whole lot about it, but I have a bad feeling about anyone messing around with such a strong spirit."

"Listen to the girl who plays at medium. Has this scared you off your little séances?"

"I'm not fooling. It was interesting at first but, with you getting hit, and it looking like that lab was the real deal…"

I wasn't about to admit to her that I had had a somewhat spooky experience myself, above and beyond getting smacked in the head by a door. "Set your mind at ease. I'll be fine."

Petra fixed me with a look, then shrugged. "It's your funeral."

Her words hung with me as I climbed the stairs. It was ridiculous of course, but…

The third floor was abuzz with students. It served to calm me. I headed straight for the door that was responsible for so much pain and inconvenience. As silly as it was, I made the final approach with caution and hesitated a bit before grasping the knob. It turned easily.

I stuck my head around the edge of the door. Stairs. Lots of them. They went up into faintly lit darkness. Hadn't Willie said something about the roof? Such must be the case. Before continuing on, I checked that the doorknob twisted readily from the inside as well.

I took the first step gingerly, as if it might open up and tumble me to oblivion. I took the next and craned my neck upward, way upward, to see the stair's terminus: a heavy looking door that stood in shadow. My heart raced.

Oh, for heaven's sake. Petra had really set my imagination free.

I stomped loudly and quickly up the remaining steps (goodness, there must have been more of them here than were completely necessary) and pushed open the door at the top.

The brilliant sun forced me to blink rapidly. I was on the

roof. Mechanical access doors broke the wall on either side of the stair door. Over to one side, and a full story down, was the greenhouse. Its panels blazed, sending beams of sunlight in every direction. I walked to the edge of the building proper, which was corralled by a foot-high safety wall that ringed the flat roof. There was an opening, through which a metal ladder fed down through it and onto a rim just wide enough for a person to stand on around the outside edge of the greenhouse's glass roof.

Covering just a patch of the panels were the red filters of which Willie had spoken. Frieda must have climbed down and almost thrown the filters into place, snapping them out as one would roll out a carpet. Why she would have attempted it herself was beyond me. Surely the maintenance crew would have had an easier time of it.

A quickly moving cloud dimmed the light from the sun. When that orb emerged, its light struck the red filter panels and sent a shaft of rose to meet my eyes.

The aurora borealis! This was what I had seen that night. I had thought it was the northern lights, but now I knew it had to have been some light from the greenhouse, playing on clear glass, then red-filtered glass. A flashlight. It must have been a flashlight's beam. But why would someone have been using a flashlight in the greenhouse? The science building was kept unlocked. I had to assume that included the greenhouse. Why not just throw on the lights?

Unless it had been someone who was not supposed to be in the greenhouse in the first place.

Brian.

What had he been doing, sneaking around in the greenhouse? What had he done? Something that brought Frieda to the point of committing murder? Or, what had he discovered? And what had he been doing on this roof that had brought him through that door in such a brown study?

I turned away from the roof's edge.

Firm hands caught me by the shoulders.

187

"Whoa there, girl. You're going to knock us both over the side if you're not careful."

"Petra! Oh, you startled me!"

"I came up to find you. The dining hall's about to open and I'm starved."

We walked back toward the access door that led to the stairs. I noticed from this perspective, a narrow catwalk that led to the aforementioned wartish protuberance housing the ventilation fan. There too was an access door, and near it, something glinted on the grid of metal that was the catwalk, right before the door.

"Wait a moment, Petra." I walked delicately across the bridge of steel, gripping the side rails. A more sturdy structure had probably never been built, but I was not keen on the feeling of open air under my feet. There was a platform outside this access door, floored in the same material as the rest of the roof, but right before it, caught in the metal mesh, was a small wrench.

Petra had followed. She leaned forward and pulled the wrench back up through the grid.

"Cool. I'm going to keep this. There was a lady at this craft show in Bardenstock, she made wind chimes and jewelry out of old tools and stuff." Petra held the wrench up to her hair. "I'm going to make me a barrette."

"Petra! That could be evidence."

"Evidence of what?"

"Of Brian's death. He had just come from the roof when he hit me, and later that night he was killed."

"You think?" She held the wrench less casually now, by fingertips. "Well, may be. I'll make you a deal. We'll let Chief Vernon know we've got it and if he's interested, he can have it. Otherwise, I'm fixing to get out my hot glue gun." She fished out a tissue from...well, from her voluminous brassiere, wrapped the wrench in it, and pocketed it.

"Now, I don't know about you, but I need some chow, and so help me, if they're serving millet casserole again, someone's

188

going to end up with a panful of birdseed on their head."

I suppose, judging from previous events, that I should not have been surprised to find that Chief Vernon was not interested in the wrench. He wasted a good bit of my time asking for the details of finding it and why I was "meddling" in the first place. After a measure of this abuse, I frankly told him that if he came to his senses, he could speak to Petra as she was the one in whose possession it now rested. And I warned him she was likely to turn it into a hair accessory soon. His response was less than cordial. Petra planted the thing in her overflowing jewelry box and, more than likely, forgot all about it.

And, I have to say, so did I. That is, I forgot just about everything outside of my schoolwork. It was October now and, along with decidedly chilly weather and an abundance of falling leaves, came midterms.

I squirreled myself away. A few times, on my way to answer Nazi Nurse's litany of questions to assess the extent of my recovery, I caught Willie tailing Frieda and I thought again of my promise to him to talk to her. The fact that I had my own reasons to talk to her was not absent from my mind either. But, though not quite as serious as murder, my studies were rather pressing. I felt badly for it, but avoided contact with anyone for several weeks.

I am thankful that Anthony respected my need for study time. He checked in on me now and then; usually I had the useful shield of a heavy book with which to ward him off. The hateful Kathy Larson followed up with my action plan and watched me like a falcon, or some such bird of prey with keen eyesight and tenacity... In any case, she seemed almost satisfied to find me so serious about my schoolwork.

It was night– don't ask me which one as they had all become a blur to me of late– when Petra flopped down on my bed, put her head inconveniently in my lap, which made it very difficult to continue reading the book I held there, and said,

"So, what are you going as?"

"Hmm?" I pushed aside a few dred locks and made an effort to keep reading.

"What are you going as– to the Halloween party after mid-terms?"

I gave up. "Halloween party? Oh, I don't think I'll be able to take the time to go."

"But you have to. What will you be so busy with after midterms?"

"After midterms?"

"Suny, I think you need to take a break. Your brain is fried. Look, Friday is the last test day and all papers are due then too. Saturday is the party. Now, you have to go, so we may as well think of a great costume for you. Something that shows off those fabulous–"

"Petra," I interjected, scared half to death of what might become of me if I allowed her to make any contribution to my costume. "I've already decided. I'll…I'll be an Arabian princess," I said without half-thinking about it. I had, after all, just been reading a children's fairy-tale book in Arabic. "Yes, I have a sari and I could easily fashion that into veils."

"Ooh, ooh, wait!" She sprang up and hauled open a dresser drawer. The now uncovered book in my lap soon became covered again, by various pieces of some outright amazing lingerie she threw aside in her search. "Here it is."

She held aloft a filmy pair of pajama pants, banded at waist and cuff. It looked straight out of Ali Baba. I must admit, it was perfect.

Petra was so pleased with herself that she'd been able to help in outfitting me, and so pleased with me that I had chosen something that would show off my fabulous… attributes, that she left me alone to finish my studies.

When I was quite done and Petra was off shopping for supplies to create her own costume, I pulled out the sari fabric and held it up to my face in the mirror.

I no longer wore a bandage on my cheek, but the skin there

was still quite new and pink. Nazi Nurse had told me I would have a scar.

I wrapped the fabric around my head and pulled it across to cover all but my eyes. Well, as much as I hated to go to parties, this one could hardly be as adventurous as the last time I had donned the beautiful silk.

Chapter 19

On the last Saturday of the month of October, midterms completed, books shut and computers powered down, the campus of Preacher's Ledge erupted in a flurry of face paint, false teeth and wigs. My own costume was tame compared to some of the absolute marvels others had created. It seemed as though more energy must have been spent on costume creation than studying in the last week.

I waited for Petra by the dining hall, the only place large enough for all of the students to gather. I shivered in my skimpy attire. She had scampered out in search of more fake blood. Her costume may have been the most elaborate I'd seen. She was plastered from head to toe in black feathers, a collar of gray ones at her throat. She had constructed a head piece that fit over her shoulders to give her a false neck that bent around her own. She was, of all things, a buzzard. A buzzard who had recently consumed an effusively bloody meal. Why she needed more blood, I couldn't fathom.

So, I waited. People passed me. An iridescent dragon, impaled of course, and accompanied by St. George. A few Albert Einsteins, a Fidel Castro, and even a wheel-chaired and bespectacled Steven Hawkings. But everyone was not quite ready, it appeared. They passed by, leaving me the only one standing and waiting for the hall to be unlocked. And turning blue, I might add.

"Hey, Suny. Awesome outfit." Todd walked up, part of a crew in brightly-colored space suits I vaguely recognized as trademarks of a particular out-of-date computer component company. Todd himself was purple. "Are you coming?"

"Thank you, Todd. I await my roommate. But it doesn't look as though they've opened the doors yet."

"What are you talking about? The party's in the science building. Everyone thought it was the perfect place for the

Halloween party, it being haunted and all."

"What! How absolutely tasteless!"

"I'll see you down there," Todd called as he was pulled away by the rest of his gang. "Save me a dance!"

I had half a mind to boycott the whole thing and go back to my room. I had already reported to Kathy that I was to attend, however. Lord only knows what she'd have in store for me if I weren't where I said I'd be after dark.

I trudged down the hill. The wind blew leaves all around me. I batted irritably at one and missed. What a travesty. Here I could be curled up in bed, warm, and finishing the last of the fascinating book on neo-socialism that I'd needed a chapter of for my midterm, and I had been cajoled into attending a pointless perversion of both the pagan celebration of Samhain and the Christian All Saints Eve. In a purportedly haunted academic building.

Some things seemed almost too much to bear.

As I crested the hill that led down to the science building, I saw Willie– dressed as Cyrano, I noted with a smile– dash from behind the husks of ornamental grass outside the door. I did not see Frieda, but he must have, as he appeared to be in hot pursuit.

Ah well, perhaps it wouldn't be a waste after all. If I could get Frieda in a corner, in the self-same building where she killed Brian, perhaps I could winkle out the truth from her, force her to confess, revenge Brian, and bring her head to Chief Vernon on a plate. With Anthony looking on, of course, eyes wide in wonder at my astute sagacity, my resolute quick-wittedness, and all without– I hardly need point out– any psi tomfoolery whatsoever.

This happy reverie put me in a brighter mood. As I made my way through the doorway of the building, which was covered in a film that sandwiched coursing rivulets of fake blood between it and the glass, I believed I might actually have a good time.

The lobby was cleared, or rather, had been cleared and was

now thronged with bodies dancing to electronic noise with a definite spooky edge. I recognized three of Todd's gang behind a synthesizer and a bank of laptops.

"Hey, there you are. They're great, aren't they? Half of tonight's music will be from their midterm." Todd pointed to a young man in a yellow spacesuit who wielded an electronic mouse. He saluted back in robotic fashion.

Todd took to gyrating up against me and then pulled on my hands. "Come on, let's tear it up."

"Not just yet, Todd," I screamed over the cacophony. "I have to find Petra first."

"What? Rocky? Okay, but you come find me after. I'm really digging your Barbara Eden."

"What?" But it was pointless. I couldn't hear and Todd was banging his head so violently, I doubted he would remember his own name at the end of the song, such as it was.

I squirmed through the writhing bodies to the stairway. Corpses, or rather life-size mannequins and dolls in various stages of torture and/or death, hung every few feet from its railing. I climbed, dead bodies spinning in the air by my side.

It was a bit quieter on the second floor. In fact, I met no one as I moved down the hall. Not having spotted Petra in the mass of dancers, I assumed she would be where she almost always was. In the biology lab. She probably couldn't have resisted a peek at her molds.

I pushed open the door to the lab. I flipped the light switch. Nothing.

I could hear nervous scurryings and a few shrill squeaks of the caged rodents.

I flipped the light switch off and on again. And again nothing to alleviate the dark.

"Petra?" I called.

A faint moaning met my ears.

"Petra? Are you there? Are you okay?"

Another moan, this one louder, and then– was that a whimper?

I ran my hands along the wire cage fronts, trying to avoid dislodging any water bottles as I made my way farther into the dark. The door into the smaller lab that housed Petra's specimens was on my left. When I ran my hand across the last of the cage fronts and felt only air, I turned and felt for the door.

Aha. The handle. I pushed.

Another moan, this one louder still, and off to my right where I remembered a window.

"Petra?" I turned toward the moan.

And there was Ambrose, the unfortunate skeleton, hanging on his stand. But, wait. How could I see Ambrose when it was as dark in here as out?

Ambrose glowed a sick green.

And then he moved.

I froze. It wasn't until I heard the clatter of the metal stand that held him fall to the floor that I found voice enough to scream.

I turned and scrabbled for the door handle, trying not to look back, but somehow unable to resist checking over my shoulder, where I saw the yellow-green shine of a bony hand reaching for me.

I screamed again and felt a hand close around my neck.

Suddenly the room flooded with light.

The hand that held me loosened and fell. "Got you!"

It was Nicholas's hand, covered in black fabric painted with phosphorescent paint in the pattern of the skeletal system, as was the rest of his body. Said body was now shaking with uproarious laughter.

"*Svoloch*!" It was all I could manage between hiccupping gulps of air. My heart hammered.

"You shoulda…you shoulda …wait–" Nicholas could not get himself to speak either, but his apparent aphasia was due to uncontrolled hilarity rather than terror.

"Get a hold of yourself!" I barked. "You nearly caused me to faint. What have you been doing, lurking here all evening,

196

waiting for some poor, unsuspecting—"

"You should have seen your face when I flipped the light on! It was even better than catching those two sophomores trying to make out by the mouse cages."

"Petra will wring your neck if she catches you in this lab. You made me so apoplectic, I could have knocked over every specimen she has in here. Now get yourself downstairs!"

"What? And miss another opportunity? Do you think Rocky will come in? That would be perfect." He rubbed his skeletal hands together gleefully.

"Right that stand, affix poor Ambrose back in place and discontinue this irresponsible jocularity this instant!" I indicated the jumbled heap that was Ambrose, tumbled next to the metal stand to which Nicholas had attached himself and thrust aside in his drama.

"Now, now. I'm just having a good time. You know, I never used to get invited to these shindigs at The Ledge. Being an outsider and all. Forgive me and allow me some fun at my first party."

"You will scare someone half to death."

"Maybe I should take a break. You want to go dance?" He came toward me and I backed away. Really. His costume wasn't helping me get over my scare.

"I was hoping to find Petra."

"But I'm a much better dancer than Rocky." Nicholas made a playful grab at my veils. "And you do look quite ravishing this evening."

I squeezed out of his grasp.

"Help me find her. Then I'll dance with you."

"Help you find who? And why the hell's my light out? I almost ran into a cage of baby rats." Petra, in all her avian glory, pushed through the door.

After they each complimented the other on their respective costumes, Nicholas had to throw the light switch again so Petra could see his theatrical reenactment of my arrival in the lab. When he was finally finished fooling around, we all traipsed downstairs.

Nicholas immediately spotted a pert and thoroughly unoriginal French maid and he left us, which was just as well as I wanted Petra to myself for a moment. If I were going to have an excuse to talk to Frieda, I needed to talk to Petra first to get her side of the…ahem, sex therapy debacle. When I brought it up, Petra was quick to fill me in.

"I tried to talk to the girl afterward, but she was having none of it. Can't say that I blame her. Though I don't know if I'd be trying to fix things up again between her and Willie, Suny. He tricked us both. I don't think I would trust him."

Before I could think to ask anything more, Nicholas compelled Petra to accompany him onto the dance floor, signaling to me that I was next. I watched them a moment. Petra's constructed neck and shoulders bobbed, making it seem that she truly was the carrion stripping Nicholas's corpse to the bone, though Nicholas appeared to enjoy it much more than a dead man might.

I decided it was time for a drink.

I threaded myself through dancers and onlookers, concentrating on preventing my slippered toes from getting mashed. It was a difficult task with all those enthusiastic rug-cutters, and I could not be blamed for running straight into a person of large stature, nor expected to do more than apologize for jostling his cup of punch.

"Oh, I am so sorry. My mistake entirely—"

"Miss Davis."

"Chief Vernon! Oh, again, my apologies."

"Don't worry about it."

"I didn't see it was you. You blend right in, don't you with that costume…uh, uniform?"

"Yes, well…"

I desired nothing more than to retreat that instant. Chief Vernon saved me the effort, however, by removing himself. He had no trouble causing the crowd to part and allow him to continue his observation of the activities.

I spotted Mahmet and a few other teachers monitoring the refreshments. He sported a schmaag, a kind of headscarf held in place by a black ringlet, but was otherwise dressed in Western attire, looking to me much like a Saudi businessman.

"Look at my Suny Davis," he exclaimed as I approached. "You have stepped out of that storybook we have been reading, walked off the page, you have. And my Kathy Larson also. She too is a princess of the Arabia. I will need a photograph. I will be the sheik with the women of his family. On my one side, the Suny Davis, and on the other, the Kathy Larson. Wait. Refresh yourself. I will return."

He sped off in search of Kathy. I tugged at my veils. The last thing I desired was my picture taken with that particular young lady. Why couldn't I have picked a different costume?

I drank thick punch. The viscosity was true to form for blood, but the addition of whatever thickener they had used didn't do as much for taste as it did for authenticity.

Mahmet scampered back, Kathy in tow, with Roger following and familiarizing himself with the controls of Mahmet's camera. Kathy looked me up and down and only half hid a sneer. She was, indeed, dressed in the Arabian style, but her costume was obviously off the rack, and not a high-caliber rack, at that.

Suddenly, I felt a little better.

Roger fiddled some more with the camera, while Mahmet squeezed us both to either side of him, a wide smile on his face. Kathy's new love looked pale and sunken in his own pajama-style pants and open vest. Twice he almost dropped the camera to keep his fez from falling off. Why Kathy had dumped Anthony for such a pallid excuse for a man, I could not say.

It was just as Roger was bleating at us to say cheese that I saw him. The dancing bodies parted for just a second and there was Anthony, resplendent in nautical finery that appeared so authentic, it could only have been that of a true sea captain from long ago. The buttons gleamed, as did his eyes when they

199

caught mine. He stopped in mid-stride and took us in. I repeated the obligatory "cheese," but I couldn't look at Roger and the camera when there was Anthony holding my gaze. I felt myself color and ducked my head as Mahmet loosened his grasp and took back his camera. When I dared look up again, Anthony was gone.

But I was not to be left without male companionship for long. Nicholas appeared and led me back to the dance floor. He was quite good. The shifting lights picked out his skeletal outline, producing a choppy rhythm of movement that matched the thrumming of the music.

Todd's buddies moved on to the electronic equivalent of a slow song and Nicholas wasted no time in clasping me to him. I noted once again that he did smell awfully nice.

Natasha, my math instructor, monitored the crowd closely. I moved myself an inch or two back from Nicholas. He allowed this, but ran his fingers up the back of my neck and into my hair.

"So," I said brightly, "Tell me about the town. It's a very nice town, I believe."

He looked intently into my eyes. "It's getting nicer all the time," he crooned.

I looked away hurriedly. Mahmet and Gilbert talked to Chief Vernon by the stairs. They talked, but Chief Vernon's eyes never stopped scanning the costumed throng.

"You should know this, if anyone does, Nicholas. What exactly is the relationship between Chief Vernon and Dr. Kennedy?"

"Why do you care about old, wrinkled love when there is new love to be made?" His waggling eyebrows were quite a sight at close range.

I planted one hand against his chest and pushed him gently, but firmly. "No, really, Nicholas. I have my reasons. So, they were once a couple?"

Nicholas sighed and removed his fingers from my hair. "Yes and no. You see, it's all the old biddies who truly run the town. Dr. Kennedy's aunt, Henrietta, is one of them and Chief Vernon's aunts who raised him too– Felicity and Hyacinth, if you can believe that one. They're all descended from the founding fathers, and they all have this crazy dose of town pride. Anyway, to hear Mom tell it, everyone just assumed they would marry– the Chief and Dr. K.– because they went to every school dance together, every church picnic. It was all orchestrated by the aunts. You know, they wanted the blood ties strengthened and all that crap. They scared away all other suitors and forced them together. So the Chief eloped to get away and Dr. K ran off to college and med. school. And that was the end of that."

He took up playing with one of my curls as I went over his tale. "So, the Chief came back with a wife and Dr. Kennedy came back to be undertaker."

"Not exactly. The Chief's wife ran away with another man right after the wedding and that's what made him come back to town. He is now a consummate bachelor. The aunts took him in again and installed him as Chief of Police."

I pondered this and flicked Nicholas's traveling fingers away with annoyance.

Todd appeared at my side and tapped Nicholas on the shoulder. While they squabbled over Todd's desire to cut in, I moved away to find a quieter spot.

Easier said than done. Finally, I headed off toward the greenhouse. I hadn't spotted Frieda yet but I had an inkling of where she'd be.

She stood guard outside the greenhouse door, encased in a dark, hooded robe, holding a scythe. She was Death.

"Frieda," I hailed.

"Oh, it's you. I thought you might be someone trying to find a make-out spot. I don't know why we can't lock the doors to the greenhouse. It's not as if we don't have enough fire doors as it is, but they have to be sticklers for policy and I'm damned if I'm going to let anyone play Adam and Eve in my greenery."

"Well, good evening to you too."

She failed to catch my sarcasm. "What are you anyway?" was all she said.

I didn't bother to answer, but silently rolled my eyes, just a bit, for the sake of my healing cheek. This was going to be a fun conversation, I could tell. I decided to jump right in. After all, I was after information and I wouldn't get it standing sentinel at her side; I had to get her to talk.

"So you're still worried about people trespassing even with Brian gone?"

"What's Brian got to do with it?" Her eyes narrowed to points in the recesses of her hood.

"Well, you said he'd ruined a run of plants, contaminated them—"

"Yeah, and even in death, he could have done more damage. If we hadn't insisted that the ventilation fan be above code, my second batch could've been history too. I told the administration they'd thank me one day."

"Thank you?"

Frieda heaved a dramatic sigh. "No one understands. I made them install the fan to cycle every five minutes, even though that boob on the board who thinks he knows everything thought it was sufficient with its capacity to have the fan cycle at the standard twelve minutes. Understand now? You see, the ratio of new air to old is increased at a rate—"

"I understand perfectly, Frieda. You think the fumes that killed Brian could have circulated down to the greenhouse otherwise?"

"Could have gotten into everything. It dissipates, but they'd have to have been sure before students could come in…" She prattled on.

Could she have felt safe in killing Brian with the acid fumes because she knew the fan would cycle them away before they reached her precious greenhouse? Why was she telling me all this? I would have to ask Dr. Kennedy about fume concentrations, about acid burns…

A movement in the greenhouse caught my eye. Ah, it was only Willie, spying on Frieda. How had he managed to get in?

"Uh, Frieda. I wanted to talk to you about Petra."

"About Rocky? I sure as hell have something to say about her. Do you know what I found in my greenhouse the day I...that is, when they let us back in after the whole Brian thing? I found a whole flat of those Amazonian herbs of hers hidden in with the overwintering annuals. If those things went to seed and blew around– hell, even with the possibility of cross-pollination– well, I'll tell you right now, she's not going to get away with unauthorized culture. I'm going to go straight to Gilbert and report her."

"That's not what I came to talk about." Enough with the cursed plants already! I proceeded to explain what had really occurred between Willie and Petra and how Petra did not have designs on him, and how Willie had indicated he'd like to have Frieda back if only she'd have him. I don't know why I even cared to try, other than I thought Willie had learned his lesson and deserved some happiness. Though if Frieda was a murderess...

"Well, I won't have him. Not only does he lie to me and sleep with her, but he actually thought at one point he might be in love with her. How am I supposed to feel about that? I mean, I'm all for trying to work together in harmony, but to date one of them?" Frieda shuddered in her long robe.

"I don't understand," I said, though a part of me felt sickened and was beginning to get it.

"She's black as coal," Frieda almost whispered. "How gross is that?"

It did more than unnerve me to have people assume I shared their bigoted positions simply because we shared a skin color. It made me queasy.

I found myself back in the lobby, but I was in no state to join in the festivities. It must have shown.

"Hey, Suny. What's wrong? You didn't have one of those

203

brownies, did you?"

It was Anthony. He was even more impressive up close, but I couldn't appreciate it fully.

"Nothing. No. What's wrong with the brownies?"

"I think some of the seniors up at The Stables baked them. They've got their own kitchen up there. Riddled with hash. Mahmet's had a couple and he's over in the corner reciting Rumi."

"I'll be sure to stay away," I said, still distracted.

"You sure you're okay?"

"Yes, yes already. Oh, I'm sorry. I'm just a bit disturbed. Never mind." I drew myself up and shook off my somber mood. "Would you care to dance?" I offered my hands.

"Uh…no…I'd better not. Just…just stay away from those brownies, okay?"

Well, then. It seemed I could do nothing more to do than go and listen to Mahmet's recitation.

The entire cluster of costumed students surrounding the Arabic instructor bore glazed expressions. They hung on his every word, though more than half of them couldn't understand any of it and could do nothing more than listen to the lyrical sounds of the ancient love poetry. For some reason, florid words of passion were not what I needed to hear right then. I broke off from the group and watched the dancers.

I broke off from the group and watched the dancers.

"Suny Davis, Suny Davis. O Daughter of the Great One." It was Diana Kowalski, the NESsie investigator. What she was doing here, I had no idea. It was obvious she too had had her share of hash brownies. Her eyes were positively bloodshot, which actually went well with her white-painted face and wraith gown with its shredded hem and sleeves.

"Ms. Kowalski." I nodded to her.

"You know, Suny Davis, I never thought I would come this close to greatness."

I felt myself tense at her sarcasm.

"I've read everything your father has written. Watched

every show he's been on. He's quite a character. Quite a character."

I remained silent, as difficult for me as that was.

"Can I tell you a secret? You have to promise not to tell anyone, especially that guy over there, that Sherlock Holmes. He's my date supposedly, though I just called him up 'cause he's a Ledge student and I wanted to get in here again, have another look around. What was I saying? Oh, yeah. Secret stuff. You can't–"

"I know. I can't tell anyone." Really.

"Okay. This is it. This whole poltergeist thing's pretty weird. It's really got me spooked. I couldn't sleep. I'm thinking you should call your father. This one actually may be the real deal. It's too elaborate to be a hoax."

I spotted Nicholas and was prepared to use him as an excuse to break away from her drug-induced nonsense when Diana made it clear that she too had seen Nicholas. And not for the first time.

"There he is again!" She gripped my arm. "That's the one I knew, not…not the other one. They look so much alike." She stopped a minute and cocked her head, her thinking obviously slowed by her altered state of consciousness.

I looked where her eyes were fixed as she continued.

"Now that I think about it, maybe I should reconsider my findings. If there's anyone who could have hoaxed that room and had reason to do it as well, it would have to be him."

"Nicholas Scarborough?"

"That's right. I remember that name now. It was about three years ago. He came to a bunch of meetings. He was super interested in how to gauge authenticity. Cornered Brad at every meeting to get him to talk about dissecting hoaxes. We all thought he was a Ledge student, 'cause he was so young. But, boy were we wrong. Brad asked him about it once and he got all bent out of shape; came damn close to saying he hated the place. What in hell would he be doing here now?"

"He's the Area Liaison, between the college and town," I

provided automatically, my brain still working on her words.

"That doesn't make any sense. After hearing him badmouth Preacher's Ledge, that's the last thing I'd expect him to be doing. Planting a bomb under the admin. building would be more his speed."

Chapter 20

I spent the rest of the party sitting on the bottom step of the stairs, thinking hard. Wildly garbed students passed me going up and down and not a few young gentlemen asked me unsuccessfully to dance. I tried to lay out what I now knew, what I had known before…the pounding music didn't help much. Eventually, it seemed only I and the clean-up committee inhabited the building.

I peeked out around the lifeless mannequin hanging by my ear. Empty lobby. It was just as well that no one had fetched me. I'd just as soon be alone to ruminate. I didn't know how to approach Nicholas, if I should approach him at all, if this latest tidbit freed Frieda from all suspicion, if…if…if…

It is not often that I feel inadequate to a challenge. I can honestly say that it is not a pleasant state in which to find oneself.

I got up and walked slowly outside. It was bitingly cold, but I hardly felt the sting. My mind was working enough to produce a heat of its own.

All this time I'd been focusing on Frieda. She was the only one I knew who really had anything close to a motive. I hadn't for a moment considered that the aim had been something other than to kill Brian. Brian himself, for something he did, something he knew. But maybe, just maybe, Brian had been an unlucky soul who happened to be available for a devious deception.

If Preachers' Ledge were made a laughingstock, if it were revealed that the administration had condoned paranormal investigations and took their findings as truth, major financial contributors to the school might yank their donations, alumni might distance themselves. In the worst case scenario, Preacher's Ledge could fail to attract the serious and sapient minds whose education was its sole reason for existence. The college could shut down.

Diana had said Nicholas hated the school. But could Nicholas hate the college so much that he would do something that could close its doors forever? Would he reveal the administration's gullibility in some sensational way? How could he do it without revealing his own guilt? Why would he hate the school so vehemently? Just because Anthony was his brother? Could that be a strong enough reason even after Anthony was gone? More to the point, could Nicholas carelessly sacrifice the life of one of The Ledge students just to set the school up for fatal embarrassment?

I thought of Brian quoting our Freshman Seminar text on the sociopath, describing the ability to feel no remorse, to not even be able to recognize the pain caused to others, because one might not be able to appreciate impending pain oneself. Was Nicholas a sociopath? Wouldn't it take more than an older brother worthy of envy to turn someone into a cold and emotionless killer?

I wasn't certain that I could picture Nicholas as such a monster. He was handsome, even likeable despite his antics and stilted phraseology. He was charming.

Such had been said too of serial killers, or so I'm told.

Now I did shiver. But how could Nicholas have killed Brian? I had felt his hands on my shoulders, in my hair...

Around my neck.

I stopped my mindless wanderings and shook my head to clear it. I was a few buildings away from Blaubury. Lights shone in some of the higher windows of Jefferson, the upperclassmen dorm to which I was closest, but mostly all the campus seemed tucked in and asleep. I was sure the hash brownies would make it a sound one for many.

I began walking again, trying not to think anymore tonight of Nicholas. My slippers were not the most practical footwear for walking on gravel, however. I soon had several stones inside them. I kicked my foot to loose them, but only succeeded in sending up a tall spray. They pinged in a shower against the building, and scattered around me, some landing painfully on my head and bare arms.

"Ouch!" I said loudly, then realized my volume and lowered it. "*Gavno*!" I whispered harshly.

Someone else was whispering as well. "Hey, Suny."

I looked up. Todd hung out his window, two stories up, impressively bare-chested, I must say.

"Todd–" I began to whisper-shout, but stopped as I realized he was not just leaning out of his dorm window– he was climbing out.

I was too amazed to move. He dropped the two stories, landing in a crouch, then walked to me, bare feet on the gravel, in nothing but pajama pants.

He took me in his arms and kissed me.

Apparently, Petra was right at least as far as kissing went. Between good dancing and good kissing, there seemed to be a correlation.

When he let me speak, I tried to protest but could not think quite clearly.

"I'm glad you threw that rock at my window. I wanted to see you. You kept disappearing on me. I never got my dance."

"Sorry," was all I could muster.

He kissed me again, and although it was quite as good as the first time, if not more so, I was over my initial shock, and felt I needed to explain myself.

When let up for air, I began, "I didn't mean to–"

"Suny Davis, is that you?" An accusatory voice came from over the way by Blaubury.

I believe the appropriate American teen term would be, "Busted."

Todd kissed me quickly, then scrambled back to his dorm, punched in his code, and tore up the stairs before Kathy could get much closer, with that stern look on her face.

I was busted indeed.

I sat in Sylvia's office Monday morning before classes. I was getting used to the chair, I can tell you.

And that was not all I was used to. I was often misunderstood and frequently found myself the recipient of misguided, though earnest, chastisement by lecture. There were a limited number of types of lecture, I've found. Some choose the stern, "This is for your own good, young lady" route. Others went to the extreme of loud and energetic defamation, almost to the point of abuse. Still others opted for the silent treatment meant to elicit sobs of confession and pleas for forgiveness. And then there were the administrators who had actually been awake in child development class, who even may have taken notes. Where Sylvia fell, I was soon to discover.

I looked resignedly around the room while Sylvia read over what I can only believe was Kathy's skewed and biased write-up of my behavior. I glanced at the chair beside me, where Todd should rightfully have sat. He hadn't been around on Sunday or I would have given him where by. Or what for... or something.

I sighed. I had been in here so frequently, I was beginning to recognize the art on the wall. There were many decent pieces and a cluster of photographs on the wall behind Sylvia's desk. These I hadn't noticed before and I inspected them the best I could from my chair. Mountain vistas, black and white studies of abandoned barns, a few of college functions and Sylvia with alumni or local personalities.

Was that Nicholas? Yes, indeed. Nicholas and Sylvia, an older gentleman who must have been a board member or alumnus, and a grizzled gentleman I knew to be a poet of the region.

Sylvia pulled me from these observations when she began to speak. She pleaded with me to understand her position. The college was co-ed, the students minors. I was a young woman of burgeoning sexuality and I would be tempted...to do what and with whom was only implied. I must comply with the wishes of the college and not let my perfectly natural, but ultimately forbidden, libido tarnish the reputation of the college, or myself. At least not so blatantly, half-dressed on a gravel pathway at one in the morning.

I was to be restricted to campus and given a curfew of ten p.m. until the Thanksgiving break.

I would have protested. In all fairness, I should have protested. But frankly, I was tired of protesting. Ah well, to look on the bright side, Kathy had remained honorable enough to keep her promise to Anthony. She had not told Sylvia of my escapades in town.

"Well, Suny, do you have anything you would like to share with me? I like to maintain an open dialogue on matters of discipline."

I looked at her. She smiled at me. Open dialogue on discipline, my size ten foot.

A knock saved me from making a perhaps unwise remark. Anthony pushed open the door.

I sank further into the depths of my chair.

"Suny," he said, nodding to me. "Sylvia."

I felt incredibly small and guilty in his presence. It amazed me. For it was ridiculous, I knew, as I had done nothing wrong, but there it was.

Sylvia filled him in on Kathy's report and on her decisions. He avoided looking at me, just stood there by her desk, clenching and unclenching his fists at his sides.

"I'll tell Mr. Davis, if you don't mind," was all he said to her. And then he walked out without a word to me.

"You really are a very lucky girl to have Anthony concerned for your welfare. He did service mentoring in town and helped quite a few…uh, lost souls find their way. He comes from such a fine local family. We're so glad to have him back in the area. And his brother on staff too. We're very fortunate."

Not so fortunate as you might believe, I thought, recalling the musings about Nicholas that had kept my sleep fitful for the past two nights.

"How did that happy circumstance come about, Sylvia? I mean…I'm so distressed that my emotions got the better of me the other evening because I am becoming very attached to the school. I would hate to see it…besmirched. Therefore, I …uh, I'm very interested in all its workings, and I can easily see how locals would want to be part of the college as well."

Whew. I expected narrowed eyes and a suspicious glare, but Sylvia was obviously in love with the school and liked nothing more than to chat about it.

"Nicholas came to me with the idea of an area liaison last winter. He was graduating high school soon and he was looking for something to do before he…well, he wasn't sure he wanted to go to a regular college. Though he could have gotten into any college– any regular college. Now that he'd finished high school, you see, but he wanted to wait, he said. So, we thought we should give him a job. I mean, it was a good idea, this idea for a job, and we thought…well, it was the least we could do."

Sylvia was flustered. She straightened the papers on her desk needlessly.

"The least you could do?"

"Well, yes. That is, you see…" She was floundering, looking pained. "Anthony was such a wonderful student, and really so mature for his age. He was the epitome of a Ledge student, of what the founders idealized. And Nicholas…well, he was bright enough. But he lacked a certain discipline. And there is only one Founders Scholarship available. We thought at the time that Brian Nelson was a worthier recipient, poor dear."

Poor dear, indeed. Imagine, two birds with one stone. Retaliation towards the college for not accepting him, and revenge against Brian for taking the scholarship that would otherwise have been his. Nicholas had orchestrated this whole thing for vengeance.

I didn't know what to do. If I called Chief Vernon, I was sure I would get much the same answer as I had about the wrench. The last thing I needed, on top of my restriction from Sylvia, was the Chief of Police calling the school to complain about my meddling. Besides, I had no proof, only a strong suspicion of motive and means. And I truly could not see how I could find out more. Without confronting Nicholas, of course. That, I was not yet prepared to do.

Anthony still roamed the campus, interviewing students, using the library. I avoided him. Aside from my typical reasons for doing so, I felt now that I would be hard pressed to keep from spilling the legumes all over him. His own brother. It would not have been easy to make small talk when I held such a damning notion.

I talked to Father right after my restriction began. That Anthony had also talked to him was clear. He knew I had been caught with a boy. In fact, the reference was "damn near time you were caught with a boy. I was starting to wonder." I hoped he had not reacted the same way when Anthony had relayed the information to him.

Thoughts of Nicholas haunted me for the next few weeks. I was lucky enough not to run across him in that time, but I was a bit jumpy. I hardly realized that I was on restriction. I actually wanted to hole up in my room. My thoughts alternated between wanting to expose him and wanting to forget the whole thing and simply continue with my studies. I no longer cared to show Anthony up, not if it meant inflicting on him the pain of a brother who was a murderer. Who was I, after all, Nancy Drew?

But it preyed on my mind. I pushed it away. I would not get involved again. At least, not unless my hand was forced. Instead, I sent a note to Gilbert asking for permission to take on another science class. Of course it was too late in the semester, but I hoped he would be impressed by my enthusiasm and would offer to tutor me. I got a flat no in response to the class request. I tried again, more explicit this time about my desire for a tutor. Another no.

This served to leave me with way too much time on my hands, time I unwillingly filled with speculation about Nicholas, about Frieda, about the circumstances of Brian's

213

death. Finally, a few days before our Thanksgiving break, I decided to make a call. I stood at the hall phone and tapped the wall nervously as I waited for a connection. Unfortunately, I got the answering machine.

"You have reached Kennedy Funeral Services. We welcome you to our family during this, your time of sorrow. Please let us know how we can begin to help smooth this transition for you." There followed the obligatory beep.

"Dr. Kennedy, Suny Davis– at Preacher's Ledge? I am sure you are aware of the um…the unwise decisions of certain officials in the death of Brian Nelson. I have become privy to some further information." I left her my number and hoped she might call before I traveled home. Someone had to listen to me and she was the closest to a sensible adult that I knew.

Todd came to say goodbye. He was leaving early for Nebraska. I had forgiven him for leaving me out in the cold to accept punishment for us both. It was easier to forgive him than I thought it might be, and I have to stress that I am sure it was because I am becoming a more flexible person, and not because he plied me with kisses. He did like to kiss me an awful lot though and, while I can't say that I didn't enjoy it, I felt that it was a fairly one-dimensional relationship we were building. One must begin somewhere however. And I was quite enjoying those kisses.

The next day, speaking of love, or rather love gone awry, I once again observed Frieda dodging Willie. I hadn't had the heart to tell him he should give up his hopes, that she wasn't worth his attention anyway. Now that I was fairly sure Frieda wasn't a killer, and now that I knew she was a bigoted, shallow little…yes, well, I'd sooner forget all about her.

Petra was staying at The Ledge over the break, as were several other students, many of them science majors at a crucial point in their long-term studies. Petra would cook them all a huge Thanksgiving feast in the dining hall, with some help from some of the faculty who lived close or had apartments on campus. I almost wished I were staying, but I

214

looked forward to a change of scenery and pace, if not to a Thanksgiving a la Magdalene, my stepmother. Last year it had been miniature roast quail and I didn't know how I would stand to see the dissection of tiny fowl again. And, despite my disappointing phone call with Father, I did look forward to at least some time spent with him.

Petra and I said our goodbyes as I packed and then she was off to meet the food distributor's truck. Dr. Kennedy had not called but I was almost relieved to be able to let the matter go for a while, as shamed as that made me feel. I had done my part, though and apparently Fate was not leading me to delve in further right now.

Anthony had called the day before and arranged to pick me up. I could only assume he had my tickets and itinerary as well since I had not spoken with Father since he had lauded my decision to loose my feminine wiles.

I snapped shut the locks of my suitcase as a knock sounded at my door.

"Come in," I called.

"Have you got something for me to carry?"

I froze, my back still to the door. It was not Anthony who stood on my threshold. I could tell from the voice.

It was Nicholas.

At that moment, I was very glad I had not yet turned to greet him. Had I done so, my terror would have shown clearly on my face. As it was, I needed to remind myself to breathe.

"Nicholas– oh, hello. It's you. I was…um…I was expecting Anthony."

"Yeah well, he's sucking up to Mom, picking up some groceries so she doesn't have to go out in all the Thanksgiving shopping madness. Are you okay?"

"Sure. Quite. Fine, really. Okay, then."

He came in and grabbed hold of my bag. Really, I had to get a grip on myself. So what if Nicholas took me to the airport? It wasn't as if he were the one who could read minds, after all. He had no way of knowing that I knew what I knew,

215

whether I knew for sure what I knew was truth or not. Or something to that effect. But I was still frightened.

Of course, there was one way I could find out what his intentions toward me were. A way to find out if he meant to do me harm. In my fear, I was willing to try anything.

I let him lead the way down the hall. I followed, but walked slowly, opening myself up to sensation. At first, it was just a muddle, like flipping channels on a television. As I passed each room on the floor, I tuned out my dorm sisters and focused on Nicholas.

And blushed madly. It seemed Nicholas was getting rather excited thinking of my...undergarments bouncing against his leg in the suitcase. I pulled back. No matter what he had done in the past, he was clearly concentrating on only one thing now.

I felt relatively calm as we wound our way down the hill to town. It had yet to snow this season and the sky was still the crisp blue of autumn. I was free from thought about my studies, free from my restriction to campus, free from–

"Wasn't that our turn?" I sat up straighter, alarmed. I knew the local geography well enough to know that we'd passed the main road that led onto the highway. Where was he taking me?

"Don't worry. I'm taking a short cut."

But I did worry. Nicholas wasn't his typical loquacious self. He was peering at the road intently. I couldn't stand the silence. If he was abducting me, was carting me off to get me out of the way, maybe I could force his hand. It would be better to struggle and escape from him closer to town, where I think I could still remember the turns we had taken.

"So," I said brightly into the silence, "are you glad to be on break, away from the college?"

"Shh. Hey, if you don't mind, I'm a bit of a nervous driver. Can the conversation wait?" He didn't look my way, but remained assiduous in his attention to the road.

"Surely," I mumbled. Can the conversation wait until when, until what? Until he had me tied to a tree in the woods, my

216

calls for help unheard?

I shifted in my seat and surreptitiously checked that my door was unlocked.

"Suny, can you stop fiddling? You're making me nervous. We're almost there."

We're what? We were most definitely not almost there. Nicholas had turned us deeper into the woods away from town.

Away from anywhere.

"Nicholas, I have to say–"

"Here we are." He turned the car onto an unmarked gravel drive. His shoulders loosened visibly. "Now, that wasn't so bad, was it?"

What did he mean? I began to panic. If I could only clear my mind, could open up to his—

What would I find at the end of this driveway?

The prettiest white cottage appeared from the midst of the trees. Fat balls of chrysanthemums made a quilt of warm color along the walkway to the door. In front of us was parked Mrs. Scarborough's station wagon.

Nicholas put the car in park and heaved a sigh. I stared at him, flabbergasted.

From under the overhang of the porch came Anthony, striding across the frosty lawn.

Before I could speak, Nicholas hopped out and went to the trunk for my bag. I was stunned, confused, bewildered…

"Suny?" Anthony opened my door for me.

"I've *krisha poehala*," I murmured, locked into my seat, adrenaline rushing away, leaving me sick to my stomach. "I don't understand. He…you…"

"Oh, hell. Your dad forgot to call you, didn't he?" He cursed again softly. "When I said I was coming to pick you up– that wasn't for the airport, Suny. That's what you thought, right?"

I nodded without looking at him, watching instead as Nicholas carried my bag into the house.

"You see, he and Bianca were granted access to some records at the University of Edinburgh. They're…well, he asked if you could join us here. For the holiday. Suny, he's in Scotland."

I know Anthony thought my blank stare was due to disappointment at Father's neglect, but he was wrong. That would upset me, I'm sure, if I gave it room in my mind. But there was no room for it. There was only enough for one thought.

I was going to spend the weekend, the *long* weekend, with a killer.

Chapter 21

Mrs. Scarborough welcomed me with an embrace and took me to the guest room, papered in small flowers. She was Portuguese. That is what I had sensed when I had been in Anthony's mind. She chattered to the boys in her native tongue, bidding them to fetch me this or that which she anticipated I might need. She was small and round with the most beautiful brown eyes, wide and warm brown like the chocolate truffles Naomi had ordered from Maxim's in Paris. Her hair too was dark, with the same wave as Anthony's, but longer, to her shoulders. She shooed the boys away and shut the door on me, insisting that I take my time to freshen up and settle in.

I did take my time settling in. This had been a surprise, to risk understating the situation. I didn't know how I could keep myself together when I knew what I knew, or thought I knew...well, when Nicholas was here, to be brief. And Mrs. Scarborough seemed such a lovely woman, and Anthony... how would I survive four days in this house?

I splashed my face with cold water in the adjoining bath and smoothed my clothes. I would just have to pretend I didn't know what I knew, or thought I knew but– Better said, I would try to act normally.

I found Mrs. Scarborough in the kitchen, making pies.

"Where is Nich– Where are the boys?" I asked.

"I have sent them out. This hovering in the kitchen, this is the last thing I am needing. But you, Suny, you sit and have pao-doce and some coffee. The boys will be back after they see who has come home from school to family."

She started to cut cold butter into flour and cinnamon with two knives. I ate some of the sweet bread and sipped my coffee.

"Your father is a funny man, not like every other man, but he lets Anthony do what is in his heart." She held her knives aloft a moment. "For this, I like him. You are sad to be away from him for this holiday?"

"I suppose one might say–"

"Tcha, no, no. Not what *one* would be saying. What do *you* say, Suny?"

"I say... I expected to be home with Father, but I am enjoying being here with you."

She frowned at me. "That is not an answer." She handed me a rolling pin as if I would know what to do with it. "That is a kindness." She plunked down a clod of dough and made rolling motions at me with her arms. "But it is not an answer. You are too much like my Anthony. Never saying what he thinks. Me, I would cry if my father did not send for me. And then I would shout." Her eyes twinkled and I could see that, despite the difference in color, they were Anthony's eyes. "But you are welcomed here to us and we will feed you well and make you laugh and then you can forgive this father."

After I had thoroughly covered myself in flour and accomplished little else, I left Mrs. Scarborough in the kitchen filling pies. I wandered into the living room. It was dim and comfortable, with an ornately carved sofa and a towering armoire in satinwood. Somehow, even with these fine pieces, it avoided feeling formal. To the right of the fireplace was an occasional table clustered with frames and statuettes. I felt drawn to it and went to examine it more closely.

The largest frame held an old studio photo of a mischievously handsome man. It was colorized in the way they did back then, but even the vaguely unnatural pastels in his face could not take away from his truly blue eyes and his short black waves of hair. This could only have been Anthony's father. If ever a man had the classic Irish combination of dark hair and blue eyes, it was he. And his teasing expression was Nicholas through and through. I could almost see the heavy eyebrows waggling.

A sadness descended upon me, and I don't think the cause was just the thought of Anthony and Nicholas being without

220

their father. I liked Mrs. Scarborough, and holidays with Father tended toward the unendurable, but still...

I tore my eyes away from the photo of Mr. Scarborough, and tried to leave my melancholy thoughts with it. In any case, it was not his photo that had drawn me to the table. She pulled me over, I think. The little girl in the frame just to the side of Anthony's father. It was the girl from the time I sensed Anthony. The picture was a school one, blue background, and she wore a quirky half-smile I'm sure was not her best grin. But she was lovely and sweet all the same. She had her mother's chocolate brown eyes, her curls tighter and cropped close. I am not a good judge of such things, but she looked to be about six.

"That's Ana."

I jumped.

Anthony had come up behind me. "Sorry."

"That's okay," I said, "I thought you were someone else."

"Like Todd?"

"What?"

"Nothing. Never mind." He picked up the photo. "She was struck by a car just outside, right by our driveway. She had just finished kindergarten."

"Oh, how horrible. I'm sorry."

"Don't let that face fool you. She was a terror." He smiled as he said it though.

My, how his eyes did shine, even in the dim light.

"I bet you were a lot the same as a child, weren't you, Suny? Torturing everyone?"

I frowned at this and then realized he was still smiling. I felt my skin flush. Anthony came closer, reached up and brushed my cheek, right above my scar.

"Flour," he said simply, softly, but he let his fingers stay, traced them over my scar, again and again.

My heart fluttered and I swallowed hard. "I was thoroughly incorrigible," I said absently.

He trailed his fingers down from my cheek, along the line

221

of my jaw. "She would have liked you. Ana. She liked people with fire." His eyes locked with mine.

"Neguinho, I need some– oh, excuse me." Mrs. Scarborough stood in the archway.

Anthony turned away, leaving a ghost of his touch still felt for a moment, and went to help his mother.

I sank to an easy chair without thought. I sat for many minutes, and every now and then, ran my thumb over my scar.

After many minutes of pointless musing, I sighed and looked over at Ana's crooked smile. I would have liked her too, I think. Such a sweet smile.

Then the photo went dark. The little face was a white negative, her lips suddenly flashing red. Red as a Popsicle stain. It shocked me back into my seat. And I heard Nicholas calling her name, calling Ana to come to him. I knew in that instant that Nicholas had been close when she died, had been there at her side, reaching…that he had laid those hands on her.

I retired early but no one seemed to think it strange.

The next day would be Thanksgiving. How would I sit at a table with Nicholas? I was tired of thinking of it. I went back over my decision to act normally. Therein lay the safest course, for sure. I couldn't let Nicholas see my doubts, my questions. But I would keep my eyes open. Open and watching for any slip on his part.

I must say, I did fairly well for a first-timer with the piecrust. If it was a bit tough, no one complained. There was turkey roasted with garlic and a potato stuffing that included black olives and another with linguica, a Portuguese sausage. I could not bring myself to eat more than a polite biteful of this last, but I did have a slice of turkey and enjoyed it thoroughly, I must admit.

And we laughed an awful lot.

Despite myself, I enjoyed Nicholas's company. It was only when a thought sailed in to remind me of his crime that I felt a little uneasy, a bit ashamed for enjoying his jokes and teasing.

Anthony was…well, he was Anthony. He was quiet, and occasionally sharply witty. He anticipated his mother's every desire and would not allow her to rise again from the table after she had sat. She had cooked, he told her. That was enough. He allowed Nicholas the stage, but was the first to step in when the conversation lulled.

And he watched me. I caught him smiling, his eyes on my face when I turned to him. And he didn't look away immediately. Maybe it was the wine. Whatever it was, it gave me a warm and nervous feeling that I didn't find annoying in the least.

Nicholas, for his part, was shameless in his admiration. He brought me to a blush several times, and his mother to tsk-tsking. At these times, Anthony held his face neutral.

I had a lot of wine too. I suppose we all did. That may have been the reason for what happened next.

Mrs. Scarborough went to lie down. Anthony and Nicholas and I cleaned the kitchen, with much throwing of dishtowels and suds mustaches, and then we retired to the den to ignore a muted football game. There was some suggestion of a poker game but it never came to more than Anthony shuffling the cards over and over. We talked about inconsequential things and drank a little more wine.

I began to get sleepy, but I was enjoying myself too much to go to bed. I stood and stretched a bit and walked to the French door that led out to the back yard. I cracked it open to let the icy air blow the drowsiness from me. The evening was clear, the moon was out. It was heavenly. I closed my eyes and let the air wash over me. It lifted my hair, caressing my neck. I parted my lips and let it come inside me like a cold drink. It was rejuvenating.

I turned back to the room and caught them both off guard. Each had been watching me, each showed their appreciation plainly. Anthony turned away immediately, saw his brother's face and then rose from his chair. Nicholas's smile only broadened at being caught. He winked at me. Anthony gave

223

me one last glance and left the room without a word.

I took a step toward him, an entreaty for him to stay on my lips. He did not see me however and Nicholas took my advance as encouragement, and that, coupled with Anthony's removal, brought him to his feet and over to me.

"You really are a treat, Suny Davis. Even after such a feast, I still have room for your delectable deliciousness." His hands, *those* hands, were on me before I could think.

I batted at them. "Nicholas, really, you are ever so kind to think so, but I am not sure if—"

My words were smothered as he kissed me.

I made what sounds I could in protest. He had my arms pinned however and my struggling was ineffectual.

So I started to kiss him back.

But of course, that was only so he would allow me a freer movement of my arms. When he loosed them to move his hands up into my hair, I got one arm between us and slammed my forearm into his throat. He gagged and sputtered and let go immediately. Unfortunately for him, I did not realize this last at the time, and proceeded to send my knee upwards and, ever effectively, I've found, my elbow to between his shoulder blades when he had doubled over. Which, of course, was only for a second before he fell in a heap at my feet.

Oh, and I was shouting all the while.

"How could you ever think I would want your murderous hands all over me? After what you did to poor Brian, not to mention your own baby sister! I am not a proponent of the death penalty, but depravity of such depth deserves little better than death. Confess now and throw yourself on the mercy of the justice system or I will make it my unswerving ambition to see you behind bars!"

Anthony had run in at the first gurgling cry Nicholas emitted. He stood before me.

"What the hell is going on?"

"Your brother is the worst sort, Anthony. I'm sorry. You will have to face it along with whatever heartbreaks you have endured before. He killed your sister– pushed her out into the road. He killed Brian, and after he had his way with me, here in your very house, I can hardly bear to conjecture what may have become of me."

He stared. Nicholas moaned.

"Are you utterly insane?"

"But it's true." I wiped my mouth on my sleeve.

"Suny, Nick tried to save Ana. He was hit by that car too and lived in the hospital for two months. Hell, he can barely bring himself to drive, he got so freaked out about cars. And Brian– why would he kill Brian?"

"He hid from you the very fact of his application to Preacher's Ledge. He desperately wanted to go, to prove you were not the only one with brilliance in the family. They did not accept him. And they gave his scholarship to Brian," I finished triumphantly. I crossed my arms over my chest and challenged Nicholas where he sat, only now recovering enough to struggle upright.

"Is that true?" Anthony asked his brother.

Nicholas hung his head. "Yeah, I did apply. And I didn't get in." He looked up at Anthony again. "But she's crazy. I never came near Brian. Why would I kill him?"

"As I said, you sought revenge for his theft of your scholarship. And you wished to spit in the eye of the school. Diana Kowalski told me you, of all people, had the know-how to set up a poltergeist hoax."

"Diana Kowal- ? That chick from NESsie? She's crazy too. I…I went to a couple of meetings and yeah, I had in mind to set up some little trap for Tony. Just as a joke. You were all high and mighty about your psychic prowess, about all the ghosts you were going to flush out. It made me ill. Everyone was taking you seriously though it was all a load of crap. I wanted to trip you up."

"But it wasn't a load of crap. It isn't–"

"I'm not getting into this again with you, Tony." He tried to stand and cursed creatively before managing the feat. "That

225

was a long time ago. I didn't do anything about it. I don't have anything against the college. Hell, Suny, I work for the infernal place."

"As a deceptive entrée into the world you wish to crumble." I fixed him with my keen eye.

He stared at me. "You– you are a loon." He continued, "Tony, I was pissed when they wouldn't let me attend so I played it off like I never wanted it in the first place. I never could even bring myself to tell you I'd applied. I begged Mom not to let you know. But now I'm there and working with everyone. I love it. I really do." He ducked his head under his brother's gaze. "I'm even going to take a class or two next semester."

Well, I don't know if I was supposed to believe this or not, but Nicholas sure had Anthony taken in.

"Suny," Nicholas said, "I apologize. I shouldn't have grabbed you like that. I didn't know you'd go ballistic on me, though. I don't think I'll ever attempt it again."

I agreed wholeheartedly with the sentiment, but I don't know if the delivery was very complimentary. He looked at me as one might at a shopping bag lady who had just asked to share one's chewing gum.

"Well, I appreciate your apology. Had I not thought you a ruthless sociopath, I might not have reacted in quite the same manner. Should it happen again–"

"Don't worry. It won't." Nicholas warded me off with one hand.

"Yes, well. Fine then. That should be satisfactory to us both."

Anthony rolled his eyes heavenward.

Mrs. Scarborough appeared, rumpled, with sleep-heavy eyes, in the archway.

"Tcha, are you boys fighting again?"

I thought it an opportune moment for me to retire.

I spent the rest of the weekend in my room. I was lucky to

be cloistered with a closetful of boxed old books. Apparently, Mr. Scarborough had been a fan of the mysteries of Agatha Christie and G.K. Chesterton. By Sunday, so was I.

I had made a thorough fool of myself. Anthony avoided my eyes at meals. Nicholas tried not to be in the same room with me at any time. Only Mrs. Scarborough remained cordial to me. The times I was not hermitted in my room with a book, I spent in the kitchen, learning how to make broa and paozinho. I found kneading to be a great stress-reliever. And I learned some Portuguese as well.

It didn't hit me until Anthony was driving me back to school Sunday afternoon, that I now had no suspect. Well, there was always Frieda. I pondered that while we drove.

Mrs. Scarborough had pressed on me a cinnamon cake and some paozinho to share with Petra. I opened the paper bag and picked off a piece of one of the rolls. I saw Anthony peer over at my parcel speculatively and I emphatically folded it shut while I chewed. He scowled and looked back at the road.

I don't know why I had dropped my suspicions of Frieda in the first place. She had motive and, more importantly, opportunity. I chewed and cogitated. Bits of Agatha Christie swirled in my brain.

We were stopped at a crosswalk in town when I spotted him. Chief Vernon was headed out of the municipal building just a block ahead.

Aha! An opportunity! I shoved the car door open, dropped the bag on my seat, and dashed across the street. I was panting when I reached him. I grasped his arm to stop his progress and made him wait while I caught my breath.

"I know you think I'm meddling–" I sucked in air. "And I know you think it was all an accident– or a poltergeist. But I can't keep this to myself anymore. I need to tell you what I know, what Dr. Kennedy knows. I need to tell you–"

"Miss Davis, let me go or I'll book you for assault and interference."

"But you have to listen. I know who killed Brian Nelson. It

227

was Frieda Montgomery."

The Chief stopped pulling against my hand and fully faced me. "Miss Davis, I am on my way up to The Ledge as we speak. If you will let me loose, I will tell you why."

I complied.

"Thank you. Miss Davis, there has been another death in that science building. Frieda Montgomery is dead."

Chapter 22

Although he protested, I had Anthony drop me at the science building. Once again, it was cordoned off with police tape; this time a wider area spreading out from the greenhouse door was also contained. An officer manned the entrance and, even after I gave numerous thoroughly logical reasons for him to allow my admission, he maintained that I was not authorized personnel.

After the Chief had told me Frieda was dead, he would hear nothing further from me and had sped off up to the college with lights flashing. Not that he needed them. There was little traffic on campus and only a few students already back from break. The bulk of them would return this evening.

I looked up at the building. He was in there somewhere. In the greenhouse, I'd wager. I thought about letting the matter drop, as Anthony had vehemently suggested I do when I had returned to the station wagon, chagrined and confused over Frieda's death. But this was my chance to prove to him...well, not to him, but to show all that I was not simply a loon, as Nicholas had called me (excusably considering his mind was fogged with pain) but a concerned citizen who wanted to be right...I mean, to see right and just things done in these cases.

Now how could I get in there and make sure that this aunt-appointed Chief of Police didn't get suckered in again?

A car pulled into the lot. The officer stepped forward to see who had arrived.

I began to tiptoe–

"Look, miss. I'm going to have to call the administration down here if you don't take yourself outta here."

I turned back from the entrance, disappointed, but prepared to rally and try to find another way to get my information. Movement from the parking lot caught my eye.

"Dr. Kennedy!" It had been she who had just now driven into the lot. I hurried forward to meet her.

229

"Miss Davis. I got your call." She walked briskly. Her salt and pepper hair was wrapped in a wool scarf against the cold. "Looks like there's more to this than anyone thought."

I gave the officer a sanctimonious nod. He wasn't flustered.

"Are you here to tell the Chief?" I asked.

"I'm here to examine the body. The district ME is out of state for the holiday weekend. I'm filling in again. Now, if you'll excuse me…"

"Dr. Kennedy, could I have a moment?" I eyed the officer. "In private?"

"I really have to get in there. And, to tell the truth…" She pulled me aside. "…while I think it's commendable of you to be concerned that your friend's killer is brought to justice, I really can't discuss the details…"

"What if I have information? I can give you details."

She pulled on her lip. "You said on the phone you had more information. Have you given it to Charles…I mean, to the Chief?"

I frowned. The information I'd meant to give her had been about Nicholas. I didn't have any new information, did I? Really, I just wanted to get her to talk to me.

"Well, uh. He doesn't tolerate me very well," I said finally. "He thinks I'm meddling."

"Same here," she muttered. "I mean, he thinks the same of me. But even so, maybe you should just leave this up to the professionals. If you know anything, write it out and give it to one of the officers. I'm sure it will be read." She turned to go.

"But Dr. Kennedy," I called. She stopped and I came closer to her, lowering my voice, "You're the only one who has her head on straight about this whole thing. You know Brian's death wasn't an accident or anything other than murder, pure and simple. And now they're going to rule this one a suicide and it just isn't so."

"A suicide? How did you know that?"

How did I know that?

She considered me from under her scarf. "Look, Miss

Davis, maybe we should talk. But not until I'm done in there. Why don't you give me your room number and I'll find you when I'm finished here."

I agreed and took myself off, feeling I'd made some progress.

When I neared the dorms, I noticed a cluster of students around the entrance of Jefferson. I craned my neck to see what all the hullabaloo was. Two officers escorted Willie between them, away from where he had dropped his suitcases pell-mell. He sobbed, so much so that one officer had to guide him by the elbow to keep him moving. They headed down the hill toward the administration buildings. Even if it looked a suicide, and somehow I was sure they would consider it such, I supposed they wanted statements from all who were close to her. Ah, poor Willie.

When I entered my room, I found Petra staring into space. She barely registered my presence.

"Hey."

"Hello, Petra. Did your feast come out well?"

"My wha– oh, dinner. Yeah, it was fine."

"What, no enthusiastic recital of the meal's decadent glory? I expected a much more excited account. I suppose you're a little down about Frieda's death. Not that I'd think you'd care very much."

She looked up quickly. "What do you mean? I didn't wish Frieda ill."

"I didn't intend–"

"Never mind."

I squinted at her. Her dreads hung in her face and, from the looks of her reddened fingertips, she'd been biting her nails. Perhaps she felt guilty for having bickered so frequently with a young woman now dead. I decided to try again to coax her out of her shell. I wanted cheering up. I wanted the normal Petra, a bouncy Petra providing a happy recounting of her culinary opus.

"So, who was in attendance? At Thanksgiving?"

"Why do you want to know that?" Again with the sharp tongue.

"Why? I was simply making conversation."

"Look, Suny. I know you were playing detective with Anthony about Brian, but you really don't want to get in on this."

"I was only–"

"No, I'm serious. I like you, sweetie. I would hate to see you get hurt." She stood and took a deep breath. "All this is getting pretty heavy. Just– just don't ask too many questions, okay?" She took in my confusion, but didn't explain further, just shook her head at me and left.

I didn't quite know what to make of that. The killer must feel perfectly safe with Chief Vernon on the case. And I don't believe my own inquiries were so blatant as to arouse suspicion. I felt in no danger. Maybe something happened over the break of which I was unaware. Why was Petra so concerned? She was definitely not her usual lively self.

I didn't get much time to think it over, however. Kathy banged on the door and demanded I verify that I had indeed returned to campus. She reminded me needlessly of my action plan, of the fact that I was expected to inform her of my whereabouts at all times. A warning that I was to control myself when in the presence of young men was also issued. And then she bade me a sarcastic farewell in flowery Arabic. I returned the sentiment, in Arabic as well, and she stomped off, ungratified in her urge to show me up, I hoped.

Then, not quite in direct defiance of her orders, but damn near close, I'll admit, I went in search of Todd.

Better if I hadn't.

I wove my way through the suitcases and other paraphernalia that littered the hallways of Jefferson. Todd had left early for the break and had meant to return early. I was sure I would find him unpacked already. In fact, I wondered why he hadn't come yet to shower me with kisses. Superficial it may be but, after the weekend I'd had, a little non-critical male attention would be welcome.

Half the doors on the hall were propped open by dirty laundry sacks and boom boxes and other post-break litter. Todd's door was cracked just a bit, so I pushed it open to see if he was *chez lui*.

He was in his room alright. But he was not alone.

"*Kakoga chyorta!*" I let out.

"Suny!" Todd exclaimed, breaking free from the embrace in which I found him.

"Rebecca! What in all of hell and creation are you doing here? And...and with Todd?"

"You sure you want the details?" She grinned at me impishly. No, actually, devilishly, evilly,

without any trace of decency or–

"Suny," Todd said and came forward. He steered me out into the hall and closed the door on Rebecca. "I'm sorry. Man, I didn't mean for any of this to happen. I got back on Saturday and there was like, no one around. And I came to see if maybe you were back early too. I was hoping– and then, see, I thought she was you. It was freaky, kind of. I thought you might be studying, and I saw her sitting in the library, in one of the study carols and I came up behind her. And, I don't know, after I kissed her neck like that, I guess I had to at least explain. When I finished talking, she...well, she didn't seem to mind too much. She came on pretty strong and, you know..."

I most decidedly did not know. And I did not know how the hell my half-sister had made her way from the Shenandoah Valley to the Berkshires in one long weekend.

"Suny–" Todd was trying to continue, but I didn't let him. I certainly did not care to hear more. I stalked off and made a beeline for Blaubury. I was fuming mad and I didn't want anyone to see me should the tears that pressed against my eyes choose to spill.

I hid in my room the rest of the afternoon. I don't know why it upset me so. Todd had been a fun diversion, but he hardly meant enough to me to produce such misery. It was

Rebecca. Here I had found a comfortable niche in an academic setting, which, despite the unfortunate incidents in the science building, I was coming to love, and that... that...fraudulent doppleganger of a supposed half-sister shows up.

As harrowing weekends went, this one was right up there with the one that preceded my arrival at The Ledge. I stuffed my face in a pillow.

At one point, Petra came back and dug through her desk and dresser, looking for something. I pretended I was asleep. I didn't want to see anyone, much less Petra, who would think me a fool for losing the one guy with whom I even came close to fulfilling a hedonistic ideal. And would she, like Todd, prefer Rebecca to me? I couldn't bear to think that the only good friend I'd ever had might cast me aside as well.

The room faded to gray as twilight came on.

I almost didn't answer the door when a knock sounded but I thought it might be Dr. Kennedy, although I wasn't sure I even wanted to see her. When I opened the door, I immediately wished I hadn't.

"Suny. We need to talk." Rebecca, glaring copper curls done up in a ponytail, stood on my threshold.

The audacity! I didn't budge.

"Look. Let me in. I'm not going to have you badmouth me all over this campus. I'll admit Todd was a cheap shot. I didn't really set out to do that to you. But it kind of fell in my lap and...well, he is a mighty fine kisser." She let a little of that Texas twang seep into this last.

"Why couldn't you have just stayed at Broadman?"

"I'm not the one who yanked me out of there! Shit, it's cold as a witch's tit up here and it ain't even Christmas. Do you think I'd try to get sent here?"

I didn't answer. I wanted to close the door in her face.

"My momma's hell-bent on me following you around. I've tried to get her to quit. Why do you think it took her so long to get me to Broadman? But you don't know my momma. When she heard you'd got sent to college– oh, lord. She's been badgering this school to let me in ever since she found out. She wouldn't even let me wait til semester break to start. After she finally got them to agree, it was adios Broadman School for Girls. Look, will you let me in? I'm damned if I'm going to stand out here all night, but you and I have got to figure this out."

I moved aside reluctantly.

She gaped at Petra's decorating. "Cool room. Is this all yours?"

"No."

She looked around some more, drawn in, I suppose, by the bright colors that shone even in the dying light. A brainless magpie, that's what she was.

"Rebecca, I don't know what you hope to accomplish by coming here." I think this was the most civil conversation I'd ever had with the girl. I wasn't sure what she was up to. "But if you think– Hey, put that down, that's Petra's."

She returned Petra's fuchsia teddy bear to the bed. "How do you like it here?"

"What? The Ledge? It's fine, thank you very much."

"Fine, thank you very much," she mimicked. My blood began to rise. "No, I'm sorry. I gotta quit that. See, I need to know if you're moving on again. I can't take this anymore. I'll make you a deal. If you stick around, I'll stay out of your way. You can even have Todd back."

"Oh, how gracious. No, thank you. Todd can find someone else to kiss, for all I care now."

"You gonna be nasty?"

"It is not I who–"

"Hell, I don't know why I thought I could talk to you. You'd rather spout verbiage than have a regular conversation."

"Verbiage? I'm surprised you know such a big word, Rebecca. In fact, I can't see how you managed to weasel into Preacher's Ledge in the first place. Did your mother convince the family attorneys that a large donation was the same as an administrative fee?"

"I'll put my scores up against yours any day. My momma put me through so many prep courses and summer schools, I'd bet—"

"Save your breath, Rebecca. I couldn't care less."

She stared at me hard, then looked away. I wasn't going to get rid of her too easily, I could see. She made no effort to leave. Her eyes lit upon my desk. She picked up an envelope.

"Munston! Shit, I should've guessed you'd have liked that bastard."

"Mr. Munston is a fine— hey, give me that letter! In fact, get out right this instant! If I want to correspond with a kind man who is a wonderful example of such an honorable profession, I will."

Rebecca dropped the envelope and smirked at me. "He's not considered so honorable anymore. And you'll be hard-pressed to keep up the pen-paling either." Her eyes twinkled harshly as she said the next. "He got himself fired right before the break."

"What!"

"Well, actually, he resigned. Can't say that I blame him 'cause they were about to axe him. Got himself accused of harassment."

"But he's gay!"

"You think I don't know that? Hell, that even makes it better. He'd have been fired either way, it being Broadman, after all."

"But that's incredible. Why would anyone accuse him? It has to be a lie!"

"Hell, of course it was a lie. But see, Suny, even in the short time she was my roommate, Morgan was a better friend to me than you'll ever be, and you're my own sister. Munston failed me on my mid-term paper and first thing out of Morgan's mouth was, 'Let's get him.'"

I couldn't believe it. What a pair of *sukas*.

Rebecca left then with a swagger, seemingly proud even of her and Morgan's destructive teamwork. It wasn't fair. What he must be going through. If ever I had considered that she could actually have been of the same blood as I...

I wrote Mr. Munston a tormented note. I scribbled page after page and soon realized that I was only relating to him all my pent up angst at every happening of the past weekend, of the past several weeks really. It was a letter I would never send, but the writing of it was cathartic. And tiring. I fell asleep in my clothes.

Chapter 23

If Petra had slept in the room, I couldn't be sure. Her bed was never made anyway. It was for the best though as I wasn't in any shape to be with anyone. Having skipped dinner the night before, I was starving. I showered quickly and trotted up to the dining hall alone, after turning back for a heavier coat and gloves, that is. It was forecast to snow. I had shoveled through a huge breakfast tray before I even said hello to anyone. Others were talking, though. There were murmurs about Frieda's death but nothing specific had leaked yet. Ghostly speculation was rampant and I felt it best that I leave before I engaged anyone directly in combat. They were all completely taken in. Ridiculous.

I was pushing open the door to leave when a voice called, "Miss Davis?"

I turned. It was Gilbert. Now what?

"Sylvia asked me to speak with you. She seems to agree with your position that you have too much time on your hands."

I attempted to roll my eyes. She would say such a thing.

"She asked that I reconsider my decision about tutoring you. Can you stop by my office later this morning?"

Great. I didn't mind Gilbert offering to tutor me– I would welcome it, in fact– but to know that he did so only to babysit me at Sylvia's request… All things considered, I should have stayed at Broadman.

After my morning classes, I made my way toward the science building. That it was open only confirmed for me that they were not considering foul play in Frieda's death. Surely they would have kept the building closed longer if they thought it to be murder. Only the greenhouse and the grounds immediately surrounding it were still roped off.

I pulled open the door. Climbing the stairs, was Petra. I began to call out to her, but she seemed in a great hurry, her backpack fairly bouncing off her shoulders as she jogged up the steps.

Students passed me on their way out to lunch. Over to my left, the hallway to the greenhouse was taped closed. I couldn't resist a closer look however. I glanced around to see if I was alone. Satisfied, I planted my toes firmly on the legal side of the cordoned area, grasped the wall and leaned forward, pressing the plastic tape taut.

I could just make out Chief Vernon's head amidst the greenery. He spoke animatedly down to someone much shorter than he. It could only be a woman. Dr. Kennedy, I presumed. Well now, she hadn't kept her word to come find me yesterday. The least I could be expected to do was to wait for her after I'd seen Gilbert, and demand an explanation for her broken promise. I was itching to see if I was right about the suicide.

I have to say, I was a bit distracted whilst talking to Gilbert. His office was just beyond the biology lab, with booklined walls, and a work table by the window. I couldn't sit still; I was too eager to intercept Dr. Kennedy before she could leave the building. I fidgeted, then stood, making a pretense of examining his photos– Gilbert with some disheveled man at an awards dinner, Gilbert spelunking in full caving gear, his face half-hidden by the mask he'd pulled down around his neck, two of Gilbert much younger, one at a microscope and one of Gilbert holding a lab rat who had been fully costumed to look like Groucho Marx. I read his diplomas, the dates on which reminded me that he had once been a child prodigy of even greater ilk than most who graced The Ledge.

He pulled me from my scrutiny. "So, what could we work on together? You aren't planning to major in any of the sciences?"

"No," I answered, fingering texts on his shelves as I moved about the room. There were several copies of books that Gilbert himself had authored with titles like "Phylogenetic Systematics: Oligotrophic Environments" and "Talking to the Past: Implications of Quantum Non-Locality" I was sure

240

Anthony and Brian would have devoured them. I could have plodded through the thick tomes but they were not my cup of tea. "I'd simply like to go in-depth on certain subjects. You know, ones that pique my curiosity more than others. To pass the time, keep me out of trouble, like Sylvia said." My hand alighted on one interesting book and I pulled it from the shelf. "Like this, the aurora borealis. I know an awful lot already, but I'd like to know more."

Gilbert stared at me, apparently unimpressed. In fact, he looked like he found the idea distasteful in the extreme.

"No? Not the northern lights. Okay. Well, any topic really. Here– physics of sound? No, well. I don't know. Perhaps you could just tutor me on your own research, or I could assist you. Or work with another student, on their research– a senior working on a thesis?"

"What do you want, Miss Davis?" He was becoming downright impatient with me.

"That's just it. I can't tell for sure." I scanned the titles in the section he kept of zoology books. Sea creatures, South American mammals…

"Maybe this isn't a good idea, Miss Davis."

He was very easily irritated, I saw.

"Why don't we forget the whole thing?"

"Ha. Funny you should say that just now." I pulled a text on elephants off the shelf.

"Elephants never forget." I smiled at him.

He shot veritable daggers at me with his eyes.

I refocused. "Please. I did want to work with you. I need something to distract my mind from all of these crazy happenings on campus."

Gilbert rose. "Why don't you come back when you've decided what you want from me. Until then…"

"Oh, alright. I suppose I should give it some thought." Maybe this had been a bad idea. Perhaps Gilbert and I differed too much in the areas of science that interested us. Quantum schwantum. It was just as well to make the meeting short. I

241

could always come back and if I left now, I could probably catch Dr. Kennedy. I made for the door.

"Miss Davis—" Gilbert let out. He took a deep breath. "The book?"

I still had the elephant book in my hand. "Oh. Could I take it, please? Maybe I'll find it interesting enough to pursue further study with you. You never know."

Gilbert gripped the edge of his desk. My indecisiveness and distraction probably seemed like a waste of time to him. I would have to think of something specific if I spoke to him again.

I dashed past the biology lab and tore down the stairs. Immediately, I heard voices. Raised voices.

As I approached the police tape, I could see Dr. Kennedy, clipboard in hand, poised to leave, the greenhouse door propped open with her foot. Chief Vernon stood just inside, his face red and controlled. I ducked back around the corner of the wall. To allow them their privacy, to be sure.

" ...never listen to me. Lillian, I don't want you sticking your nose into all this. You are not the official ME—"

"I'm a damned sight better than Perkins, if his last report is anything to go on."

"Lil, you didn't even get to read Perkins's report. You're in over your head."

"Don't call me Lil. And it's you, Charlie, who's in over his head. If you would just read my report on Nelson—"

The Chief lowered his voice to a hiss. "I did read the damned thing, Lil. And I know what you think. I...I can't get into this anymore with you. Just stay out of it. You don't understand."

"I understand one thing, Charlie Vernon. You haven't changed one little bit. Still stubborn and close-mouthed. I have half a mind to call the State's Attorney...or someone." She said this last as she walked away, letting the greenhouse door hinges squeak shut on the Chief. She ducked under the tape and passed me without noticing. She went to the stairs but, rather than ascending them, she plopped herself down on the bottom step and put her face in her hands.

I watched her a moment. Afternoon classes were already in full swing so there was no one just milling about. I could leave her in peace to muddle through, but in her position, I would have welcomed a comrade in arms, someone of like mind, prepared to crusade for truth…

"Dr. Kennedy?"

She started, then collected herself, running her hands through her tangle of hair made wilder by the greenhouse's humidity.

"Oh, Miss Davis." She heaved a big sigh.

"I…uh…I hope I'm not disturbing you."

"Oh, I'm disturbed alright. But it's not you. I need a drink," she muttered.

"In times of great discombobulation, I find a warm cup of chamomile tea to be a great stress reliever."

Dr. Kennedy looked at me sharply. "Did you say tea?"

"Why, yes. You see, the amino acid tryptophan is found in appreciable amounts in chamomile, much as it is in turkey, and containing such—"

"Miss Davis, you do have an alibi for both deaths, don't you?"

"Alibi? Why yes— whatever for?" Surely, she could not think…

"You just seem to know an awful lot about this case that no one else knows."

"I assure you, I have not a murderous bone in my body. I much prefer to deal with conflict by engaging in mutual discourse—"

She held up a hand. "Stop. Okay, look. You have some information, and if the Chief doesn't want to hear it, I guess I should. It'll give me more meat for my official complaint."

We took the doctor's car and headed into town. I only felt a mild pang of anxiety about leaving campus without letting

Kathy know. I was no longer restricted to grounds, however, and how long could a cup of tea take?

The doctor gazed longingly at The Hangar as we passed it, but we continued down to The Dive. This cramped but warm establishment served bagel sandwiches and soup, and salads too if anyone could bear to crunch cold lettuce on such a brisk day. They also provided a variety of warming libations. Of the non-alcoholic sort, mind you. It was the unofficial Ledge hangout where locals dared not tread. The walls were covered in bumper stickers, magic-markered poetry and some near art-quality graffiti.

It was empty of customers when we arrived. Dr. Kennedy and I ordered mugs of tea and sat at a booth in the window.

"So tell me what you know about Frieda."

Uh-oh. "Well…it looks like a suicide…"

I needn't have worried. Dr. Kennedy, without question, needed to vent.

"Well, sure it does, on the surface. You find a teenaged girl splayed out on the tile floor of a greenhouse, vomit at her mouth, broken mug shards all around her. And then throw in a poem, identified as in her own hand, not precisely a suicide note, but definitely written in depression. Analysis will probably come back saying the tea was made with some poisonous herb and you could take that all to be suicide. Charlie adds in that her grades were not great. She'd actually failed her mid-term science evaluation. And what's more, she just lost her boyfriend. Looks like suicide, doesn't it?"

I shrugged.

"My point exactly. Maybe yes. Maybe no. But you pull back a minute and look at it in context…then maybe it's a different story. But does Charlie see that? No. Can Charlie see anything Aunty Felicity and Aunt Hyacinth don't want him to see? No. If they say, ooh, ooh, another ghostie for our collection, is he going to say boo to them? Oh lord, I'm making puns and I don't even realize it. This is just too much."

Dr. Kennedy unzipped her purse and pulled out a liquor

miniature. She dolloped a bit in her Earl Grey. I pretended not to notice. I heartily agreed with her vehement condemnation of those who believed they saw "ghosties." That I had seen some… disturbing apparition that a more gullible soul would have described as such an entity was something I would not share with her. I recapped what we knew instead.

"So, Frieda has been poisoned in her greenhouse. And the body was found early Sunday afternoon, ruling out the vast majority of students. Do we know who was present on campus over the break?"

Dr. Kennedy produced her clipboard. "I snagged a copy of this when the Chief was passing it out for officers to get statements."

I glanced over the list, but not knowing many of The Ledge students yet, the twenty or so names meant little to me. "Do they know if anyone has a connection to her?"

"They've probably got all the statements by now, but I haven't seen anything compiled. And, like I said– like you said, in fact– they're treating it as a suicide. Did she confide in you? Why did you think suicide?"

Chyort! "Yes, well…actually, I thought anyone trying to frame it as suicide would think that the bitter pill of her romantic disillusionment may have…along with her bad grades… uh, proven sufficient motive for…that is…um… what they did not know, however is what I do know, that she was no longer distraught over her loss of Willie. In fact, she would not take him back, even after it was made clear to her that he desired a reunification. To leave a poem of unrequited love as a suicide note would be the last thing Frieda would have done."

Dr. Kennedy took a moment to process all of that. I didn't blame her. I hardly knew myself what I had just said. She leaned forward. "So, if you know her so well, what do you think could have been a motive for her murder?"

I considered for a moment. From what I knew about Frieda, she spent all of her time in that greenhouse. And as

245

noisome as I found her to be, I had not heard that she was particularly good at creating enemies. More than any of us is, that is.

"To be honest, I don't know her that well at all," I began. "I just had cause to know of her romantic quandary. Perhaps, looking at it in context, it has some connection to Brian's death?"

Dr. Kennedy pounced. "My thoughts exactly. Now, you had some more information for me about that…"

"Uh…yes, well." I couldn't tell her about Nicholas. She would think me such a *durak*. Wasn't there something else I'd wanted to tell her, anything that didn't involve Nicholas? The wrench. That was it. "There was a wrench. Yes, Petra and I were up on the roof… seeing where Brian had come from when he first struck me with the roof access door, that is…and we found a wrench on the walkway to the fan housing room. A small wrench. And Chief Vernon didn't care to see it—"

"Wait a minute. Back up."

I did and related all that led up to the wrench's discovery.

"Brian had been on the roof?" Dr. Kennedy tapped her pen on her lip.

"And so had Frieda."

"Yes, yes, but there's something in that…"

I watched her. Outside, it had begun to snow lightly, and though Dr. Kennedy seemed to be watching the flakes drift down, I knew she was not seeing them. I too took to watching the snow and thought. Brian had been disturbed by something when he came down from the roof. And he had gone out of the building to…to what? To talk to someone? To get something? And the wrench. Had he had it with him the first time? Had he brought it back with him to the building? Had it even been his? Because we knew he had returned to the building after I had run into him. He was killed in the chemistry lab, after all. Could he have gone back to…to do what? To meet someone?

It was all a muddle. If only I could get it clear in my head.

Dr. Kennedy picked up her clipboard and flipped through the papers on it.

...lividity...time of death...hypatic toxicity...

I clamped down on my mind. Sensing bits and pieces had never led anywhere useful. Not ever. If it had been of any help, I would've known Nicholas was taking me home for Thanksgiving, would've known he couldn't have killed his sister, or Brian...

There had to be some way to connect the dots without resorting to the tried and untrue. Perhaps a list.

One, Brian had been on the roof. Two, he left and came back to the chemistry lab for some reason. Three...wait, wait, back up. Did he go to the chemistry lab? That was where the body had been found but...

"Dr. Kennedy!" I startled her out of the snowfall reverie to which she had returned. "Yes, that must be it. The contusions on his heels. Could those have been made by dragging Brian's body from somewhere else?"

She shook her head. "They were much too deep– the tissue damaged– it had to have been a repeated trauma, hit over and over..."

"But stairs! What if he had been pulled down stairs?" I remembered just how tortuously many stairs there were leading down from the roof.

Dr. Kennedy stopped her pen from tapping. "It's possible...if there were a lot of them..." I nodded. "...but I'd have to say he was alive, at least for some time after. In addition to the fact that we know he died from asphyxiation, the blood in the tissues, the extravasation–"

"Yes, yes, but he could have been knocked out up on the roof, then dragged down to the chemistry lab. Someone had been in the greenhouse earlier in the week, sneaking around in the dark– I saw the flashlight beam. What if he'd discovered something, and went to the greenhouse roof... to spy maybe? And was caught, and knocked out, and dragged..."

"And then beaten with flying objects and ultimately killed

with acid fumes?"

It sounded crazy but there was something there.

"I'll give you the dragged down the stairs part." Dr. Kennedy pulled out some typed pages and scribbled in their margins. "If his shoes had come off in the stairwell from being pulled...that's the only way I'll believe those contusions could have occurred. I suppose someone could have put them back on him. But why all the poltergeist stuff? Why not just kill him and get it over with? And why do it at all? And who?"

"Could it have been Frieda? Did she know the Chief was predisposed to believe in poltergeists? Who else could he have been spying on?"

"I don't know, but then why was she killed? Unless it really was a suicide. Maybe out of remorse for killing him?" The doctor capped her pen and dropped it in her purse. "We don't have much to go on in either case."

"There weren't any clues you haven't shared with me? I mean I know, officially, I shouldn't be told much, but the official case here is being completely mishandled."

"Gotta agree with you on that one. There's really nothing else, though, nothing unusual. Just a broken mug, a melodramatic poem, a dead body. Pretty standard." Dr. Kennedy took her last swallow of tea. As she put it down, her mouth twisted into a scowl. "Except a pretty perverted napkin."

"What?"

Dr. Kennedy unclipped a few photos from her board. She shuffled through ones I'd probably rather not see, and handed me one.

"The tea tray she'd brought from the science lounge was spilled. There was a sugar shaker, a spoon. The napkin was under the tray on the floor. Can you make them out? The photo's kind of grainy; it's one I took myself."

I could see them just fine. Peeking out from behind leafy vines were round little naked men frolicking all over. All over Petra's bandana.

248

Chapter 24

I could not for a minute believe it was Petra. I said nothing to Dr. Kennedy about my ability to identify the bandana. She thought Frieda had been using it as a napkin and, until I could figure out how it had gotten in the greenhouse, I would remain mute on the matter.

The doctor offered to take me back to The Ledge, stating that she had some things to write up now, but I declined. I would call out one of the town's two taxis. I needed time to think and I couldn't face Petra while I had any doubts in my mind about her.

Dr. Kennedy left. I drank another cup of tea.

Petra had no reason to kill anyone. Did she? I started with Brian. They had been friendly. She had cried about his death. The person who had killed him was a base creature, unfeeling, and for whom Brian was a threat. Wasn't that the way it worked? Dr. Kennedy and I had surmised that Brian had been spying on someone in the greenhouse from up on the roof. But Petra's work had been in the biology lab with her precious molds.

Although, that had not been her first project.

Her initial thesis had been based on Amazonian herbs that, when fermented just so, had antimicrobial properties. And hadn't Frieda said she'd found those herbs hidden in the greenhouse, despite the cancellation of Petra's original project? Could Brian have noticed this, as well as contaminating Frieda's plants, whilst traipsing through the greenhouse unwelcomed?

More importantly, I realized, Frieda had told me of her intention to tattle on Petra, to expose her clandestine propagation. And Frieda had just been killed.

I must have been missing something. It could not be so.

I paid my bill and walked out into the snow. The flakes were fat now and streaming down, quickly enshrouding all the shops and the street in white. I headed toward the garage where the taxis were to be had.

Granted, Frieda had been killed, poisoned with what we suspected was a tea steeped from…poisonous herbs. But no, surely Petra was not the only student familiar enough with horticultural toxins to know how to make such a tea.

I would come at it from a different angle. It was thought to be a suicide, framed to look like one. The killer had to have access to Frieda's work, her writings, to get a copy of that poem. The killer had to know it would make sense when investigated, in light of Frieda's break-up with Willie…

Ooh, well…I suppose I had to admit Petra did have some special knowledge there.

But…but…anyone who knew how often Frieda was in the greenhouse could have made use of her absence to raid her room for potential suicide note material.

It wasn't looking good for my roommate. This was knowledge Petra had as well. In fact, being in the science building so much herself, she probably had noticed the pattern of Frieda's schedule.

I stopped on the sidewalk, not wanting to come up with any more reasons why Petra might be a better suspect than most. I had walked past the garage without realizing it. It was now about four blocks behind me. No matter, I still wasn't ready to go back to my room anyway. I would walk a bit more and, although it didn't look promising, I would puzzle this out.

I allowed that it could be construed that my roommate had a motive for each crime, if some of my and Dr. Kennedy's speculation proved correct, but what about opportunity?

Petra had remained at The Ledge over break. Well, there was that. Aha! Petra had been with me the evening of Brian's death, had been with me for dinner, had been with me at the mall…except for the two hours when we had split up to pursue our own tastes in shops. Petra hadn't purchased anything other than the dress I convinced her to buy. That had occurred after we had reunited.

250

And it had been her idea to split up and meet again later. Yikes.

Forcing these thoughts from my mind, I looked around and noticed that I had walked clear out of town. The snow was getting deeper. I glanced back at the lights that were just now coming on behind me. It was a good mile back to the garage now and not much farther than that up to The Ledge. Certainly I would be fine if I just kept going. I gauged that the snow was about four inches deep at this point. I was less trusting of the old sedans that served as town taxis than I was of my own boots for safely maneuvering the hill road's curves. There wasn't much wind and I wasn't cold in the least. Well, just a tad on my toes and fingers. And nose. That was a bit frosty.

But Petra. I had to be sure. As I trudged, head bent now against the assault of snow, I thought of her. It wasn't in her character. She was so bubbly, so full of life and ready to commit herself to helping others. I stopped a second. How far did that commitment go, though? Could she weigh the lives of two students against the possibility of developing a new drug with the potential to save many? To save millions? What if it were stronger than any of the drugs now used to fight fatal diseases? Could that be justification? Could Petra see that as justification?

The wind picked up and snow blew into my face and down the collar of my coat. My fingers were needled with cold now and my feet felt like clubs in my boots. I could not even see the town below me anymore. I was surrounded by wind-whipped trees and gray twilight through streaks of white.

I believe I've said before that sometimes I wonder at my own judgment. But, in my defense, I had never experienced snow like this before. It was a far cry from the lazy flakes that had drifted past the window of The Dive.

The warm, toasty Dive.

It did me no good to ponder such things. I turned back to the thoughts that had distracted me from the cold in the first place. Maybe they would continue to do so.

But my resolve to discredit the notion of Petra as suspect was fading. She had not been herself of late. Was she disturbed at killing once again? Was it finally getting to her? And hadn't she warned me to stay out of it?

I like you, sweetie. I would hate to see you get hurt.

She knew enough from years of séances and other paranormal shenanigans to conceive of a poltergeist hoax. She may even have known of the Chief's connections, through his Aunts, to NESOPsI. She had lived here for almost four years. She knew Anthony, had maybe discussed such things with him.

I was still stuck on how she could have managed to pelt Brian with...oh, it was awful to think of it. Dr. Kennedy had said the pattern of bruising was odd, but if we were right that she had knocked him out and dragged him down the stairs...

How had she managed to hit him with anything if he'd been knocked out cold on the floor? He was obviously hit while standing, which made the poltergeist theory so plausible in the first place.

Headlights shone around the bend; a car was coming down the hill slowly. I thought about flagging it down, but I had to be close now, right? And they were going the wrong way.

The car passed but then skidded as it slammed on its brakes and pulled into a careful U-turn. The headlights blinded me for a moment. Then I could see a pale face through the rapidly batting wipers. In the contrasting light and dark, it appeared almost skeletal. The impression was fleeting however, and I felt relief at recognizing the face as Nicholas's.

As he pulled the car to a halt beside me, I made a connection that only furthered Petra's damnation.

Ambrose.

I repeated the name to Anthony when he shot out of the passenger door and came to me.

"What? Suny, are you okay? We've been looking for you for hours since Kathy reported you missing. Why are you walking in this? You could have called me. Even if you'd thought you'd get in trouble, you should've called me."

He led me to the car and, I have to say, I felt a little disoriented. I couldn't feel my feet or hands and the blasting heat of the backseat stung my face.

"She used Ambrose, you see. His stand really. Like you did, Nicholas." The words came out slowly and I barely realized I was forming them.

The brothers glanced at each other in the front seat.

Anthony said, "She's worse than I thought. Let's get her back to the dorm where she can get out of those wet clothes. You going to be okay to keep driving, Nick?"

Nicholas swallowed and nodded. I could see his shoulders set determinedly as he turned back to the dusted windshield.

I closed my eyes after that and concentrated only on trying to still my chattering teeth.

Nicholas let us out at Blaubury and went to park. Anthony carried me from the car and up the stairs. I would have protested but I couldn't seem to feel my feet to walk. I fought him a bit when he tried to carry me into my room, though. Would I be able to face Petra without letting my suspicions show? But I needn't have worried; she wasn't in the room.

Anthony gingerly removed my boots. I felt woozy and was of little help. My fingers wouldn't work to unclasp my wet jeans. It was a good thing my cheeks were already pink from the cold because he had to help me peel those off as well. When he had my feet soaking in a bucket of warm water from the laundry room, and I had managed to get the rest of me wrapped in a sensible flannel nightgown, he sat at my desk and let me have it.

And how, to use a colloquialism.

"No matter what else goes on in that head, there certainly isn't an ounce of common sense! First you go off without informing Kathy, or even me or Petra, or anyone. Then you walk...*walk* home in a snowstorm? Not even dressed adequately? I can't save your butt all the time, no matter what your father has asked me to do. And I certainly can't be with you every second. I have my own work, my real work– you have to rein yourself in, Suny, or your father's just going to have to find someone else to–"

"Is she okay?" It was Nicholas. He had a steaming mug in his hand and, after sniffing it tentatively, my desire for warmth won out over my new trepidation over hot drinks prepared by others, and I took a sip.

"She's fine," Anthony said dismissively. "She just needs a leash, is all."

"Now, now, big brother. Have you let Kathy know we found her? I can see not. Would you rather I did it? After that, I'm heading up to The Stables to crash with some of the guys. I don't want to head back down that hill in this. I don't want you to try it either. Mom's station wagon isn't four-wheel drive. I'll call her and tell her we're stuck." He turned to me. "Be good now, Suny. And don't hurt him, no matter how gruff he gets with you, 'cause I know you could. Promise?"

I couldn't have stopped shivering long enough to hurt Anthony if I'd tried.

Anthony continued to harangue me after Nicholas left until, minutes later, Kathy burst into the room.

"*Inti mafish much*! Did you think you could sneak out again?" She pointed to my head. "*Ma fish kahraba.*"

"Your fish what?" Anthony sputtered, trying to get between Kathy and me, cringing as I was on the edge of my bed, feet still soaking.

"She said, 'There's no electricity, no power,'" I supplied, pointing to my own head.

"That's right, you *humara.*"

I narrowed my eyes. "*Ahhlass*, Kathy. If you know what's good for you."

"I will not shut up and don't try to threaten me. I'm recommending suspension. You forget, I'm the one in charge here."

254

"Oh, really?" The rest of me was waking up along with my thawing toes. "Not for long if the Admin finds out about the extra special tutorial you've been giving to Roger."

"Wha– I...I don't know what you're talking about." Her eyes shifted to Anthony, and then back to me. "Sure, I tutor Roger, but that's part of what I do here. He's not the only one who pays me to help get through Mahmet's advanced classes."

"So now you're a *sharmoota*?"

"How dare you, you little *kelbeh*!" Kathy colored and clawed at Anthony, trying to get past him and at my throat, I suspected. I shivered, and it wasn't only from my chill. Kathy's petite frame was rigid with fury and I hoped Anthony could hold her.

Anthony managed to maneuver her out the door. He locked it for good measure. Even then, I could still hear Kathy shouting epithets that would have made Mahmet blush. Anthony turned back around to me.

"Oh, listen to that. She just called you a bastard."

Anthony glanced at the door. Kathy finally tired, or ran out of profane Arabic, and her voice faded down the hall.

All the adrenaline left me. My head hurt too from the angry picking I had done on Kathy's mind. I should have controlled myself better, even if I was suffering from hypothermia.

Anthony noted my sagging posture. "Lie down now. I'll dry your feet." He put socks on them too and pulled my covers up. "I'll talk to Kathy."

"I'm not worried about her anymore." And I wasn't. It was Petra who concerned me now. "Are you going up to The Stables with Nicholas?" I asked meekly.

"Do you want me to stay until you've fallen asleep? I don't think Kathy will come back. I do have to call your father again, to let him know that you're safe, but that can wait. It's only, oh, about midnight in Scotland." He smiled down at me. I had to cast down my eyes to keep from blushing.

"I'm sorry, Anthony. I don't try to..."

"Hush, Suny. It's okay. I'm getting used to it." He turned

255

off my light, sat on the floor, and leaned against my desk. "Close your eyes," he ordered.

I did. I dared not peek. It was comforting to have him with me when I thought Petra might return any minute. I thought he could hold her off, even though she was much bigger of frame than Kathy.

I giggled despite myself, thinking of Anthony manhandling Kathy.

"What?" came Anthony's inevitable query.

"I'm sorry. Nothing. I was just thinking about Kathy." I opened my eyes. He looked away to the darkened window, lamplight showing driving powder in the slits in the blinds.

"So...she and Roger are definitely..." He let it trail off.

"I'm sorry about that too, Anthony." He closed his eyes to my response. "I...I think she's crazy."

He opened his eyes and looked at me. He opened his mouth to speak, but all that came out was, "Go to sleep, Suny."

I closed my eyes obediently.

"Thanks, though," he said quietly after a moment.

I snuggled more deeply under the covers and drifted off.

I awoke some time after midnight from a terrific nightmare. I had been stampeded by elephants in the snow, searchlights blinding me, Anthony calling my name, looking for me in all the wrong places. I woke sweating and sitting on the edge of my bed before I was fully awake.

Anthony was still huddled on the floor by my desk. He snored with his mouth open, head thrown back. He would awaken with a serious crick in the morning. Petra's bed was still empty. I pulled her chenille throw off and laid it across Anthony's legs.

The aftermath of my dream hung with me. Petra. It had something to do with Petra and the whole mess. I forced myself to lie down, but I knew I wouldn't sleep for a while. How could I be sure it was Petra? I knew I didn't, in my wildest suppositions, want it to be her, my only friend in the whole world, but I had to consider the evidence. Could I tell Dr. Kennedy about the bandana, try once again to relate to the Chief my suspicions? My latest suspicions, that is. How would he ever believe me when I'd been so wrong until now? The bandana was one thing. She had loaned it to me weeks ago but I hadn't even worn it. Was the bandana enough evidence to convince the Chief? To convince Dr. Kennedy even? What else was there?

The wrench. Could that really have been evidence? I remembered how Petra had reached past me for it before I could pick it up. Had that been intentional? Had she recognized it as something she'd dropped? Something Brian had dropped? It couldn't have been what she knocked him out with; it was too small. But it had to have some significance in all of this. Fear that I would find a clue such as that even may have been the real reason she'd come up on the roof behind me and...

tried to push

...startled me. Oh, no. Not pushed. Could it have been? I rubbed my shoulders, remembering her firm grasp on them.

I flung aside my covers once again and stepped carefully around Anthony to get to Petra's dresser. I opened her jewelry box and felt through it.

The wrench. It was gone.

If I had reserved any doubt as to the wrench's significance, that doubt was now gone as well.

I woke up in the morning late for class. Anthony had left; only a scrawled, "Call me if you need anything," propped on my desk bespoke his presence. The snow had stopped, but the sky was still gray. Even to my inexperienced eye, it looked like this was a temporary lull between spates of snowfall.

Classes weren't cancelled. They never were, I had been told, as most of the faculty lived close by.

When my classes were over for the afternoon, I trudged

through the snow to Blaubury. I had avoided returning to my room during the day, choosing to visit the library instead of risking an encounter with Petra had she chosen to finally come back to our room from wherever she had been spending her nights.

I crept down to the end of the hallway and eyed our door. It was closed. I approached it slowly and, upon reaching it, put an ear gently to the wood and attempted to still my heart and breath.

I heard nothing.

Still cautious, I turned my key in the lock and warily pushed the door open.

Empty.

I sagged at the doorframe in relief. Everything was not exactly where it had been, though. A new set of dirty clothes thrown on her bed and some wet socks on the radiator showed she had been here and not too long before.

I sat on my bed. I couldn't keep on sneaking through my day. What if she did sleep here tonight? How could I be sure that she, having killed two fellow students already, would not kill again? Even if I weren't in danger...

I like you sweetie.

...someone else could be.

Oh, why Petra, why? Could it really be you?

I wished I could be even more certain than the mounting evidence against her caused me to be. As much as I hated to, I actually found myself considering using my... my...well, my abilities to see if I could tell if Petra truly was involved. But would it help? I was the first to disbelieve the validity of such doings. But I couldn't simply accuse Petra of two horrible murders without being as sure as possible that she had committed them.

In the past weeks, I had opened myself to sensing more often than I had in all of the years since I had decided to close off that part of myself. But each of those times had been in a moment of stress, of fear, of fatigue, of anger. I had not given myself time to process the sensations, the images. No wonder I hadn't been able to interpret them fully or to understand them clearly.

I tossed several furry things off Petra's bed and sat down. I pulled her chenille throw around my shoulders and tucked my feet under me. I had come to love Petra along with all the wondrous and unexpected things that The Ledge had to offer. I so much didn't want it to be her.

I slowed my breathing, willing myself to relax. I closed my eyes. I opened them. Leaning sideways, I grabbed a gaudy rhinestone tiara from her bedpost and popped it on my head and closed my eyes again. From head to toe I was ensconced in Petra.

I opened every pore.

A quick flash of people in masks, green and purple beads, gold.

Petra must have worn the tiara for some Mardi Gras celebration. I wrapped the blanket tighter around me and leaned back into the plethora of cushions that enveloped Petra every night.

Dead white rats heaped in the bottom of a cage…Brian laughing, the laughter becoming a snort, then a cough…a beautiful woman with smooth firm skin the color of brown lentil dahl, hair white in a halo…a dark form lurking, raised arm in silhouette, something bulky extending where the hand would have been…a plant nestled amongst summer bright flowers, its green fading to brown, to black, to chalky ash…Frieda, blue eyes narrowed, ice white hair around her face… face that grimaced and cursed, lips sneering…fading…and oh, the anger…rippling through, waves of it crashing…

I struggled up and stood. It was more than I could take. I had never felt such searing rage, such base and cruel malevolence. Could this be the emotion that brought Petra to kill? I pulled the tiara from my head. I felt sick. Sick and saddened. That Brian and Frieda were strongly present in Petra's mind lately I had no doubt. And the plant. Death had wafted around it like swirls of smoke from a funeral pyre.

In light of my deductions from the night before, all of my

259

sensation only served to be the glacage sur le gateau. I had to go to Dr. Kennedy and hope that identifying the bandana as Petra's and telling her the wrench was missing would be enough to get her to do something serious. Something immediate. I still wished I had more physical evidence she could show to someone, something more than conjecture.

I went to Petra's dresser again. It was easy to see that the wrench was not in the jewelry box. I searched her drawers and desk for good measure. I even burrowed into her bed again to look beneath pillows and the mattress itself. Finally, I sat on the floor by her bed. I knew it wasn't in the room. I'd looked everywhere.

Except the trashcan. I reached under Petra's desk and pulled out the can.

Only paper. I was about to shove it back under the desk when I sensed…something. I dumped the contents on the floor beside me.

Rough draft after rough draft of typed abstracts and reports tumbled out. Apparently, Petra was a perfectionist in her work, despite her tendency toward slatternliness otherwise. But what was this? A crumpled notecard. I smoothed it out. Scrawled in pen, barely legible, was the following message:

I have given some thought to our conversation of the other day. Please meet me in the biology lab at six this evening.

It was dated this same day. Who was this from? To whom had she spoken the other day? Or wait. Was this a note to or from Petra? I didn't know her handwriting. She typed all her work. I turned over the card. An engraving of Mt. Billington in all its snow-capped glory graced the front flap. The name of the college and its seal were printed underneath. Petra had a box of these cards. I had seen it, nearly empty, when I had searched her desk. But then again, I too had a box of these same. They sold them at the bookstore.

To Petra or from Petra? From whom or to whom? It could be something she'd received, read, crumpled and tossed. Or, I thought as I picked up rough drafts of her school work and stuffed them back in the waste can, it could have been a first draft of a note she herself had composed and recopied. It was rather hard to read the writing on this draft.

Either way, I bet I knew where Petra was going to be at six o'clock this evening. I looked on the wall at her Felix the Cat timepiece, its tail swinging as pendulum. It was nearing five o'clock now. I would gather some supplies and go see what I could see.

From the Blaubury stair landing window, I watched from five-thirty on as scattered drifts of students made their way up to the dining hall. By six o'clock it would be full and I expected people would linger over a second mug of something hot rather than brave the cold before forced to do so. The science building would be empty for a while. Or rather, near empty.

When it was time, I pushed out into the night. It had begun to snow again, this time in full force from the beginning. The wind howled through the open spaces between buildings. I did not even try to find a path. They were never shoveled, I'd been told. I just set my own course and crested the hill before the science building with little problem aside from chattering teeth.

I patted the bag that hung over my shoulder. I couldn't see it in the early winter dark, but I knew what it contained without checking as I'd done that task obsessively while waiting as Felix's tail had ticked back and forth. It held a mini-recorder, my digital camera, some paper and pencils. Nothing super high-tech but then, I was not sure what to expect from this rendezvous, nor what it might require other than careful observation and recordation.

The lobby was as well-lit as it always was, the stairs bright as well, and yet it seemed dark and ominous. When I thought about it, I hadn't been here after sunset except during the Halloween party. Perhaps it was only the transference of that atmosphere to this occasion. In any case, I trembled a bit as I put each foot on each step of the twisted stair. I could not guarantee that it was only the remnants of the cold that made me do so.

The door to the biology lab was closed, but not locked. Despite the college's policy of leaving everything open, I didn't know if Petra or her contact would have locked it. As silently as I could, a millimeter at a time, I pushed the door open. When it was more than a few inches ajar, I knew for sure the lights had not been turned on. I reached my hand in for the switch, then hesitated. What was I doing? Would I announce my presence and glean what I could from the element of surprise? Or would I sneak through the dark to the inner lab where Petra and her contact certainly must be?

I chose the latter and slid myself through into the gloom. Once again, I let my hand run along the cages on the left hand wall. But something was wrong. I felt the water bottles hanging clasped to the wire mesh, but something else obstructed my hand, something thin and square– the door. One of the cage doors was open. I pushed it shut by feel, hoping not to crush anything trying still to make good its escape. I ran my hand along the next cage and took a step forward.

A horrific squeaking rang up from the floor. *Chyort!* I had almost crushed the poor creature. But then I felt another square of metal protruding from the plane of cages, and moving forward more rapidly, I felt another and another. Again a squeaking rang up from the floor, but I knew my feet had not touched anything this time. I froze. Again a squeak, a scurry, a scratching, another squeak.

And then something crawled over my foot and tried to climb into my boot.

I scrambled backward for the light switch. I threw it on.

And screamed.

Hundreds of pink eyes and flesh-colored noses took note of me in the sudden glare. But they were not responsible for producing my scream.

Sprawled face down on the floor, blood matting the coils

of her dred locks, was Petra.

Before I could lean down to bat away the half dozen fat rats who sat on her back and legs, I heard the hinges of the inner lab door open.

I turned, but not in time. A footstep came, a sharp pain on the back of my skull, and then there was nothing.

Chapter 25

It was cold. And loud.

On regaining consciousness, these were my first thoughts. I could see nothing for the first few moments but I knew instantly where I was.

The sound of the fan's cycling had startled me to sentience. It was immeasurably louder here in the housing room than when heard in the hallways of the science building below. Its thrumming, and the accompanying whoosh of air was like a banshee wailing. Perhaps that was why they chose to enclose it rather than let the fan exhaust freely on the roof. Or maybe that was another odd, yet unquestioned decision on the part of the architect who had designed the structure. In any case, the walls of the housing room were riddled with venting grates. Through these a bit of reflected moonlight came. The snow must have ceased but the night was still way beyond brisk. I was sure the frigid air would come through the grates even more readily when the air currents changed as soon as the fan cycled off.

And it could do so none too soon. The flooring was the same metal grating as the catwalk, with shadowy exposed metal pipes and ducting below. It vibrated tremendously, making me feel as if the whole thing might just jitter off the roof and send me down into the snowy valley with it.

My head was tender but not bleeding. Whoever had hit me had not done so too vehemently. Seeing the rats all over Petra's prone body had been almost enough to make me faint of my own accord. A relatively minor blow was all it had taken to send me off into senselessness.

Petra! The vision of her came back to me and I let out an involuntary cry. Her head had been bloodied. I hadn't been able to tell if she was alive or not before I too had been struck down. Was she still bleeding on the lab floor?

No, she was not. She was bleeding here in the fan housing room with me.

I had crawled around the monstrous protuberance that was the fan itself, in an effort to locate the door. Instead, I found Petra. She was still breathing. In fact, when I lifted her head to check the extent of her wound as well as I could in the near darkness, she let out a moan. Good. That was a good sign. And her head seemed not to be bleeding so freely any longer. My fingers came away with blood already thickened and clotting. I wiped them on the sleeve of my coat as I removed said garment. Petra was in only her clothes and there was no telling how long we'd been outside of the building proper, out in the cold. Or how long we would remain here. I covered her as well as I could.

Having clambered over her procumbent form, I quickly found the door. It was locked, of course, and only a key would unlock it. I felt along the walls for a light switch of some kind, but there was none. After another few minutes of searching for something, anything, to add dimension to our dark and lonely circumstance, I slumped against the wall and huddled close to Petra to share with her what warmth there was still left in my body. I no longer even had my bag so I could record our last wintry moments for posterity.

The fan cycled off. I nearly began yelling for help now that there was some chance of being heard, but thought better of it. Was it sensible to draw attention to the fact that I was conscious, or more so to wait and spring unsuspected on our attacker, should said person return?

But what if our attacker did not return?

I pushed the question aside, or rather, replaced it with an alternate one. Who had it been? I hadn't gotten a look before I had been bludgeoned.

Well, it hadn't been Petra. That, I knew for sure. I stroked her locks away from her face. Had I not been the recipient of a blow myself and awakened to find us both locked in a cold and isolated place, I would perhaps still have believed that

Petra's contact had knocked her out in self-defense. The evidence against her had been so strong. Even what I had sensed… I blushed there in the dark. What a *dubiina* I was to think that anything I'd sensed had any interpretable meaning at all. I had to admit I was relieved that she was not the culprit. I tugged my coat more firmly around her and tucked it under her shoulder to hold it close.

I hugged myself around the knees and shivered. Who had it been? I was sure it was the same person responsible for all of the crimes. That only made sense. But who else had anything to do with Brian and Frieda? And was Petra part of that list, or had she just been suspicious and gotten herself tangled up in it, as I had? I glanced down at her unconscious form. There was no way to ask now. I would have to assume she was part of the group of victims.

Brian, Frieda, Petra.

I closed my eyes and concentrated. It was like one of Father's intuition-building lists. Make the connections, I heard his voice tell me.

Brian…Frieda… Petra…

Willie! Could it have been Willie? He had thought Brian and Frieda had been having an affair, he had been with Petra who had rejected him ultimately, and so too had Frieda. Had she told him she would not have him back over the break? Had they quarreled after Thanksgiving dinner?

Wait. That was no good. Willie hadn't been at The Ledge over the break. I had seen him myself, returning with his suitcases. Surely they would have checked that he had truly been where he was thought to have been at the time of Frieda's death. Even Chief Vernon could not have been so remiss as to neglect that possibility, suicide ruling or no.

There had to be another connection. They were all science students, had all been ones to come to the building frequently to check on projects, all had the same advisor…

Gilbert. Gilbert had–

A scratching of a key came against the metal door.

Before I could decide whether to feign senselessness or to scramble to my feet to attack, there he was in the doorway, a gun trained on me.

Gilbert indeed.

"Ah, sleeping beauty awakens. Good. I was going to have to try some ammonium carbonate…you know, smelling salts."

"I know what it is, you fiendish man. I also know what hydrochloric acid is, and what hypatic toxicity is. As do you, apparently."

He chuckled. "It never ceases to amaze me, the insight of such young minds. Though, I'd have to admit, you did catch me a bit off guard when you strutted into my office like that and started spouting off about auroras and elephants and sound… What a clever way to blackmail someone. I'm wondering now if you are still interested in trading your silence for something or if I will have to…well, why don't you tell me how you figured it out. I have to admit I'm curious. I didn't really believe it was possible that you might have some real psi talent, judging by what a farce your father is, but after that performance in my office, I had to know if you had reasoned the whole thing out– as if someone could have figured out my plan on their own– or if you somehow… just knew." He let the door bang shut behind him and pocketed the keys. "That's half the reason I sent you that note to have you meet me here this evening. If Petra hadn't shown up with all her accusations and threats it could have been a much simpler meeting, just you explaining it all to me, and then I…well, I still insist that you satisfy my curiosity."

He prodded the tip of the gun in my direction, indicating that now was a good time to begin my explanation.

There was only one problem. I truly didn't know what in all of creation he was blathering on about. I had to think fast. Wondering if he would lose patience and just shoot me didn't help to get my neurons firing. At least not productively. What was he talking about, blackmailing him with elephants? I had taken his precious book from him, had even read some of it in the library when I had been avoiding returning to my room. It wasn't a scandalous book. How could I possibly blackmail him with it? What else had he said? Auroras? Sound?

I closed my eyes to relieve myself of the portentous sight of the barrel of his gun. Connections, connections. Auroras, elephants, sound. Auroras…elephants…sound…

A flash of memory of Father at a conference lectern came to me…a question had been asked…

And, as if in answer, the fan kicked on again.

"Infrasound," I bellowed over its noise and stood, approaching Gilbert despite his threatening posture. "Low frequency sound waves below the human ear's threshold. They cause psychophysiological effects in humans and other creatures. Fear, anxiety, body temperature fluctuations, even blurred vision from retinas vibrating in harmony with the waves. Elephants use it to ward off enemies and to communicate amongst themselves. And the aurora… sometimes it produces such effects. Whole regions of people seem to suffer malaise at times of great solar activity. And the fan…"

The vision of white haze floating down the hall at me, inexplicable fear, a shiver.

"When I was a child, Father corresponded for a while with a British professor who had been experimenting with infrasound after an improperly installed exhaust fan caused similar apparitions and anxieties in his offices." Why hadn't I thought of that sooner? But then, I never took Father's interests and correspondents seriously and I had been only ten or so.

Gilbert nodded to me.

I went on. "You must have realized that was what was going on after the reports had come in of people seeing ghosts. And you…" The pieces were falling together, but I hardly believed my own words as I said them, "…you used it, didn't you? You didn't fix it because you wanted the science building empty at night so you could…"

Gilbert beamed encouragement. I was a star pupil, it seemed.

"…so you could be alone in the night here to work on Petra's experiment. You did the same thing to Anthony. Shot down his thesis so you could later use his idea for your own research. That's how you wrote your book on quantum non-locality, isn't it? But Petra's…you couldn't wait…"

Gilbert bellowed over the fan's noise. "The students who gathered the plants on the Amazon expedition last summer only brought back so many samples. I had a drug company executive already interested and he wasn't going to wait around forever. Eventually, they would have sent their own team down. Petra wanted to look at the process holistically, getting the fermentation right, mimicking the conditions the indigenous peoples used. I knew I could isolate the active ingredient faster than she could bumble through including all the anthropological nonsense. But I couldn't do it out in the open. I had to do it when no one else was around. And with these damned open facility policies Sylvia loves so much, I was hard-pressed to find the solitude. Already I'd had to knock out one student who almost stumbled upon me. The ghost sightings were a god-send."

"And you couldn't let them end."

The fan cycled off again and I could hear his reply with an eerie clarity.

"Exactly. When Brian came to me and said he'd figured out why the ghost effects were produced, I knew I had to do something. He wanted to experiment with it before fixing it, but I couldn't expect him to keep it quiet. The boy was always talking; he never shut up, ever. And he was sure to mention it to Scarborough."

"So you met him up here, Brian thinking you were going to adjust the fan in some way…"

"He had a plan, to take measurements of how it was now installed, then fix it, to see if the apparitions continued, then to take it a step further by reinstalling it the way it had been to try to reproduce the standing wave– the infrasonic wave. He had grand ideas of then testing all of the NESOPsI alleged haunted sites locally. And with Scarborough around, I knew it would happen. I couldn't let him do it. I was too close..."

I stood nearer to him now, trying to ignore the gun. If I could get him to keep talking, to forget the circumstances...

"And a poltergeist fit right in." There were only a few feet between us now.

"I came up with that after Brian left my office. I'd pulled out Scarborough's research since he was suddenly back in town. You can never be too careful. He had all kinds of crazy articles he'd copied for me when he was a senior. I had a file so thick, I could have made Brian's death look like anything from a werewolf attack to spontaneous human combustion. And Brian was such a loser. If you knew anything about poltergeist theory, and our bumpkin of a police chief sure as hell did, it would look perfectly natural. It was a nice logistical puzzle, though. How to do it, I mean."

Gilbert looked at me as if we were simply standing around having a chat. He smiled. "We used to dress up our lab rats. I won first place in grad school for my Groucho costume. The kids here do that too, though not so much with the lab animals– those are my babies. But your friend there–" He waved the gun nonchalantly in Petra's direction "– Rocky, she treats that skeleton in the lab like he's her date to the prom, talking to him all the time, calls him Amberly, or some idiocy. I got to thinking that his stand would be perfect for holding an unconscious Brian upright while I... Well, you know the rest. I knew there would be noxious things spilled, so I figured if the poltergeist–" he let out a chuckle, "– if the poltergeist didn't kill him, the fumes would."

"But you had to be in the room too."

His eyes lit up in the dim light. "You didn't figure that out? I thought for sure the way you lingered over the photos in my office that you knew that as well."

I thought back, but all I could remember was the rat with the thick black mustache.

"Perfectly natural for a serious cave explorer to own his own gas mask. Well, I can see you understand now. And it was a good thing I brought it because that boy was a bit stubborn. When I checked him there on the floor, after the cabinet–"

I winced.

"– the bugger was still alive. And this damn fan–"

I jumped as it whirred to life again. So did Gilbert, just a bit.

He raised his voice above the noise, "– the damn thing was extracting all the fumes from the acid I'd spilled before it could get to high enough concentrations to kill him. And I wasn't going to mess with the fan's setting and risk destroying my ghost. In the end, I had to do it manually."

I moved even closer to him, trying to appear as if I were straining to hear his words.

"After that, things went pretty well. I isolated the active compound, a metabolic inhibitor– well, you're not interested in all the details. But it went well. Only a few rats died in the first trial back in October. They all survived the second trial before Thanksgiving. And then Frieda had to go and find the plants."

"So you killed Frieda as well as Brian," I shouted above the din.

"Yes. I had to."

Oh, how I pined for my mini-recorder!

"She came to me after she found the plants. I couldn't risk that she'd let Rocky know she'd found them. Rocky would know it was me because I'd confiscated all the specimens. But I guess Frieda got to her before I could get to Frieda. Rocky had it all figured out."

He glanced over at her and I sprang. I knocked the gun out of his hand with a chop to the wrist. It skittered away into the darkness beyond the fan. I twisted and brought my elbow up to meet his nose. It did so with a satisfying crack. But I had underestimated Gilbert. Despite the pain of his broken nose (and oh yes, I was sure I'd broken it if his cry, louder than the fan, was any indication) despite this, he had the presence of mind to lock me in the crook of his arm. He pressed hard against my throat.

The fan cycled off and left a heavy silence, filled only by Gilbert's labored breath and my occasional gurgles.

"It's too bad I can't just kill you now. But I've got a streak going, and I'm damned if I'm going to let you push me into something that I can't frame as an accident. You see, I'm going to leave you here. Let them think you two were trying to channel the science building ghost and the door shut on you, even though you'd propped it open after picking the lock. You huddled together for warmth, but the stormy night got the best of you. I really wish Petra hadn't bled so much. I had to come back to do something about that, to provide some cover story for that bloody bump on her head–"

"You're gonna have to think of something better than a cover story now, Gilbert."

Petra struggled into the light, her hand the only steady part of her as she held Gilbert's gun, pointed straight at him.

"Let her go," Petra said in a seriously scary tone.

But Gilbert's grip on me only tightened.

"You think you can hit only me?"

"I'm from Louisiana, honey. I've shot reptiles almost as ugly as you from much farther away. Don't think I don't remember how."

Gilbert loosed me and I breathed in raggedly. Petra didn't move a muscle, but kept the gun leveled on Gilbert.

"Get his keys, Suny."

I held them up for her to see. "I had already procured them whilst he had me in his grasp. There is something to be said for Father's enthusiasm for slight of hand, after all. Had you not roused yourself and obtained the gun, I would have–"

"Suny, open the damn door."

"Right."

I turned to do so. But Petra must have relaxed a bit at that point because, the next thing I knew, Gilbert was rushing her, Petra was screaming, "Run, Suny, run!" and then a shot rang out. I could hear no more after that as the fan kicked on again and I was, as suggested, running out of the door, leaving the keys behind me, and stumbling across the snow-covered roof. The moon illuminated the space, but I was panicked, disoriented. It took me a moment to see where the roof access door was among the other mechanical access doors.

And that was a moment too long.

Gilbert appeared in the fan room doorway, no gun in sight, but no Petra either. He shook the catwalk as he ran, and broke right to cut me off before I could reach the door to the stairs. Instinctively, I knew he would reach it before I did. He did, and clamped his hand on the knob possessively.

"Oh, no, you don't. Give me a chance to catch my breath, and then I'm going to make sure you don't go down these stairs until you're carried down in a body bag."

I swallowed hard and backed even farther away from him. Granted, I could use a bit of aikido now and then, but its effectiveness in my application of it was in direct correlation to the amount of surprise it met with. Gilbert wouldn't be surprised any longer. I backed up farther again while he collected himself and let go of the doorknob. He took a step toward me and I took a step back. He took another and I, the same.

"You better watch your footing, missy. You don't want to fall off the roof, now do you?"

I looked backward. The snow was so deep, I could barely make out where the low safety wall edged the roof. I shivered.

"Or maybe that would be a good idea. Young woman flings herself off a roof after killing her roommate—"

Petra! I shook my head. I couldn't think of that now.

"Oh yes. One good shove will do it, I suppose." Gilbert advanced toward me and I scurried backwards.

"Wait," I sobbed. "Don't push me. Please. You win. I'll jump. But at least let me do it myself. I…I couldn't stand to have your hands on me again, even if just for a moment."

Gilbert stopped and crossed his arms over his chest. "You

can't offend me now. You're the one who's going to die. Suit yourself," he smirked. "Jump."

I glanced behind me and took another step back in the snow. I shuddered against the cold wind and flexed my hands to bring the blood back to my fingers. I looked back again and took yet another step. The greenhouse roof lay below, thinly covered with a crust of snow and ice that had melted in the sun, then had refrozen at nightfall. I looked at Gilbert. How he would gloat to see my body crash through those panes now that he had isolated his active ingredient and no longer needed the tropical heat the greenhouse had afforded his specimen plants.

I swallowed hard and squared my shoulders. Gilbert took a step forward.

"No. Don't come any closer. I will make good my promise." One more quick glance behind me. "Goodbye, cruel world," I sang out into the darkness and leapt backward.

I sailed downward for what felt like way too long, then reached out with both hands and slapped my frozen fingers around the icy metal rungs of the ladder attached to the outside wall. As quickly and as quietly as I could, I clambered up the dozen rungs I'd fallen. Just before I reached the top, I saw what I had so hoped I would see. Gilbert's boot was on the edge of the roof, the rest of him crouched, eyes peering through the dark to see where I'd landed. I lunged up the remaining rungs and cracked my forehead into his kneecap. At the same time, I let go of the ladder with one hand and slammed my fist up to Gilbert's crotch. No one would blame me for…well, for making sure that the force of that blow was extreme.

Gilbert let out a strangled cry. His hurt knee buckled, and I do believe I saw his eyes actually cross as he doubled over in pain. I grabbed onto his coat collar as he lowered his face toward mine and I heaved him further off balance and off the roof over my shoulder. He fell down and down and…

I did not turn to see his descent. I was satisfied well enough to hear the shattering panes of glass below me.

I drew in a jagged breath and wrapped both arms around the ladder rungs. I hugged the icy metal and just tried to breathe.

Many minutes later, a voice came from above me.

"Suny, are you going to hang out there all night?"

Brown.

"Anthony."

"Come on up here."

I climbed the last few rungs and let him pull me up the rest of the way. He held me at arms length, looked me up and down, then pulled me to him, wrapping his arms around my frozen form.

"You're shivering."

"I believe the appropriate American teen expression would be, 'No, duh,'" I whispered into his coat.

He untangled from me and took his coat off, enfolding me in it. He tried to make me walk, but I stopped him. "How did you know...? Where did you come from?"

"We were downstairs when we heard the crash. The Chief has had Gilbert under surveillance since they found Frieda, but just enough to know where he was at all times. When he didn't come out of the building for so long...and neither did you or Petra, they finally got the okay to come in and start looking. I...I was just making sure..."

"I'm okay. I'm...I'm not so certain about Petra."

We turned to see the fan housing room, where two uniformed police officers were working to open the door.

Chapter 26

"Enough with the temperature taking, already." Petra took the thermometer from her mouth and brandished it at the Nazi Nurse.

"You have a serious twitching laceration on your shoulder. Should it get infected…"

"Infected, my big black butt. With all those horse pills you make me swallow six times a day? Now…" Petra grabbed a glass of water from her tray and gulped it down. "Now, I'm thirsty. Go do something useful like getting more water. Pretty please," she added.

The Nazi Nurse stomped out. Petra turned back to me. "I don't know how you stood her so long. It's only been two days and I'm going to throttle the woman already."

"Well, one must be patient with her. She means well. After all, you are suffering from second impact syndrome and a gunshot wound."

"Ha! What a crock! If they were really worried, they would've kept me at the hospital. The thing only grazed my shoulder. And if Gilbert hadn't slammed me up against the wall at the same time, I wouldn't have any second impact bullsh–" Petra broke off and glanced over at the other bed where her grandmother, who truly did have skin the color of brown lentil dahl and a halo of white hair, slept soundly after her long flight from Louisiana. "Anyhow, the bullet only made me hit the wall, which knocked me out and kept Gilbert from shooting me for real. Though I still don't know why he didn't just shoot you when he caught up with you. Not that I'd want him to…"

"They found the gun inside the cage…you know, the protective cage that covered the fan's blades? He must have pushed you so hard that it flew out of his hand and fell through the caging."

"Okay. I know he would've made sure he'd killed me if he'd

had the time– I made him so furious in that lab when I let him know the gig was up - but what I still wonder is how he could think to kill so many people and believe he could claim to have isolated the antimicrobial agent and get all the glory that started with my experiment. People knew about it, knew what I'd started out to do."

"He was cocky alright. He did succeed in stealing Anthony's work, after all. But that wasn't the plan here, Petra. He was burnt out, I believe one would say. He'd driven himself so hard since he was a child that he had nothing left to offer by the time he was thirty. It wasn't an altruistic desire to share his gifts with other young geniuses that made him teach at The Ledge. He needed ideas. And he thought you all would burn out too. That's why he didn't care too much about killing such brilliant talent. He figured you would all snuff out soon, just as he had."

"Yeah, and I bet the prospect of fame and moula didn't hurt either."

"Moula maybe. But not fame. He could never have succeeded in being named in any research on your plants. You're right, too many people would have recognized the study. He just wanted the money. He planned to scurry off to Mexico and spelunk to his heart's content."

"That's sure where he belonged– in a deep, dark hole." Petra reached back with her good arm, flipped her pillow over, and settled back into it. "How do you know all this, Suny? Did you wheedle it out of him before I woke up?"

"Uh…" How did I know all of this? *Chyort!* "…uh, that's right. When you were still…knocked out, one might say. But I'm surprised you didn't know, spending every night hidden in the lab, watching him since Frieda died. I guess finding that note he sent me made you realize that he was about to get nasty again."

"I'd have been an idiot if I hadn't figured it out. First, Frieda tells me she found my plants, then she ends up dead with some fake suicide poem. Gilbert probably just pulled that out of the portfolio she submitted for her mid-term literature grade. He was her advisor. He had access to all of that. And besides, those dead rats in October exhibited signs of–"

"Stop. Say no more. If I never see another rat, it'll be too soon. After seeing all of them crawling all over you–"

"Now you better stop, Suny." Petra shuddered. "I know he let them loose to get rid of the evidence that he'd been testing the antimicrobial on them, but–" She shuddered again and pulled her sheet up to her chin.

The Nazi Nurse returned then with a whole pitcher of water. Along with her came Dr. Kennedy, who immediately checked Petra's pupils and took her pulse and pressure. Petra didn't seem to mind and the Nazi Nurse stalked out in a huff. Before she could close the door, a veritable parade squeezed through. Chief Vernon and Sylvia took in the crowd around the bed and went to finish their conversation by the window. Anthony sidestepped Dr. Kennedy and came up to Petra's side.

"Hey, Rocky. How's the hero?"

Petra snorted. "There's your hero, Tony," she said, pointing at me. "I'm just the dolt who's good at getting herself knocked around."

Anthony looked at me, then away towards Petra's grandmother, who was snoring as loudly as ever I'd heard Petra snore.

"Your grandmother came up to congratulate you, though."

"My gran came up to make sure I was getting quality care so she didn't have to medivac my rear end down to the bayou. She took one look at that battleaxe of a nurse, and gave into jetlag, satisfied. But hey, Suny, you're the one who should be given the key to the city, or to the college at least. Is your dad flying in from Scotland to see that his hero is okay and to take her out on the town?"

"No."

"Oh."

The room got quiet.

Anthony filled the void, "But I...I'm taking her to dinner for him. At...at Chez Marguerite...as a reward."

I stared at him. He was?

"Ooh, la, la, Suny girl. That's one schwanky joint."

"What is that?" Sylvia broke away from the Chief, leaving him to fend for himself against Dr. Kennedy, who looked desperate to talk to him.

"Nothing, Sylvia. I'm just taking Suny to dinner...at her father's request. Sort of a...a surrogate thing."

I frowned at him. He didn't look at me.

"Well, good. Maybe I should foot the bill," she said. "On behalf of the college, that is. Not only did you save yourself and Petra, Suny, you saved the reputation of the school. And provided me a replacement for Professor Gilbert. I did a phone interview with Mr. Munston just this morning. He'll be joining our faculty right after the winter break."

This news did make me smile. I would be thrilled to be around Mr. Munston again. Surely he would agree to be my advisor. And, as an added bonus, his continual presence would serve to make Rebecca positively livid.

"I'm off," Sylvia announced. "Rocky, I'll be back to escort your grandmother to the dining hall at five-thirty, if she so desires. Right now, though, I have to meet with Nick and this Diana Kowalski person. And for that, we owe Ms. Davis another thank you. They're proposing a joint study with Preacher's Ledge and the university to test all the local haunted sites for infrasound. Suny set them both on the scent, in Brian's memory is how she explained it to me, right Suny? I'm so glad Nick is finally taking some kind of study seriously."

"Yeah, or someone," Petra added and winked. "That Diana Kowalski may be just what he needs to get serious. As for me, I just want to get out of this bed for good. Someone'll be hard-pressed to get me back into one for a while. Unless he's really good, that is." She smiled. After a moment, the smile broke into an even wider grin. "Though, you know, after enough grieving time, I may just give Willie another try. He was getting

280

pretty good there after a while. And he was such an eager student." She waggled her eyebrows.

I blushed and moved to the other side of the room. Anthony stayed with her and talked about whether or not she would consider attempting to replicate Gilbert's work.

I sat on the foot of Gran's bed. I wanted to talk to the Chief, but he and Dr. Kennedy were…engaging in quite animated discourse and I couldn't find a way to break in.

"– really think I chalked it all up to a poltergeist?" the Chief was saying.

"You've always done whatever you thought your aunts wanted. Why not this time? You're the one who ruled it an accident."

"Not officially. I just passed that around here to the administration, staff, and students. We thought we'd let whoever killed Nelson relax while we searched through it all some more. He was bound to give himself away."

"Let him relax? Let him kill again, you mean." The Chief stared at her hard, then looked away. Dr. Kennedy reached out a hand to him. "Oh, Charlie, I didn't mean that– I know you didn't want that to happen…"

He slowly turned back to her. "We were still investigating the first one when the second one occurred, you know, still gathering evidence even…"

Suddenly I knew where the wrench had gone. Chief Vernon had sent someone in to get it, not wanting to clue us in, to involve two students any further than they'd already gotten themselves involved.

"…you could have told me," Dr. Kennedy was saying.

"Why? So you'd get all puffed up knowing you found everything the ME found? Perkins doesn't need you for competition. He's a fine District ME and we don't need another half-baked coroner snooping around."

"He is a fine ME, fine enough to recognize that I'm a damned good coroner. In fact, he's invited me to brush up on my pathology so he can recommend me to the state ME for appointment after he retires next year."

"What!" Chief Vernon bellowed. Everyone in the room looked up. Gran stirred in her sleep. I patted her foot and she settled back down. The Chief narrowed his eyes at Dr. Kennedy, who allowed a smug look to creep onto her face. He lowered his voice, "That means I'd be working with you all the time?"

"Unless you can do your job well enough that we don't have any more crime around these hills. Get used to it." Dr. Kennedy nodded to us all, informed Petra she'd be back to check on her later, even if Dr. Benslow was around, and left.

I rose to do the same, but Chief Vernon laid one beefy paw on my shoulder.

I spoke before he could, "I have to commend you on your insightful investigation, Chief Vernon–"

"That's not what you were saying last week."

"Well, I…I–"

"But I have to thank you for flushing out Gilbert. Damn fool thing to do, but it took guts. We had him surveilled but we had Willie under suspicion too until we could verify that he really had been home over the break and on the plane he said he'd been on. I guess we weren't watching Gilbert close enough. We could have saved you and your roommate a couple of knocks."

"You never suspected Petra?"

The Chief threw a glance over at Petra, white patch of gauze on her crown. "No. Maybe if we'd had all the info you had… If all this had turned out differently, I would've had to book you for withholding evidence."

If all this had turned out differently, I'd not have been here to be booked. But I didn't say this to the Chief. I had kept things to myself that I shouldn't have, but then, I had tried to give him evidence before, and I thought him a bumbling keystone cop, obsequious to his crazy ghostchasing aunts. This too, I did not relate to the Chief. I only smiled as he turned to go.

"Oh, I almost forgot," he said to Petra. "I need you to sign this statement that you recognized the bandana, et cetera, et cetera." He handed Petra a sheet of paper and a pen.

"Hey Chief, when do I get my bandana back, anyway?" she asked. He mumbled something about evidence and left. Petra and I had already figured that the bandana must have fallen from my pocket when we'd been up on the roof together and Frieda had picked it up on one of her obsessive trips up there to check her red filters and had kept it. Petra had also forgiven me for letting that little piece of evidence lead me on to think such horrible things about my best friend. In fact, she had told me she didn't blame me in the least and after listening to my reasoning, wondered why the hell she hadn't been cuffed and dragged down to the station by Vernon himself.

Anthony and I bade Petra our farewells and walked out of the health sciences building together. It was still bitingly cold, but the sun was bright, dazzling off the sheet of snow on the ground.

We walked a ways across campus, not speaking. Anthony's breath came in little plumes of mist and I thought, with each one, that he was going to say something. Finally, as we neared the building that housed the mailroom, he stopped under a tree.

"Well, Suny, I've got to hand it to you. You were right and I was wrong. No poltergeist after all. I knew there was a reason Brian showed himself to me after his death—"

I gaped at him.

"—but I thought it was a kind of sad suicide message. I guess now it was more like a plea for justice. I get these after-death messages sometimes, you know. But you- you figured it out and never used your abilities at all."

I didn't correct him. After all, I don't suppose trying to sense Petra's involvement counted. I had misinterpreted her sympathetic thoughts for Brian and Frieda's plights and her rage at Gilbert as indication that she was the culprit. Anthony did not have to know this, however. If anything, it proved again to me that he was wrong. My "talents" were worse than useless. I would vow now to abandon them forever.

Really, I would.

"Anthony, now that I'm off my action plan– Kathy must have told you, or Sylvia– I guess Kathy's not speaking to either of us… But did you really mean…that is, are we really going…"

"To Chez Marguerite?" He let a half-smile creep onto his face. "I suppose we could. If Sylvia's paying anyway. Just to make up for your father…"

It was then that I saw Rebecca emerge from the mailroom building with Todd. She stopped mid-stride and stared at me, standing as I was next to Anthony. Anthony with his quirky, attractive half-smile. She scowled, dropped her bundle of mail (letters only from her intrusive mother, no doubt) and grabbed Todd, kissing him passionately. She broke off, leaving Todd a bit flabbergasted, but not unappreciative, it seemed. Rebecca put her hands on her hips, challenge in her eyes.

Well now, if she thought…

I threw my arms around Anthony's neck, gazed lovingly into his startled sapphire eyes, and kissed him like I had never kissed Todd. Somewhere in the middle of it, he began to kiss me back and I forgot all about the scheming half-sister trying to show me up. I forgot about Gilbert, about Petra, and Frieda, Nicholas, and Brian. I forgot about snow and cold and fathers in Scotland…

And then Anthony pulled away from me roughly.

"What the hell was that for!"

I looked over his shoulder. Rebecca had stomped off over the snow. Todd scrambled after her, the mail he had retrieved for her spilling from his arms.

"Oh…just a thank you…in advance, for dinner."

Anthony looked uncomfortable. "Suny, I–"

"Oh, don't tell me…"

"No, really. I think I should say… you're a lovely young woman but I… I work for your father, you see… and you're only sixteen–"

284

I glared at him. Convenient for him to say that now, after he had kissed me back so fervently. Not that I really cared– I had acted impulsively, spontaneously. It meant nothing at all to me. Really. At the very least, I didn't need his fumbling excuses. The nerve…

Suddenly, a tree limb above his head snapped and teetered and then, in not quite a straight line, it fell. It clipped Anthony on the shoulder. Inside me, some tension I'd been holding snapped as well. I felt lighter, satisfied…

"Damn, that hurt! Suny!" Anthony cried, rubbing his shoulder. "Hey, did you do that? Come back here!"

But I had walked away and I wouldn't come back this time, no matter how much he called.

"Don't believe in poltergeists, huh?" he called after me.

But I didn't really listen to what he said. I was busy trying to decide what dress of Petra's I would wear to Chez Marguerite. Something seductive, something tempting…

Something that might get me another kiss. Or at least make him want to give me one.

Whether I let him or not was a completely separate matter.

About the Author

McLean Jacobson reads, writes, and teaches in Columbia, Maryland. She is the proud recipient of the Malice Domestic Grant for the first Suny Davis mystery, *Extrasensory Deception* (then titled *Hypothesis for Murder.*) She loves to read about paranormal and psi research, psychic personalities, and anomalous events. Share your own experiences with her through her website McLeanJacobson.com!

Connect with McLean Jacobson on
Twitter @McLeanJacobson
Facebook https://www.facebook.com/mclean.jacobson.3
and on her website: McLeanJacobson.com

Acknowledgements

The support of many people made the creation of this book possible. Thanks especially to Michael, Sadie, Jacob, Aryn Kestel, Rob Gutro and Sterling Wilson for their support, including design and publishing expertise. Also thanks to Wonderland Book Arts and freepik for images and design. Most of all thanks to Cally Roosa who edited and designed this book.